Haven

Safe Haven

A collection of linked stories

Susan Dugan

For Laura, Theresa, Margaret, and Kara

CONTENTS

Rose (Walsh) Trambeaux, 1897-1992

Annette (Trambeaux) Shea, 1932-

Colleen Shea, 1955-

Annette

High Hopes

"And he's got high hopes …" Gerry and Annette Shea and their five-year-old daughter, Colleen, sang along with Frank Sinatra to the blaring radio ad, heading up the big hill in their 1957 Dodge in the dwindling light. Past the stone Presbyterian Church on the corner, illuminated from within, where silhouetted figures could already be seen driven to their knees in a last-ditch effort to prevent the world from going to hell in a hand basket via the election of a Roman Catholic president. They had just dropped off the last precinct lists Gerry had been calling to rally reluctant voters after driving people to the polls all day, along with a set of Kennedy/Johnson signs Annette and Colleen had waved throughout the long, dank afternoon at the corner of Main and Cherry, striving to convince Rocky Ledge's predominantly Protestant, Republican population to take a chance on Jack's "new frontier."

Jack, Jack, Jack, thought Annette. She enjoyed repeating the name in her head. Like everyone else she knew, she referred to him by given name, as if on intimate terms. As if she might at any moment find herself on a first-name basis with a millionaire, sitting down to dinner at some swanky club in the city; rising for a casual spin on the dance floor. His kind eyes with that tissue-paper crinkle of pain around the edges cast a spell on you from behind the TV screen; pregnant Jackie with her breathy voice elegant and serene at his side. Annette smoothed her new hairdo, a bouffant, just like Jackie's. Everyone said she resembled Jack's wife with her dark hair and eyes, courtesy of her French Canadian father. From a distance, at least, until her mother's broad face and snub Irish nose shifted into focus.

"Again, sing it again!" cried Colleen, as they pulled into the driveway.

"We need to feed you and your brother so Mommy and Daddy can get ready for the party we're having," Annette said. "You're going over to Michael and David's house tonight, remember?"

"Those children are absolute monsters," Colleen said.

"They're not so bad," Annette lied.

"I want to be at the party with *you*, Mommy," Colleen said. "I want to watch Jack win. I worked my fingers to the bones all day. I deserve it."

Annette caught her husband's eyes, the flicker of a smile that ended in a frown. He shrugged and shook his head.

Jack had actually shaken Colleen's hand when Gerry drove those folk singers with the stringy hair—unsanitary young women who did not shave their legs or armpits—to a rally in Poughkeepsie, instantly transforming her into a miniature fanatic on the Senator's behalf. Graced with a photographic memory for lyrics, Colleen lay in bed each night belting out the likes of *If I Had a Hammer* and *Blowing in the Wind* in a perpetual effort to stave off sleep, ever fearful of missing the next transforming scene in the unfolding drama of her life. She was not your run-of-the-mill five-year-old, needless to say. Currently she wanted to vote, build a bomb shelter, star on Broadway, fly to the moon, and raise a gorilla, not necessarily in that order.

"You have school tomorrow morning, remember?" Annette said, hoisting her daughter out of the back seat.

Colleen's small strong thighs gripped her mother's waist. She cupped Annette's chin in her hands, eyes wide and beseeching as Ingrid Bergman's in *Joan of Arc*, the movie Colleen had watched with them on TV, miraculously adopting the saint's persona as her own so that every request of her mother was now framed as an argument for immortal justice; leading Gerry to refer to her privately as "Colleen of Arc."

"Please, Mommy. This is a once in a lifetime moment."

Gerry laughed.

Their lives had become but a series of once-in-a-lifetime moments in the past five years. Children did that to you.

"Jack is on the right track, Mommy," Colleen said, sealing the deal.

Really, she was putty in this child's hands. She needed to pull Dr. Spock down off the shelf before she had hopelessly spoiled her daughter. "You can come for a little while, if you're a good girl and go in with Daddy while I go get Timmy."

Colleen kissed her mother on the cheek over and over again with a wet, smacking noise.

Annette handed her to Gerry and headed across the street to Alice and Joe's to retrieve their son.

When no one answered the side door, Annette let herself into the darkened kitchen and called out, inhaling the perfume of fresh-baked cheese straws cooling on cookie tins on the stove. Alice had strong opinions about food, particularly what passed for cuisine in suburban America. Béchamel-splattered recipe cards lay scattered about the kitchen counter. Now and then— Alice absorbed in perfecting a cheese soufflé or salmon aspic or tarte tatin—Annette would find her friend's boys wandering the neighborhood in their pajamas shooting with their little bow and arrow sets of a late summer morning, disarm them, and feed them Cheerios and grilled cheese sandwiches until her friend's latest culinary seizure had passed. Knowing she would reap just rewards as the recipient of Alice's Michelin-worthy masterpieces.

"Alice," Annette called again. Her eleven-month-old son, Timmy, staggered out of the glowing hallway on his stubby legs, colliding with his mother's calves.

Annette scooped him up, planted a kiss on his ruddy cheeks, and attempted to smooth his flyaway hair, pale and soft as the silk on a cob of corn between her fingers.

"Ma," he said, poking her throat. Unlike Colleen who began speaking in phrases at eight months, Timmy had made no effort at speech besides that one endearing syllable. Annette suspected it could be years before her son—more than content to allow Colleen to serve as his personal translator—uttered his first sentence.

"Alice," Annette called, again, her nostrils confirming the suspicion that her son needed changing.

"We're having a bath," came Alice's voice from down the hall.

Annette carried Timmy into the bathroom, like most of the rooms in this house identical to her own save for the color of the tiles; white with navy blue accents instead of pink with green.

"Welcome to paradise," Alice said. She knelt on the bathmat, reaching into the soapy tub to let out the drain. "Say hello to Mrs. Shea," she added, standing and handing her boys towels. She wore pedal pushers and a clingy sleeveless top. Weather and seasons did not seem to register on Alice who often showed up in sandals and a sundress for a Christmas party, flaunted black boots and velvet at Easter Mass, and had no respect whatsoever for the largely unspoken rule prohibiting the donning of white before Easter or after Labor Day. She strode to the beat of a different drummer, Alice often claimed—invoking Thoreau in self-defense, a faraway look in her eyes—as if literally obeying the inner cadence of said musician.

"Hello, Mrs. Shea," chirped Michael and David, tiny replicas of their father with eyes like little bullets, velvety brush cuts, and freckles so abundant their hides seemed crafted of calico. "Hello, Mrs. Shea," they repeated, in their sing-song voices, beaming up at her like perfect little altar boys in training, as if the bath had somehow scalded away the base natures that kept their mother perpetually on edge. The boys had recently coated the walls of their room with Vaseline; shredded Alice's mink stole for hamster bedding, and painted their faces with Methiolade to match the Indian headdresses Joe had bought them. The brush cuts followed Michael's thankfully aborted attempt to scalp his brother with a butter knife.

"Now go get in your jammies," Alice ordered. "They're on your beds."

The boys careened out of the room naked and shivering, launching into a series of screeching laps around the hallway.

"Any word on turnout?" Alice asked. She stacked the plastic boats and measuring cups on the edge of the tub, half-heartedly swiping at the gritty ring left by the draining water with a washcloth.

"Looking good. Joe said to tell you he'd be home shortly."

Alice and Joe were the only other Catholic Democrats on the block. The two couples had immersed themselves in the campaign, dragging their kids to rallies throughout the county, helping coordinate the motorcade with Harry Truman at the old Haverstraw High School; stuffing envelopes, knocking on doors, and manning phone banks.

Alice stood, holding her back with one hand and herding tendrils of bottled blonde hair into the headband from which they had escaped with the other. She rubbed her luminous green eyes, underscored in the florescent light by dark crescents. She hadn't been sleeping again, Annette suspected. She could go for weeks on end like that. "It's the only time I have to myself," she would say, joking, but her exhaustion tugged at the skin covering her delicate facial bones, drew her lips together in a hyphen that did not seem to move, even when she laughed.

"If you don't get in your jammies this minute I'll tell Kathleen you can't watch The *Flintstones*," she yelled, over her shoulder, in her sons' general direction.

The boys stampeded into their room and slammed the door.

"It's exciting," Annette said. "I really think Jack can pull this off. I wouldn't have believed it six months ago, but."

"Oh, Annette, the world is changing," Alice said, seizing Annette by the shoulders.

Timmy hid his head in his mother's neck, as if at the very thought of it.

"We are just so lucky to be living right now, to be a part of this generation." Alice threw out her arms as if addressing an auditorium full of skeptics. "Sometimes when I'm lying in bed staring at the ceiling, listening to Joe snore, thanking God for these two *perfect* children, my whole body tingles with the feeling that we're right on the threshold of something so thrilling, something that will leave us completely transformed." Her voice had dropped to a whisper. She leaned forward, head bowed, a teller of secrets. "Alive in a whole new way, you know?"

Annette nodded, could not help herself, rearranging a squirmy Timmy on her hip, thinking about Jack's speech at the Democratic convention, America's "new frontier." Marveling at Alice's talent for articulating concepts Annette had only just *begun* to register. She thought about tackling unemployment and school segregation, closing the missile gap with the Russians, getting this country moving by making new, better, *intelligent* decisions. She thought about Jack and Jackie, the haloes they seemed to balance on their handsome heads, the electricity they so effortlessly exuded, all that boundless promise. Was that what Alice meant?

Timmy reared back in her arms. She almost dropped him. "I better go feed these kids," she said. "See you in a bit."

Halfway down the driveway, Annette turned back to find Alice standing outside on the cement stoop, bare arms backlit by the yellow porch light, exhaling a ladder of cigarette smoke in air on the verge of birthing snow, squinting off into the distance through the thickening mist as if trying to discern early-breaking news.

Disappearing in a cloud of Old Spice, Gerry walked across the street and set Timmy free with the Cudden's monsters and Kathleen Bennett, their sixteen year-old next-door neighbor, returning minutes later with Joe and Alice swathed in a sheath the color of Flamingoes that illuminated her creamy shoulders. Colleen was already downstairs in the recently finished basement batting at clusters of red-white-and-blue balloons and loops of crepe paper she had helped her father string from the low ceiling while Annette bathed and fed Timmy. Even the promise of ice cream sundae fixings at Alice's house had not persuaded her to join the other children.

"I don't blame you one bit," Alice said, descending the stairs with Annette and Colleen. "I prefer my company, too."

"You're boys are a menace," Colleen whispered.

Alice nodded gravely. "Exceptionally well said."

Annette bit her lip. She had often said the same thing in Colleen's presence, but, fortunately, so had Alice.

Alice set the cheese straws and a plate of homemade pate and water crackers down on the long folding table Annette and Gerry had borrowed from the county Democratic headquarters. With little more than a dozen active members, Rocky Ledges could not afford its own venue—the Shea's home had become the unofficial clubhouse. But even though they entertained a lot, it always made Annette nervous.

"You think the food table's OK here?" she asked. "Where should I put the hats and the noisemakers?"

Alice rested a reassuring hand on her friend's shoulder. She breezed about the room folding paper napkins into Japanese fans, arranging plastic cups into concentric towers, and artfully displaying bowls of chips, onion dip, and the platter of cream-cheese-and-olive stuffed celery Annette had thrown together early that morning. Alice had wanted to major in fine art but the grandparents who raised her after her parents were killed in a car wreck would only fork out money for a nursing degree— *something to fall back on, you know*—should she fail to marry a reliable provider.

Their attempt to foist the day's prevailing wisdom on their granddaughter backfired, however, when Alice dropped out after only one semester to waitress at an exclusive Manhattan club. She took up guitar and landed a job singing in a coffee house on her nights off. That's where she met and fell hard for a beat poet who fled to California in the middle of the night several months into their affair, leaving her in bed to face his landlord pounding on the door, insisting she hand over three months back rent. And then a cousin in Nyack set her up with Joe. A manager at the Gypsum plant, he liked pizza and beer and baseball, seemed so reliable compared to the city men she'd been dating. *Something to fall back on, you know.*

"I thought I could marry into sanity," she'd once confided to Annette, sitting on a chair in her kitchen, hugging her knees to her chest, and shaking her head at the folly of it.

Annette sat very still. She had never had a friend bare herself so. It gave her hope that her own nagging sense of something missing might one day work its way up her throat and into words.

The doorbell rang and Annette dashed upstairs, leaving Alice to finish working her magic. The Clooneys and the Margiones, bearing Chex Mix and a bottle of Seagram's, had driven over together. Annette took their coats and Gerry and Joe accompanied them downstairs to the built-in wet bar—Gerry's pride and joy—courtesy of his Christmas bonus last year. About to head back downstairs herself, Annette nearly tripped over Colleen lurking behind her. The child retracted the thumb from her mouth but not soon enough.

"I didn't have my thumb in my mouth, Mommy," Colleen said, before Annette could launch a good scolding.

"You're tired; maybe I better walk you across the street."

"I am not at all tired."

Really, she would argue with a saint. It could drive you insane. And she hated to go to sleep—every single nap and bedtime a whole new battle.

The doorbell rang.

"Can I answer it?" Colleen asked.

"OK; that will be your job. You answer the door and tell the people to put their coats on our bed and come downstairs."

"Yes, *M'am*," said Colleen, clicking her heels together and saluting like Shirley Temple.

"Use your best manners and no thumb in your mouth." Annette swatted her lightly on the bottom, the child's crinoline springing back against her palm.

Downstairs, most everyone had donned plastic top hats with red, white, and blue Kennedy banners glued around the brims. Annette grabbed one but it didn't fit over her newly teased hair. She fingered the campaign button on her navy blue shift. Colleen raced downstairs and curtsied for the Connors. Annette handed them hats and placed one on her daughter. It swallowed Colleen's head and she staggered around in circles, giggling, arms outstretched. "I can't see, I can't see," she chanted.

"Open your eyes; open your eyes," Gerry called, from behind the bar, one of the many routines they had perfected from the *Three Stooges* show.

Annette drifted to the phonograph set up on a card table and placed the needle down on one of the 45's they had borrowed from Kathleen the babysitter—*Tonight's the Night* by the Shirelles. They had turned the TV volume down; the polls hadn't even closed in California and the East Coast returns had just begun to trickle in. Annette could not help swaying a little to the music.

As usual everyone had bee-lined for the bar where Gerry and Joe stood mixing whiskey sours, gin and tonics, and 7&7s like pros, telling jokes involving priests and rabbis beneath a dangling neon Budweiser light—a gift from Annette's older brother—complete with revolving Clydesdales.

Rene Connor already sat enthroned on a bar stool popping stuffed olives and maraschino cherries like candy, tasting and turning up her nose at the many concoctions the boys whipped up for her review.

"Any bets on how many votes Jack will take in Rocky Ledges?" Rene's husband, Mickey, asked.

"Well, there are the twelve of us," said Bob Margione.

Annette laughed.

"Oh, you," said Rene. "There are more than twelve of us Catholics, for Christ sake. They'll all be voting for Jack."

"If they remembered to register," said Alice.

"How many in Our Lady of Sorrow's parish?" Rene asked.

Gerry shrugged. "Three, four hundred."

"There you go," Rene said.

"Three, four hundred out of six thousand," said Joe. "Not too bad."

"I have half a mind to vote Communist next time just to drive our founding fathers crazy." Alice threw back her head, exhaled a Slinky of smoke rings. "Just think, the *Reds* crawling up the bonny banks of the Hudson."

"They would shit their pants," Gerry said, choking on his drink. He handed Annette a gin and tonic.

"I wouldn't go around joking about being a communist, if I were you," said Marie Margione.

Alice's eyes narrowed. "What are they going to do—black-ball me from the Daughters of the American Revolution quilting circle? We're already blackballed folks, in case you haven't noticed."

Rene twisted her pillow-like lips.

"More libations, warden." Alice handed Joe her empty glass.

He set it down on the bar. A swift volley of troubled looks passed between them. They had been fighting again, Annette suspected, or, rather, Alice had been fighting. Joe did not fight. Joe disappeared.

"I think I'll go see if there's any news yet," he said, heading off toward the TV.

"Good idea," said Rene Connor, staggering off on her stilettos behind the prow of her exposed chest, the pink lady she had finally approved sloshing around in her glass, pale blue chiffon jiggling Jell-O-like around her hips.

Alice shuddered.

Annette could not figure out why Alice let people like Rene get to her.

"I cannot abide fools," she'd once stated. An unfortunate policy that could ruin your health in a town like this, filled with generations of Revolutionary War descendents growing more inbred and intolerant each day along with a throng of vapid newcomers like Rene.

"Dance with me, Daddy." Colleen stood, tugging at her father's sleeve. Gerry had never quite warmed to dancing, especially the formless style recently gaining in popularity, but, like his wife, could seldom resist Colleen. He handed his drink to Annette and set off toward the Margiones and the Clooneys and the newly arrived McDuffys, now undulating in the corner to his daughter's current favorite tune, aptly entitled: *You Talk Too Much.* Annette's father had once danced with her, too; how quickly our dancing days are over.

"You OK?" she asked, plopping down on a stool beside Alice. Alice smiled. "Just tired."

Annette patted her back. "Maybe you need to eat something."

"Thanks, Mom, but I think I'd prefer another drink."

Annette reached into the ice bucket and dumped a handful into Alice's glass, added gin and tonic, and refreshed her own.

"Have you ever had a real conversation in this town?" Alice asked.

"Define real."

Alice laughed. She twirled the ice in her glass with her index finger. "Talking about something other than toilet training, husbands, TV, and what's on sale at the A&P—the God-damn price of peas."

Alice suddenly looked like she might cry. She would turn thirty in a couple weeks—a milestone that still loomed several comfortable years ahead of Annette—maybe that's what was really bugging her.

"*We* have real conversations," Annette said. But even as the words left her lips she wondered if it were true. Because Alice talked, really, Annette just listened. Unwilling to dwell on the sudden feeling she had somehow failed them both; she rested her palm on Alice's wrist. "Come on," she said, after a while. "Let's go check out the returns."

Annette and Alice drifted toward the opposite wall. With only a small percentage of votes in, Kennedy and Nixon appeared neck and neck, Walter Cronkite said. Outside the Kennedy Hyannis Port compound a reporter stood holding an obviously malfunctioning microphone, little smoke-like puffs—a testimony to plummeting temperatures—emanating from his soundlessly moving lips.

"... expected to be so close we may not have a winner until tomorrow morning, some Kennedy campaign staffers predict," he surmised, as the faulty equipment rumbled back to life.

"Well, that's just crazy," said Rene, tossing her head. "How could *anyone* on God's green earth vote for Nixon after those debates. I mean, the man is positively sour looking. Who wants a president that looks like a hound dog?"

Annette and Alice traded glances. Half those voting for Jack would do so based not on his proposals but on his movie-star looks. It bothered Annette, when she thought about it too long. But like everything else these days, it *really* bothered Alice.

The volume in the room seemed to rise all at once; the way noise at parties often does, as if God held an audio knob in his hand intent on drowning out any more Rene-like observations. Annette smiled to herself at the thought of it.

Across the room, Gerry and Joe sat on folding chairs holding their drinks, as if engaged in real conversation, oblivious to Colleen leaning against her father's knees. Annette wondered as she often did if the men ever confided in each other about their worries, their hopes, or their marriages.

"Wouldn't you like to be a fly on the wall just once?" she'd asked Alice.

"Now that would be one bored-to-death fly. Let's see, a treatise on Micky Mantle's batting average, the merits of Budweiser versus Miller, Marilyn Monroe's chest size, what have I left out?"

She supposed she was right. Gerry never seemed to have any idea what was going on between Joe and Alice. Of course, he had served on a PT boat in the war just like Jack; had been trained to give only his name, rank, and serial number. Remained a proper soldier.

Annette glanced at her watch and rose. "I'd better get that kid of mine to bed. I mean, it's almost ten o'clock."

Alice nodded; gave a little wave.

"Come on, Missy." Annette took her daughter's hand.

The men didn't seem to notice.

"You think they can really make a go of that new city baseball club next year?" Joe asked, as they slipped away.

Annette smiled to herself; made a mental note to repeat her findings back to Alice.

"I'm not sleepy yet, Mommy," Colleen insisted. But she allowed her mother to lift her without a struggle, her body doubling in weight as it relaxed in spite of itself against Annette's shoulders.

"Nice talking to you as always, Colleen," called Alice, as Annette carried the child upstairs.

She helped Colleen wiggle into her pajamas.

"Read me *Charlotte's Web*, Mommy."

"No story tonight, remember—that was part of our deal."

Colleen sighed. "Is the window all the way closed?" she whispered.

Annette went to the window and locked it. Ever since Colleen had to get down under her desk and cover her head with her arms as part of the regular bomb drills the government now required of all public schools she'd been obsessed with nuclear war. She had seen some documentary on TV about fallout following the bombing of Hiroshima and become terrified that radioactive waste would somehow sift in through the windows while she slept.

"No one's going to drop any bombs, I'm telling you."

"What about the Russians?"

"The Russians don't want to drop a bomb on us. I mean, if they did, we'd just drop one back. They don't want to die."

"I'm too young to die," Colleen said.

"Yes, you are."

"You are, too, Mommy."

"That's right."

"But Grammy says the Russians are heathens and there's no telling what heathens might do."

Annette rolled her eyes. Her mother did not seem to grasp the insensitivity of sharing her ideas about Biblical predictions of Armageddon with her impressionable granddaughter. Promises of heavenly salvation did little to assuage a child's fear of losing her immediate family in a mushroom-shaped poof of smoke.

"Grammy doesn't know everything," said Annette. "No one is going to drop any bombs on any of us. I promise. I'll be right downstairs. You are very safe, OK?"

Colleen nodded solemnly, but did not look convinced.

"Just think; when you wake up, Jack will be president."

"Can I have the light on, Mommy?"

Annette kissed her on the forehead, turned on the small night-stand lamp, and switched off the overhead light.

"Leave the door open?"

"Just a crack—sleep tight, now." She knew better than to add the part about bed bugs.

"See you later, alligator," called Colleen.

"In a while; crocodile." Annette pulled the door almost shut behind her. Party noise wafted up the stairs. Colleen would not be sleeping any time soon.

Downstairs, Annette caught up with her husband, behind the bar again tending to ever-thirsty guests. Rene had begun slurring her words but was still, sadly, comprehensible. "What kind of Catholic girl makes chopped liver?" she asked Annette, stabbing at a cracker.

"Sounds like a setup for a joke," Gerry said.

"It's pate," said Annette. "French—very elegant."

"Oh, yeah? Take a whiff." Rene held her cracker up to Annette's nose. "It's chopped liver, alright, already. I grew up in the Bronx, remember?"

Annette opened her mouth, but shut it again. *If you can't say something nice*, came her mother's voice in her head.

Gerry's brows knit themselves together across his high forehead. No one could understand how Micky Connor with his heart of gold had ended up with the likes of Rene.

"Seen Alice?" Annette asked, standing on tiptoe to peck at her husband's cheek.

He shook his head.

"Any word yet on the tube?"

"I doubt we'll hear anything tonight." He handed her another drink. "They're calling it the closest race in American history. Cronkite said Nixon might demand a recount if it's as close as they're predicting."

Annette sighed. "Jesus. How are we going to get these people to go home?" she mouthed.

Gerry shrugged.

Headed for the TV to check on the situation herself she almost tripped on Alice's red stilettos. "My ruby slippers," she called them, like Dorothy's in The *Wizard of Oz*. There's no place like home, thought Annette, sipping her drink, eyes scanning the room for signs of the slippers' owner to no avail. She picked them up and wandered from group to group asking after Alice. She wasn't upstairs, either. The gin hit her all at once and, slightly woozy, Annette dumped it in the kitchen sink. She stepped outside, still carrying her friend's shoes to clear her head in the chilly air and found Alice standing barefoot on the stoop, smoking a cigarette.

"You're exhausted," Annette said. She pressed her palm to her friend's forehead as if taking her temperature.

"Yes."

"Jesus, Alice, you'll freeze to death out here. Come on, I'll walk you home and tuck you in. You just need some sleep."

Alice nodded, leaning on Annette for balance as she pulled on her shoes.

Kathleen was sleeping on the couch when they walked in.

"Go lie down," said Annette. "We can pay her tomorrow."

Annette sent Kathleen home and checked on Timmy sprawled out in the middle of the Cudden's guestroom bed. As usual, he had kicked off all the covers but still seemed warm as a baked potato when she pressed her palm to his cheek. Both her children ran like little Easy Bake ovens. She covered him anyway.

The monsters were sleeping, too, in twin beds against opposite walls, Michael clinging to a small metal gun from the cowboy outfit his grandfather bought him for his fourth birthday.

Annette slipped into Alice's room. She lay in bed wan and fragile in a translucent pink slip, collarbones jutting anvil-like beside the gully of her throat. She'd been losing weight, Annette knew, but hadn't really noticed how much until now. "The kids are fine, sweetheart. Can I get you anything?"

"Water, please."

Annette returned and handed her the glass.

"When you wake up, Jack will be president," Annette, said, as if comforting yet another child.

"You think I can dream my way out of here?"

Annette rested her hand on Alice's forehead again. "Sure, you can. Want the light off?"

Alice shook her head. "I hate the dark."

"Sweet dreams," Annette called, shutting the door.

She checked on Timmy one more time before heading home.

Colleen was still tossing and turning and singing "This land is your land ..." as Annette passed her room but Annette decided to ignore her. You could not make a person sleep, she told herself, not a big person or a little person. In the bathroom, she took two aspirin and ran cold water on her wrists to ward off the hangover already cranking down on her temples like a vice.

Downstairs people had begun repeating their jokes, their stories, and pausing every few minutes to ask each other what was happening on TV, as if in need of constant translation. Annette poured herself a club soda and allowed Gerry to pull her into his lap.

"I could pull a few fuses." Gerry nuzzled her neck. "Fake a power outage." He ran his palm up her thigh beneath her skirt, stroking the skin between her silk stockings and girdle. Her brain barely registered the weak pang of desire passing through her. She struggled against the weight of her eyelids as her husband's strong thumb massaged the hills and valleys behind her knee. Alice's voice came back to her then, echoing like the lyrics of a song stuck in your head:

"You think I can dream my way out of here?"

Instantly revived; she reeled off Gerry's lap; dashed upstairs and across the street propelled by a mounting suspicion; pushed the door of the Cudden's house open and headed for Alice's bedroom.

"Alice," she said, rummaging in the covers.

Her friend did not move or respond in any way.

"Alice!" Annette shook her by the shoulders, patted her cheek, pressing her ear to her mouth. She seemed to be breathing, if shallowly. She grabbed her clammy wrist and pressed her fingers to a faint pulse.

"Jesus Christ, Jesus Christ." Like a prayer she invoked the name—a prayer and a curse at the same time. She dialed her own phone number. It rang three times before Colleen answered

"Shea residence," as if she were twelve, as if it were three in the afternoon; "Colleen speaking."

"Colleen, listen to me. I need you to go downstairs very quietly and tell Joe I need to talk to him right now over at his house—will you do that please—*quickly.*"

If Colleen was shocked to have received a phone call from her mother and avoided a lecture about still being awake she did not let on.

It seemed forever before Annette heard Joe's voice on the phone, an eternity before he appeared in his bedroom. Annette had opened all the windows and pressed a wet washcloth stuffed with ice cubes to Alice's forehead as if trying to freeze her into consciousness.

"I don't understand," she said, massaging a limp hand. "She didn't have that much to drink, did she?"

"She had more than enough if she took those pills that God-damn doctor gave her." Joe foraged in the nightstand drawer and held the orange plastic medicine bottle he retrieved up to the light. "I don't know how many were in here, but it's empty."

"I'm so sorry. I didn't know." Annette thought of Alice sitting at her kitchen table in short-shorts hugging her knees:

"I thought I could marry into sanity."

Jesus Christ, Jesus Christ.

So much for the baring of our souls, Annette thought. "I called an ambulance," she said, as if reading lines someone else had written.

"Forget the ambulance. We'll make it faster if I drive. Give me a hand, will you?"

Annette helped Joe bundle Alice into the camel hair coat she inherited from her mother, and settle her into the back of their Oldsmobile.

"I'll take the kids over to our house to sleep. Call us when you can."

Jesus Christ, Jesus Christ.

She watched Joe peel out of the driveway before heading inside to gather up the children.

"Nothing like a little accident to perk up a campaign party," Gerry said, carrying a bag full of trash into the kitchen.

Annette stood at the sink. "What if it wasn't an accident?"

"Jesus, Annette, that's a helluva thing to say." He dropped the bag on the linoleum floor. "What about Joe and the kids?" he demanded, as if merely acknowledging the possibility that Alice might have wanted to take her own life amounted to an assault on her family. Which, maybe it did.

Annette dried her hands and hugged herself to keep them from shaking, swallowing the torrent of words flooding her throat, hoarding them for the long overdue *real conversation* she would have to have with Alice tomorrow.

"That woman needs to go see a priest and get her head screwed back on right," Gerry said. "Joe's an F-ing saint. She doesn't know how good she's got it."

A vision of her mother asking her father to pull up the car and take her to the priest engulfed Annette. It happened whenever they disagreed. Father LaCroix always could get Rose's head screwed back on right. Annette had never envied her mother at all but she envied her now; envied her simple, relentless faith, a faith that suddenly seemed impossibly naïve this November morning in 1960 on the edge of a new frontier that somehow didn't seem all that new anymore.

Jesus Christ, Jesus Christ.

"Since when did my best friend become 'that woman'?" Annette said, her voice low, confessional.

"What?"

"You better get some sleep," she said, arms stiff at her sides now, fists balled like one of those Irish step dancers that performed at the church last Saint Patrick's Day.

Gerry rubbed his eyes; rubbed and rubbed. He did it all the time. That man could rub out anything. "Christ, I can't believe I have to go to work in a couple hours. You'd think Nixon would have the decency to concede so we could all get a good night's sleep." He bent over and kissed her Jackie-like hair.

In the living room, Annette checked on Michael and David, sleeping foot-to-foot on opposite ends of the couch. After she'd returned from Alice's and settled the children in Gerry actually *had* pulled the fuse supplying current to the basement. People shuffled upstairs, glanced in horror at their watches, and stumbled out to their cars. Joe had called not long ago to report that they'd pumped Alice's stomach and needed to keep her for observation at least 24 hours. He would stay in the waiting room and call them in the morning.

Annette headed for Timmy's room next; replacing the crocheted blanket her mother had made over her son's scissoring legs before looking in on Colleen. The child lay on her side, back to the door. "Where have all the flowers gone," she sang, making shadow puppets of her hands on the wall in the dim light. "Long time passing ..."

Annette sat down on the side of the bed. "What are you still doing up?"

Colleen flipped over to face her. "I don't know, Mommy." The child pressed her hands to her temples and squeezed her eyes shut; as if trying to get a better take on all the interference going on inside her head. "This is a test of the emergency broadcast system," she said. "This is only a test."

Jesus Christ, Jesus Christ.

Annette slipped off her dress and stockings, dropped them on the floor, scooted out of her girdle, and climbed into bed. "OK if I sleep with you?"

Colleen turned over and melted into her mother's torso.

Annette turned off the nightstand light.

Colleen patted her mother's bouffant. "Go to sleep now, Mommy. When you wake up, Jack will be president."

Rose

Irony

She did not know what to make of him.

From her perch on the piano bench in the sitting room of her brother Joseph's house in Waynesburg, New York, she watched him out of the corner of her eye. He stood in the foyer; stooped over to prevent his head from grazing the ceiling, a hand-knit navy scarf obscuring his mouth. The hair spiking out his nose had iced over. He huffed beneath the scarf; stamping his boots, brushing snow from his mittened hands, and gazing down at her sideways across the horsehair couch and chairs and spindly walnut table. His eyes were soft and brown and over-sized, like a cow's.

"Rose," her brother said.

She snapped the lid on the console piano she'd insisted on taking with her from her childhood home despite her father's opposition shut. (They had spoiled her—everyone said so—it explained everything.) Inhaling a breath of dignity she did not feel; she rose. Her hand flew to her throat to caress her mother's broach. With her index finger she traced the raised filigree profile embedded there. She longed to pop it open to retrieve the tiny hank of golden hair nestled within, and tickle the wishbone of her cheek with it as her mother once had. It was all she had left.

"Rose," her brother repeated, and she retrieved the wayward hand. She clasped them both together in front of her and assumed the position of the good girl she had always strived, but not always succeeded, to be.

"This is Victor Trambeaux," Joseph said. He swept his arm through the air like the maitre d' at the French restaurant in Albany Allen had whisked her away to that long afternoon of their courtship, before her father caught wind of their plans. She should have married him on the spot, right there at City Hall as he begged. God would have understood; she was almost sure. They could have married for real in the Church after Allen converted. He would do anything for her, he said; and everything. His emphasis on that word had left her trembling.

Victor Trambeaux yanked off his scarf and matching cap, bowed his head, and studied the floor like a row of sums. She had never seen such large feet. To muzzle the silence wailing around them she stepped forward, extended her hand, and opened the small, sculpted bud of her mouth—her best feature—that had inspired her name. To her surprise, her mother's voice—calm and certain and with only the barest whiff of her parents' brogue— spoke in her behalf. "My pleasure," it said.

His hand enveloped hers with a not unpleasant pressure as his eyes continued to examine the oddity of his feet.

Joseph beamed, swollen in the corner.

His wife, Marta, tottered out of the kitchen grasping a tarnished silver tray of coffee and her specialty pinwheel cookies filled with raisins and dates. "Welcome to you, Victor Trambeaux," she said, placing the tray on the table. Her hands buzzed through the air; engorged dueling hummingbirds. "Come set a while and have a sweet."

Rose lay in bed watching the flame from the milk carriage burn its way along the dark street outside her window; ricochet off the dormered ceiling. She had taken to awakening hours before dawn; unable to fall back asleep; consumed by a litany of regrets. She wiggled in the narrow feather bed until she had sufficiently swaddled herself in the quilt Marta had sent her for her sixteenth birthday. The quilt she had slept in blissfully every night back in Braeburn. Before mother died, her brother Raymond took over the farm, and her father decided to make a full-time job of destroying her future.

After a while, the shadows on the wall coalesced into a moving picture show of her life. She watched as images of her mother— stooped over the egg house in her baggy woolen coat, irreverent corkscrews of hair springing off her forehead; churning butter between muslin-gowned knees; rocking and knitting at the fire, ears poised to capture every note of her only daughter's etudes— reeled in her head. She could see herself bent over her desk at the schoolhouse. Dipping her pen into the inkwell and scratching out sums; rising tall to recite Longfellow, Emerson, and Dickenson; and even that most revered of Shakespeare sonnets:

Shall I compare thee to a summer's day?
Thou art more lovely and more temperate ...

Her longtime teacher, Miss Williams' vigorous nodding the best applause she would ever receive; Miss Williams, who strolled with Rose across the schoolyard during recess day in and day out painting faraway worlds with the brush of her tongue. Worlds where women marched in the streets to win the vote, wiped out disease, wrote novels, and argued the law. Tantalizing, secular, evil worlds, light-years away from Braeburn.

"Teacher's pet," Allen teased, after finally gathering the courage to speak to her at all; he later confessed. Walking home from school that day three years ago when she'd glanced up, caught her breath, and found herself really taking him in for the first time; this childhood friend and neighbor, closer to her own age than any of her older brothers. They'd grown up together playing hide and seek in the silos, sledding, skating, and swimming in the frigid hole where the river turned its prodigal back on its source for good. Once, when she was nine, Allen had plucked her out of the ice just in time. He dragged her back to his house and let her steam-dry by the fire to avoid her father's wrath for venturing where forbidden. With his piano-player fingers he fed her splinters of his mother's brittle pilfered from a tin hidden above the coat cupboard in the foyer. She hadn't thought a thing about it, but now. He stood beside her a half-foot taller, his jaw grown square and prickly, green eyes merry; full lips curled in a smile that seemed to imply a whiff of something sweet and secret between them.

The stain of a blush crept across her pale cheeks. She bowed her head.

And now the lights on the wall shifted again, months ahead. To find Allen and Rose traversing the river bank hand in hand, a picnic basket swinging in the light May breeze. Scrambling down on the flat, mossy rocks to lay out the blanket and the lunch his mother had packed them: a bundle of cold chicken and a jar of pickled beets. Potato salad and a thermos of lemonade and half an apple pie he had pilfered from the pantry. They chewed in silence; watching the water foaming over the dove gray rocks as if they had never seen so fascinating a sight. Until Allen vaulted to his feet, plucked a bouquet of violets from the loamy shore, knelt down, and offered it to Rose. Lifting her hand to his mouth and pressing his lips against its sinewy surface.

She gasped at the unexpected jolt of pleasure. There were violets everywhere.

He laughed. Then he lifted her face to his and kissed her hard on the lips. Later she could not even wager how much time passed before she came to her senses.

Would Victor ever kiss her, she wondered, pressing her cheek into the flannel pillowslip as if trying to cushion the prickly thought of it. They were to be married, Joseph said. He had asked for her hand, although he had not asked *her*. A point she had tried to raise with her brother.

Joseph had made a little stop sign of his palm. "He is a good man, Rose. A simple, decent, country man; honest as the day is long."

"A Catholic man; you mean," she said. She could not seem to help herself. It was Miss Williams speaking through her this time. She seemed, these days, but a mouthpiece for other people's voices.

"You need a husband, Rose," said Joseph, in his gentle, sales-man voice that had cajoled local farmers to buy more cradles and plows than anyone in the county.

"I could teach," she said. "I have a high school diploma. I wouldn't have to depend on you and Marta."

"It's not the money, Rose." He patted the flap of hair that ill-concealed his prematurely bald scalp and sighed, as if he knew his next words would pain him. "You're high strung, always have been. Just like Mama said."

She turned her back on him then, wrapped her arms around her rib cage and dug what was left of her nails into the bone.

"Rose," Joseph said, not unkindly. He was her favorite, only seven years older. Back in Braeburn when they were young, he had dragged her around on her sled; taught her to ride their old mare, Lucy. His hand touched down lightly on her shoulder before springing away as if singed. "You need a man to take care of you—ballast; a family, children, someone to love."

She gulped back the words that came rushing up her throat like a kind of sickness she could not control; her *own* words this time, true words: *I had someone to love.*

She paused, and swallowed them back. "I don't love him, Joseph," she said.

He did not appear to hear her. "You will be a great mother, Rose. You can have the children Marta and I could not, bring us all the joy that's been missing in our lives."

She reached under her pillow and drew out the letter she'd taken to storing there. Her father's words disguised in her brother Raymond's scratchy script. Daddy had never learned to write but he knew all too well how to dictate. She ran her fingers over the single white page embellished with a raised silver *MC*; mother's stationary. Still too dark outside to read, but she had memorized the contents:

Dear Rose,

It's been a long, cold winter here. Rory Inman froze to death in the fields when his horse caught his leg in the fence. Carrie Paulson lost her baby girl Edna to the measles. Raymond has built a new chicken house and taken up selling eggs in town.

I thought you would want to know that Allen Peters has engaged himself to a distant cousin in Albany.

We are all grateful to be well and hope to find you the same.

As always,

Your father

She stuffed the letter back under the pillow. Marveling at the ease with which her father mixed word of Raymond's new enterprise with limbs, dead babies, the eggs of chickens, and shattered dreams. She reached out and pressed her palm against the cold window; kept it there long after her teeth began to chatter, as if coaxing the icy dawn down the tunnel of her wrist, her forearm, her shoulder, her breast; to have its way with her heart.

She did not think her spine had ever stood as straight as it did now, flush against the couch in Joseph's sitting room. Victor sat still as a corpse at her side. The clock on the mantel boomed in the stillness as she watched the frail second-hand crawl across its moon face. *Mother Mary help me*, she prayed in her head, over and over. Still, Victor sat clenching and unclenching his swarthy hands. He was nearly her age; Joseph claimed, but looked at least a decade older. As an only child he had been deferred from the draft to run the family farm after his father died last year.

"Joseph said you had something to ask me," she blurted at last, unable to bear it any longer.

He cleared his throat, rose, bent over, and tried to kneel but his large limbs knocked into the coffee table upsetting the cream. Flustered, he stood; misshapen giant's foot catching an already unstable table leg and upturning it on its side. His feet slipped out from under him; his elbows flapping in the air akimbo; and he landed on his bottom with a thud that rattled the china on its rack and in her teeth.

"Mercy," she said, darting to his side, and kneeling down.

"I'm so sorry," he said. "You must think I'm some kind of fool. It's just that I'm so nervous, and you're so lovely, I …"

"Shhhh." She had never heard him string so many words together. His voice was deep, with a bit of a French accent evoking the comforting scent of Miss William's lavender perfume, the moments when she'd inexplicably launch into that exotic language. Rose had always wanted to study French but her after-school farm chores prevented it. Maybe Victor could teach her.

He stared up at her then; straight into her eyes for the first time with a look so lost and pleading she might have cried as she'd been longing to all day. For no reason at all her mind drifted back to the French restaurant that day in Albany. They'd sat among smartly dressed city folks at a candlelit table set with linen napkins and ponderous silver. As if born to the good life Allen ordered bowls of fragrant onion soup topped with melted cheese followed by goblets of chocolate mousse. In a corner by the multi-paned window a man played a stringed instrument Rose had never seen before. A cello they called it, carved from exquisite varnished wood, its back curved unnervingly like a woman's beneath her chemise. Well, she was done with that fairy tale.

She gazed down on Victor. He was not Allen. She did not love him. But he was a simple man, a country man, a good man. *Thy will be done*, she whispered in her head, addressing the God of her childhood. The God to whom, prior to Allen, she had pledged her devotion. The God who had seen her through her brothers' deaths, her mother's loss, her father's tirades. The God she'd nearly forsaken for the elusive pleasures of this world.

For the first time in months the picture she carried of Allen in her mind—the one his father had taken at his graduation with him sitting on a chair in a suit and tie, hair slicked back and eyes boring into you—began to fade back into the ether from which it sprang.

Marta scurried in, breathless and wringing her hands. "What on earth," she said, taking in the scene on the floor.

A sound whistled in Rose's throat; a sound she felt hard-pressed to identify. A sound she hadn't heard herself make in an awfully long time.

To her astonishment, Victor threw back his head and laughed, too.

They married in the middle of May at Saint Andrew's in Waynesburg. Victor's cousin Maurice and Marta stood up for them. Her father came up for the wedding but Raymond could not leave the farm. Her three other brothers had died of scarlet fever one by one, year in and year out—even though mother had never stopped speaking of them as if they still lived; setting places for them at supper—along with her stillborn sister, June.

Some neighbors of Joseph's attended along with Victor's mother, Annette, who had moved into a little square house down the road on their property in Lauraville to make room for the newlyweds. Annette's sister Andrea, her daughters and their husbands and children, and Victor's godparents who lived several miles from the Trambeaux farm all came. Victor's paternal aunts and uncles still lived outside Montreal and could not make the journey.

Rose dragged her eyes away from the mocking violets embroidering the jade grass outside the church window and took her father's arm.

He walked her down the aisle in excruciating slow motion, rheumatism locking up his knees at every other step, kissed her cheek as decorum dictated, and handed her over to Victor. She searched his face in vain for the approval she naively expected to find but he only turned abruptly away. He rubbed his palms together in front of him as he hobbled back to the pew as if washing his hands of her once and for all. She might have been back in school the way she repeated the vows Father LaCroix recited. She kissed Victor as instructed. She did not meet his eyes.

The wedding party and guests retired to Joseph's where Marta had a cold lunch of boiled ham, stewed tomatoes, deviled eggs, and homemade rolls waiting. Victor's mother provided the wedding cake, a three-layer affair with boiled frosting decorated with miniature daisies that matched Rose's bouquet and the flecks of gold in her eyes. She plucked at the bunched up waist of Marta's wedding dress that no amount of altering could force to conform to the longer, leaner contours of Rose's frame. At last she slid a knife into the cake's creamy folds. She prayed that God might spare her from asking too much of this life, from the Devil's Food greed still flowing at the center of her own dark nature.

Children raced through the house and out into the yard. After a while they rolled up the carpet and cranked up the Victrola Joseph had bought Marta for Christmas and danced to *You Made Me Love You* and *Alexander's Ragtime Band* and *Pack Up Your Troubles in Your Old Kit Bag*. To her astonishment Victor proved a handy dancer; spinning and twirling her round the floor with a light assurance that belied the embarrassment of his frame and feet. Rose followed him tirelessly, hoping to stave off the inevitable reality of their wedding night until Marta ended the festivities with a piercing whistle that halted the revelers.

"Time to throw the bouquet, Rose," she said.

Returning from the hen house with a basketful of gritty eggs, Rose paused a moment on the steps leading up the back doorway. A sudden dizziness washed over her. The chickens were hers. She could milk a cow, of course, but she had a way with chickens and now, mistress of her own coop, could even raise the axe and chop off a head when the time came without incident. Hoisting a hatchet with ease; pinning a neck to a pine stump. Reciting a Hail Mary slowly and surely, even as the beheaded fowl hopped about seconds more, controlled from afar by its phantom brain. Mother would be proud.

After a while she threw back her head and drank in the muggy, late August breeze that bore the promise of Lake Champlain. A scent she had already come to identify with summer after two years but miles from its banks. An aroma that recalled Victor, surprising her with an overnight visit there for her birthday in June, the honeymoon they'd never had.

They'd stayed in the vacant home of his dead father's cousin twice removed, away on a trip to Saratoga to visit his son. They bathed in the frigid water, helplessly swatting the black flies suckling their tender flesh. Later, after dinner, itchy and sunburned, they lounged in Adirondack chairs in the moist air over a pitcher of cold tea and a bowl of wild strawberries. Watching sailboats cut through the chop gleaming like frosted iron beneath a wanton sun that refused to set. Rose tried once again to prod Victor into remembering the language of his birth, the language his mother insisted he renounce; the language his parents had spoken only to each other. A secret bedroom language he had not been privy to.

"Parlez-vous Francais," he said, tickling her bare feet resting against his knees. "That is it. I don't even know what it means."

Lazy as children, giddy with unfamiliar idleness (Victor had talked his godfather into the following morning's milking in an unprecedented fashion); they tumbled into bed at last. And Rose, all tangled up in the midnight light, lips stained with strawberries, had opened to her husband in a way that had not happened before or since. The baby she knew she was carrying had been conceived that night.

In the kitchen, she set the eggs on the edge of the sink and lifted a tea towel from the bread rising on the counter. She had just floured her hands to knead it when the doorbell rang. "For heaven's sake," she said, aloud, wiping her hands on her apron before heading for the door and attempting to stuff tendrils of hair back into the net she used to rein her wayward tresses in.

She was not dressed for visitors. Whoever could be calling in the middle of the day, in the middle of the week; she fretted?

She did not know what to make of him.

He stood on the threshold taller than ever but with shoulders grown wider and a heavier jaw; eyes that matched his uniform still merry despite the dark brows that had, in consternation, stitched themselves together all of a piece across his forehead.

"I am back," Allen said.

Back, she repeated in her head, not knowing he had gone.

Her thoughts chugged away from her. It wasn't until her eyes fell below his waist that she noticed the cane he carried in his left hand, biting into the slatted wood of the porch and drawing her attention to the peg leg jutting out the hem of his pants. It wasn't until she saw that false limb that it dawned on her what he meant, where he was back from.

She couldn't say how he ended up seated at their kitchen table or how she came to brew coffee and set out plates of gingerbread from yesterday's supper. She could not remember speaking or moving but there he sat, Allen, her childhood friend, her alternate future, broken like a beloved childhood toy. He talked incessantly about how he'd shipped out soon after she left with a half dozen boys they'd known. How it gave him a sense of purpose after he'd lost his. His voice trailed off.

(She should not allow him to talk of this, she knew she should not, but still, she could not speak. Her tongue as paralyzed as the day she watched her mother bleed to death in a vain attempt to pass her final son from a collapsed womb.) Allen spoke of how they died, the other boys they'd known. Blown to bits they could not gather up enough of to bury. The word "smithereens." How lucky he'd been.

His voice cracked wide open on that last part and he bit into his fist. She had never seen him cry. Not even when his older brother cut off the tip of his ear lobe that time trying to give him a haircut in the barn.

She handed him a tea towel. Her palm made little circles across his back.

What with both her brothers too old and Victor deferred, the war had seemed a distant, unlikely affair in the papers and the few moving pictures she'd seen; grainy and dreadful. Hopelessly romantic in ways only stories seen from vast, safe distances can ever be. The weight of her own naiveté and self-centeredness descended on her as she sunk into the chair beside him.

"And your wife?" she asked.

He mopped his face with the towel. "My wife?"

"You were engaged to a cousin in Albany, my father wrote me …"

"What in the world?" he said. "I shipped out not long after you left, Rose. I couldn't think of what else to do when you wouldn't answer my letters. I was going to be drafted anyway and I figured I might just as well. Why didn't you answer my letters?"

"Letters," she repeated. Her stunned mind rummaged for the proper word to describe the situation in which she now found herself. She recalled the story Miss Williams had read them about a poor young woman who had nothing to give her husband at Christmas. She sold her beautiful hair to buy him a chain for his watch; meanwhile he sold his watch to buy combs for her hair. *Irony*, Miss Williams called it. Rose thought about the letters her brother obviously had intercepted, and the letter her father had written to carry his lie. Irony. She had never before partaken of that word in her own life but now felt certain she would taste it repeating on her until the day she died.

"Rose," Allen sputtered. He took her hand "Are you happy?"

For the first time since he'd arrived she thought of Victor. He would be cutting hay, still; navigating fields gleaming and braided with it, the sun a lucky penny in the sky. He and the hands he'd hired for harvest would be heading in for dinner directly and she hadn't even put on the potatoes.

"Victor is a good man," she began, reciting Joseph's lines. The script she had somehow agreed to.

"Rose," he said, lowering his voice. "I could still take you with me. I *know* you still love me. I *know* you didn't choose this."

"Allen, don't," she said, rising.

He caught her wrist. "We don't have to live in this world. Jesus, Rose, it's not even *real*. We can sail across the sea and start all over. There are other worlds. Places where none of this would matter one bit. I've *seen* them."

For a long moment, her thoughts jumped the ship of his words. Cruised out the front door across the atlas Ms. Williams had spread out on the wall in the schoolhouse that had imprinted itself in Rose's brain. With what determination had she stabbed straight pins into that map at eleven years old: Paris and London and Rome.

"I'm married, Allen," she whispered. Her hand subconsciously slipped into her apron pocket to caress her still flat abdomen.

He pushed up out of the chair, lips clamped shut; the little muscle at the side of his jaw flexing.

She followed him to the door.

On the threshold he turned and met her eyes. "It was supposed to be me," he said. "I wish it had been me."

She watched him hurry out to the waiting carriage and driver she had not noticed before, moving far too fast for his severed limb. She shut the door behind her.

In the kitchen she stoked up the stove, peeled the potatoes, pumped water into the pot, set them to boil, and cut the leftover pot roast into long strips. Stirring the gravy his parting words echoed in her head and for the first time she realized they might have a different meaning. She thought he meant it was supposed to be me that married you but now in a sweaty confusion erupting in her solar plexus she realized he might be talking about the shells that took the others instead of him on a battleground somewhere.

The heat of the stove, the smell of the gray meat, Allen's hollow, pleading eyes, a world larger and more indiscriminate than she had ever have imagined, ambushed her. Covering her mouth, she made it to the sink just in time.

Colleen

Signs

Here's another reason why I hate my brother Timmy. My best friend Laurie and I built these snow houses today in my backyard so the good cloud people would want to come down and visit. The houses are pretty small but the good cloud people are probably invisible so size doesn't really even matter. We built 10 houses. Each house has two rooms—a bedroom and a kitchen. In the bedroom, we molded a little snow bed. In the kitchen, we made a little stove and sink and a table with two chairs. We left the roofs off the houses so we could move things in and out easier and also so the good cloud people could lie on their backs and look up at the stars in case they got lonesome for home. We stole some old socks my mother uses to polish shoes and laid them on the beds, and pretended they were tiny sleeping bags. We put one walnut and one butterscotch candy my Grandpa gave me at Christmas on each kitchen table so they'd have something to eat.

Then, who comes waddling over in his giant snowsuit like a baby abdominal snowman but my little brother Timmy. He hurls himself backward on top of the houses like he's trying to make an angel when all he's really trying to do is squish them. So I start screaming at him and he starts screaming at me and my mother opens the window and starts screaming at *both* of us like she always does when *he* does something wrong.

"What's going on, you two?" she screams.

Laurie rolls her eyes at me, digs in her pocket, pulls out a red jawbreaker, bites off the cellophane, and pops it in her mouth. I roll my eyes back. "He ruined our houses," I scream up at my mother. I cup my hands around my mouth so the scream won't escape.

"I'm sure he didn't mean it! He doesn't know any better, Colleen. Come on up here, Timmy, and play with your sled."

Mommy always says the same thing when Timmy has ruined something—that he doesn't know any better. I wonder if there is something wrong with his brain. I try to imagine his brain. I think it must look like a dark woods full of pricker bushes and poison ivy and spiders. It must smell like a pile of old wet towels mixed up with wet dog and worms. Now Timmy gets this stupid little smirk on his face—the same one he always gets when mommy rescues him—and sticks out his tongue.

"Ewwwww!" Laurie cries. Green snot has started streaming out of Timmy's nose. He sticks out his tongue and licks it up in a truly disgusting fashion. Then he stomps off.

Laurie holds out her mitten and hands me a jawbreaker. I take off my mitten with my teeth so I can unwrap it and pop it in my mouth. It practically sets my whole mouth on fire and makes my eyes water. (I really don't like the way jaw breakers taste but I like the idea of them, so I eat them anyway.) We kneel down in the snow and start digging up all the houses and the candies and the nuts and the socks and building them back up all over again from scratch. Daddy and Timmy come sliding down the hill on *my* red saucer that no one even asked me if they could use which is just typical. So I close my eyes and pray for the Virgin Mary to stop me from wanting to take my brother's head in my hands and bash it against the side of the house. I have not made my first Confession yet and if the Commies bomb us or something while we're sleeping I will have to go to hell if I don't stop daydreaming up ways to kill him. But Mother Mary must be busy with some other kid because nothing happens. He is still driving me crazy and I still have murder on my mind.

In bed, I try to remember the words to the Apostles' Creed. I have Catechism tomorrow and Sister Scholastica might pop a quiz on us at any time. If you can't remember the Apostles'

Creed, she takes down the yardstick from over the blackboard and smacks your knuckles with it. It is the only time we get to see her hands. The rest of the time, she keeps them tucked into her black robe. She has hands so white you can see right through them, hands like a dead person at a wake. Brandon Duffy says she keeps a couple of knives up her sleeves, too, but I don't believe him because everyone knows he's a big fat liar. Also I don't think God would let the nuns use knives on us; unless you did something *really* bad like maybe actually kill your baby brother.

"I believe in one God, maker of heaven and earth, and in his only son, Jesus Christ, Our Lord. Born of the father ..."

I just about always get stuck on this part about the birth. The way Jesus got born makes no sense at all. Last summer, Laurie and I found out how babies really get made by the father sticking his penis in the mother. Only Jesus didn't get born that way. As far as I can tell, Jesus' father, Joseph, never did the stick-in thing to Mary. Instead, this angel came down and tapped her on the head with a magic wand or something and presto! Jesus started growing in her stomach like a flower. It doesn't seem fair, if there's this whole other magic way to make babies, for God to make everyone else do this truly disgusting stick-in thing. That is just my opinion but I don't see why everyone can't just get some help from an angel. Maybe if you pray hard enough, and stop going around sinning sins all the time, and become a saint like Joan of Arc, God will give you some kind of break.

I just cannot stop thinking about this. If married people do this stick-in thing, and nuns like Sister Scholastica are married to God, does God ...? It must just make God so sick he wants to puke! I close my eyes and press my hands together and try to think Joan of Arc thoughts and finish the Apostles' Creed.

"... suffered under Pontius Pilot, was crucified, died and was buried ..."

But somehow, my mind starts gallivanting off to the snow houses and the good cloud people maybe coming down for a visit while I am sleeping. They only come when you're asleep which is kind of sad. I have another sad thought—Laurie isn't making her first Communion with me because she's a Presbyterian. Sister and Grammy both say that means she can't get into heaven *ever* because she never even got baptized in the One Holy Catholic and Apostolic Church to get rid of her original sin. You don't even have to do anything to get original sin except be born. So no matter how good Laurie is, they will make her go to Limbo, which is where they also send babies who die before they get baptized. Limbo looks a little like heaven, except for God isn't walking around there handing out his grace, which is a *big* difference. You can't be happy forever without grace. If I were Laurie, I wouldn't even bother trying to be good.

I wonder if the baby seed that died in my mother last summer went there after they flushed it down the toilet. If it did, it will have to live all alone in Limbo until Laurie gets there. Sometimes I wish I didn't have to be Catholic and remember all these prayers and say goodbye forever to my best friend when I die. But then I cross myself and push these devil thoughts away and recite the "Act of Contrition" to myself. It starts like this: "Oh my God, I am heartily sorry." But then I start thinking how last week in Catechism, Sister called on Brandon Duffy to stand up and say the Act of Contrition and here's what he said: "Oh my God, I am *hardly* sorry." We all just busted out laughing and Brandon got the yardstick again and had to go stand in the hall. But now, every time I go to say the Act of Contrition, all I can think of is, "Oh my God, I am *hardly* sorry." Like Brandon Duffy has planted some kind of devil's seed in my brain.

So I give up trying to say it. Instead I make a list in my head of ways to improve myself. I will love my baby brother no matter what cockamamie thing he does next. I will not sass back my mother no matter what cockamamie thing she tells me to do. I will act self-reliant and set the table and make my bed every single day. Then I say a prayer for Laurie and the baby seed and the baby bird we buried alive because my mother said it was about to die anyway which just goes to show you that just because people are grownup does not mean they have any idea what they're doing. I pray for the people from the land of good clouds to visit while I am sleeping and leave a sign they came, a sign that they are winning over the bad clouds maybe, anything at all to give us something to keep us going down here.

The next morning, before I go to the bus stop, I race down the hill in my backyard to look at the snow houses. Everything looks exactly the same except for two walnuts are suspiciously missing. My heart starts beating fast and my whole body tingles, like when your foot falls asleep and then finally wakes up. I charge up the hill and into the street with my books and my lunch box, and run down to the corner as fast as I can. I can see the yellow school bus coming and if I miss it one more time, I am in deep dog doodoo as my father likes to say. They call school buses yellow but they are actually orange; no one I have asked knows why. I get on the bus and find a seat next to Mary Jane Ferris.

"Hi," she says, hanging her head like someone who just got slapped. Laurie thinks Mary Jane is stuck up but I think she's just afraid of other kids. Her mother never lets her play with anyone and keeps her locked in the house like a prisoner. When she does let her out, she yells at her to put on a hat when it's hardly even cold. Then, some gang of big kids comes and spits on her and swipes her hat and runs away with it. So you can see why she's just about afraid of her own shadow. Still, sitting next to Mary Jane means I won't have to talk and that's exactly what I want—a little peace and quiet to help me think over the cloud people's sign. While I think, I lean my forehead against the cool bus window and squint so the sunshine on the snow passing blends together in this pink and blue and white rush, like a ballet tutu.

When I get to school, I go to my classroom and sit down at my desk next to Laurie's; lean over and whisper the good news in her ear. She bites her lip and says nothing. It just about drives me crazy when she does that.

"So, what do you think?" I ask.

"Well, I guess it *could* be a sign. But it could also be that someone stole them. Some brother or some big kid or some squirrel. We need to get proof."

"How can we get proof?"

But the bell rings and in comes Mrs. Appleby. She makes us all shut up and starts handing back our arithmetic tests from Friday which is no way to start a Monday morning if you ask me.

We are lying on Laurie's bedroom floor cutting out Princess Grace paper-doll clothes from a book Laurie got for Christmas. Princess Grace used to be a movie star but then a prince fell in love with her and she got to be a princess. Laurie's sister, Ellen, who just turned 15, pokes her head in the room.

"What are you two little nut balls doing now?"

Ellen has a body like a Christmas tree. She hates our guts because she's going through a very difficult stage. She has gooey pimples on her face plus she's fat so she can't help but take it out on us. Now she lumbers over and picks up the paper Princess Grace dress Laurie just cut out. A shiny green gown with a tight waist, a giant skirt, white fur at the wrists and neck, and a big hood trimmed with white fur. It has gold princess hair drawn around the inside of the hood like a ruffle; with ears tucked into the hair, and two giant emeralds in the ear lobes.

"Looky here," says Ellen. "Look at this precious little hood. Does it detach? It must detach. Let's see." And she rips off the hood with a quick twist of her wrist. "Oooops. What do you know; I guess it doesn't detach. My mistake. What a crying shame."

"Mom!" Laurie screams. "Mom!"

"Scream all you want pecker head. She's not home. *I'm* taking care of you, little sister. Aren't you the lucky one?"

Laurie beats on Ellen's legs with her fists. Her moon face turns pink as strawberry ice cream. She tries to bite Ellen's leg, but Ellen just laughs and kicks her off like a dog.

"I'm telling!" Laurie screams. "You're gonna get it!"

"Telling what? It was just an accident. A simple mistake anyone could make." She laughs some more and lumbers away.

After she leaves, Laurie gets up, slams the door, and pulls her desk chair in front of it. She sits back down and punches the floor. "She makes me so mad! I just hate her!"

I know exactly how she feels. In my mind, I start to say the Act of Contrition but it still comes out, as "Oh my God, I am *hardly* sorry" so I decide to change the subject to try and cheer us up. I decide to try to talk again about the sign and getting proof from the good cloud people. "We still haven't figured out a way to tell if they come when we're sleeping," I say.

"Because we *can't.*"

"What?"

"As long as they're outside, we can't prove they came."

"Yeah, well. We can't move the snow houses *inside*. My mother would kill us."

"Here's what we could do, though. We could write them letters asking for a sign and put them under our pillows. Then, on their way back, they could fly down and leave us a sign under our pillows."

"Or, in the letter, we could just tell them that if they take the letter, that will be the sign. Make it easy."

"I don't know. Ellen said a sign has to be something someone leaves, not something someone takes away."

"But Ellen hates our guts. Plus she lies." There was no arguing with that.

"OK. Let's go get some paper. Let's put away these dolls and write some letters."

Here is the letter I write:

Dear Good Cloud People:

We hope you like the houses we made, and the food. If there is some other kind of food you want, we will get it for you. Maybe we could come up and visit you sometime? Things are not going so well down here. Are you anywhere near Limbo? Well, thanks a lot. And please remember to leave a sign.

Yours truly,

Colleen Shea

P.S. Here is some perfume you might like to have called Chanel Number Five. Well, that's all for now.

Here is Laurie's letter:

Dear Good Cloud People:

If you cannot leave us a sign, then take this letter with you. If it is gone, we will know you were here. That will be the sign. Here is some more perfume called Faberge. If you see the bad cloud people, tell them about my sister Ellen. Maybe they will want to come take her. Thank you very much.

Yours truly,

Laurie Wright

We fold up the letters around the tiny sample bottles of perfume we stole from my mother. She used to sell perfume to other mothers but it didn't work out so now she has a whole briefcase of samples stashed away in the back of her closet underneath her sewing. We decide we will each put the letter and the perfume under our pillows every night and wait for a sign.

That night, instead of a sign, I get the bad dream again. The Russians have dropped the bomb. First there is a flash so bright I can't see anything for a couple of seconds. Then the whole sky fills with this gigantic mushroom cloud. Then everything goes dark. I get up out of bed and feel my way down the hall to my parents' room but my parents are missing. I go into Timmy's room, wake him up, and take him by the hand. He starts crying, of course. Plus, we have to stop every few steps so he can pull up his pajama bottoms that always fall down. We walk outside barefoot in the dewy grass. I don't know why it is never winter in my dreams. I keep calling for my parents but it just gets darker and darker until I can't see anything. I mean totally pitch black. I remember this movie we saw at school about "radar-active" fallout that comes raining down after the bomb explodes to kill any people it didn't get the first time. So I turn around and try to find my way back to the house but I can't see anything and Timmy keeps tripping and blubbering.

I wake up and open my eyes and the shadows on the wall bounce around like a cartoon mushroom on one of those Green Giant TV commercials. My heart goes beat, beat, beat like a Ricky Ricardo bongo drum. I am lying on my side with my back to the door afraid to turn over. What if I turn around and there is this bad cloud person standing over me holding a hatchet and wanting to kill me because he found out I gave the good cloud people food and perfume? After about a hundred hours, I turn over very slowly and … look. But all I see are shadows dancing around like the flames of a campfire on my closet door. I sit up and lift up my pillow. I squeeze the folded note in my fist; feel the cool, hard perfume bottle inside. I press it to my hot cheek. It is almost morning by the time I fall back to sleep.

After school, I put on my snow clothes and boots and walk up the hill to Mrs. Brownson's house. Mrs. Brownson lives in this giant house made of stones at the end of our street. If you look at the stones up close, you can see chips of gold and silver and even some diamonds in them. If you squint your eyes at them on a sunny day they glimmer like jewels. When I was little, I used to think Mrs. Brownson was a queen in a castle and we were her subjects. But then when I turned six, I found out she got rich by marrying this man who got rich by buying up a bunch of steel mills and then dying.

So I go up the walk to Mrs. Brownson's house and climb up all these steps, all the way up to the big wooden door that looks like a castle door in a book of fairy tales. I scramble up on the black iron railing and reach over to the middle of the door to grab the heavy knocker with its mean lion face. It takes me a while to get my balance right. I grab the handle and knock, knock, knock on the door and wait. Pretty soon I see Mrs. Brownson's silver head looking out this tiny window in the door so I scream out: "Mrs. Brownson! It's me, Colleen Shea!" And she must hear me because she turns her head to where I'm kind of clinging to the railing and almost smiles. I know Mrs. Brownson is not the world's biggest smiler, so even a little smile goes a long way and means she is glad to see me. Daddy says she hardly ever smiles on account of she is German and they don't believe in it. Only she is not the same kind of German who went around killing everybody in sight during World War II, my mother always points out. It seems there are good and bad Germans. Just like cloud people.

"Why, Colleen!" Mrs. Brownson opens the heavy door. "How good of you to visit."

I jump down off the railing and go through the door and take off my mittens and shake her hand.

"You're just in time for tea. Eric, come and take Miss Colleen's things. And set another place for tea, if you please."

Eric is Mrs. Brownson's servant. He always wears the same thing—a black suit—like a magician. He is very tall but he has tiny feet and wears pointy black shoes. He has a mustache that looks like he drew it on with a magic marker. He combs his hair straight back on his head and pastes it down with Brill Cream.

"Miss, Colleen," he says, and does this fancy little bow. He takes my coat and my mittens. I sit down and he helps me pull off my boots so I won't leave puddles on the shiny wood floors. Mrs. Brownson has already seated herself back in the parlor—I can see the top of her curly, bluish hair peeking over the straight-back sofa that has wooden legs with hooves on the bottom like a horse. Quietly, I take a little running start and slide in my stocking feet across the gleaming floor, coming to a stop just before I hit this giant rug. The floor is so smooth and fast I never even get splinters. I tuck my hair behind my ears and walk around the front of the sofa; sit down next to Mrs. Brownson and fold my hands in my lap like a lady.

A low round wooden table with matching hooved legs already has been set for tea with a blue-and-white China tea pot and dishes. On one of the dishes, Eric has placed all different kinds of cookies—sugar, ginger, and round Russian teacakes that look much better than they taste. From far away, the plate looks like a giant flower. I notice right away a row of lemon bars—my favorites.

"Some sweets, dear?" asks Mrs. Brownson. "Go ahead and help yourself."

I take a napkin and tuck it in the neck of my sweater. Then I take a little plate and on it I put two lemon bars and one macaroon—so as not to appear too greedy. Then Edward comes with another teacup and Mrs. Brownson pours me a little tea and fills the rest of the cup up with milk from a matching blue-and-white pitcher. The late afternoon sun streams through the high windows turning everything in the room bright yellow, even the giant black piano that is so beautiful it makes me just want to cry. Mrs. Brownson catches me looking at it.

"Would you like to play this afternoon, dear?"

She likes for me to play the piano even though I don't know how and have to fake it because once she had a daughter who played the piano but then grew up and got killed in a plane crash. But I don't want to play the piano today. Today I have more important business with Mrs. Brownson.

"No thank you, Mrs. Brownson."

"Well, how have you been, dear? How are your studies coming?"

When Mrs. Brownson says "studies" she means school. I figured that out a long time ago. "Pretty good," I say. "I had all A's on my last report card except for arithmetic. I got a B in arithmetic."

"Very good, Colleen." She pats my knee. "And what have you been reading?"

"I am reading some Nancy Drew books my cousin Alice who is eleven let me borrow. Nancy Drew is a girl detective; a very smart and brave one. I might want to be a detective when I grow up if they won't let me be an astronaut."

"You are a very smart girl," says Mrs. Brownson. "You can do anything." She looks away, across the room to a little table full of pictures in golden and silver frames; pictures of her daughter who died. And some other pictures of her son Peter who grew up and moved to Seattle and never came back.

"Mrs. Brownson," I say, clearing my throat and brushing cookie crumbs off my fingers and on to the plate in my lap. "I have a very big favor to ask you."

She seems to snap out of it then and turns her head back to me. "A favor? But of course, dear. What is it?"

I put down my plate on the table and fold my hands in my lap. "Mrs. Brownson," I begin. "I was wondering how much room you have in your bomb shelter? I was wondering if you might have room for a few more people when they drop the bomb."

"My bomb shelter," she repeats, staring into space like she is in some kind of dream. "More room for whom?"

"For me and my family. Just my mother and my father and my brother and me. None of us are fat or anything. We wouldn't need much room."

Mrs. Brownson just looks at me for a little while. Then she puts her hand on my forehead like she is checking to see if I have a fever. She brushes away my bangs. "I think we would have enough room. I'm almost sure we would. Would you like to go take a look?"

This is going a lot better than I had hoped. "I would like that very much."

"Eric," cries Mrs. Brownson, "fetch our coats. Miss Colleen and I are going on an expedition."

I shove the rest of a lemon bar in my mouth and Edward brings all my clothes back again and helps me put them on. He helps Mrs. Brownson into a brown fur coat and high-heeled boots trimmed with brown fur and a matching muff. We go outside and down the steps and around and down to the driveway. Half way up the driveway toward the garage, Mrs. Brownson puts a key in the lock of this secret door covered with ivy vines that leads to the bomb shelter. We go through the door into this secret passageway that smells like a basement and then through this other door and down these stairs into the bomb shelter. Mrs. Brownson lights a kerosene lamp on a table in the middle of this room about half the size of a real basement. It feels cold, but not like freezing cold. Four metal cots with white-and-gray striped mattresses have been pushed up against the walls. One wall has been completely lined with shelves full of canned food and big jugs of water. "Come," says Mrs. Brownson.

I follow her to a door at one end of the room. Inside are a tiny bathroom with a toilet and a sink with a plug. "You have to fill it up with water yourself," she says. "If they drop the bomb, there won't be any water." She shows me a small closet filled with more bottles of water, a first aid kit, white sheets, and gray wool blankets. Back in the main room again, I study the food, mostly giant cans of Campbell's soup and peanut butter. Also, small cans of white asparagus. I have never seen or tasted white asparagus but it must be one of Mrs. Brownson's favorite foods in the world because there are like a million cans of it.

"So, what do you think, Colleen?"

"It is a very nice bomb shelter," I say, even though it is the only one I have ever seen except for on TV.

"Well then, you and your family are perfectly welcome to join me," she says. "Only, I don't think there will be any bomb. I really don't think it will happen." She blows out the kerosene lamp; leads me up the stairs by the hand and out into the January air that smells like cold, wet sheets. "Will you come back up for more tea?"

"No, thank you." I look up at the sky. The setting sun has left behind a wavy line of orange with a purple stripe through it, like a piece of ribbon candy. It is later than I thought. "Thank you Mrs. Brownson," I say. "Thank you very much."

I start running down the street but a film of ice has begun to form again on the road, forcing me to slow down. Well, at least we will have some place to go when they drop the bomb. We will just have to share cots and learn to like white asparagus.

For four nights, Laurie and I have been putting our gifts to the good cloud people under our pillows before we go to sleep, but still no sign. On Friday, Laurie invites me to sleep over. Maybe if we sleep in the same place it will make it easier for the good cloud people to find us and leave us a sign.

After school, we play paper dolls—Princess Grace and also Sandra Dee. Then Mrs. Wright calls us down to dinner. The Wrights eat dinner in a dining room that looks just like the Cleaver's on TV. Mrs. Wright even wears a dress and a fake strand of pearls. But Mr. Wright doesn't wear a suit, just a sports shirt and slacks. He is always laughing. He looks like Santa Claus must have looked before he got old and grew a beard and got sent to the North Pole.

I sit next to Laurie, right across from evil Ellen. Mr. and Mrs. Wright sit at each end of the table. Everybody starts passing around plates of food.

"Do you like lamb, Colleen?" asks Mrs. Wright.

I am not sure I have ever eaten lamb, but since I am a guest, I say yes, and help myself to a big piece. I spoon a wad of mashed potatoes, which I love, and a small pile of peas, which I hate, on to my plate. I wait for them to say grace but no one does. They just all start digging in. So I say it in my head. I am about to pick up my fork when it hits me. This is *Friday*—the day they killed Jesus. Catholics do not eat meat on Friday if they want to stay out of hell.

"Is lamb a meat?" I ask.

"Yes, Colleen. It's somewhat like beef. Here, have some mint jelly. It brings out the flavor." Mrs. Wright reaches across the table and spoons a blob of bright green jelly on my plate. I take a bite of mashed potatoes and let it dissolve in my mouth, stalling. I know eating meat on Friday is a sin, only I can't remember what kind of sin. If it is a venial sin, then I will only have to go to Purgatory if I die between now and my first confession. But if it is a mortal sin and I die before my first confession, they will make me go to hell. Forever! But if I say I can't eat the lamb, Mrs. Wright won't understand because she's a Presbyterian and only gets to go to Limbo no matter what she eats. She will think I don't *like* the lamb and that would hurt her feelings and be rude which would also be a sin.

"What's the matter Colleen, cat got your tongue?" asks Mr. Wright. He reaches over, tries to tickle me under the arm, and busts out laughing.

"Don't you *like* the lamb, Colleen?" asks Mrs. Wright. "You haven't even tried it?"

"Yeah, don't you like the lamb Colleen?" asks Ellen in that way she has that let's you know she hates you even though she hasn't really said anything bad.

I smile. My heart pounds. I pick up my fork and cut a small piece of lamb and dip it in the jelly the way Laurie does, close my eyes, and pray to the Virgin Mary to save me. They're all looking at me. I put the lamb in my mouth and start chewing. It tastes different from anything else I've ever tasted, but good different. "Delicious," I say, and cut another piece. Now that I have sinned, I might as well eat the whole thing. So I go ahead and finish the scariest dinner of my life, praying to God I will not die before my first confession which is probably also some kind of gigantic sin.

Laurie and I each lie in twin beds across from each other in Laurie's room. I am sleeping in Ellen's bed. Ellen has gone to sleep in the guest room. The house is dark. Everyone else has long since gone to sleep.

"Which do you think is farther away?" I ask. "The land of the good cloud people; or the land of the bad cloud people?"

"The bad cloud people, of course."

Laurie always seems so sure about everything. I wish I could be like that but the truth is; I just don't know how. "Why?"

"Because, if the bad cloud people were closer, they'd be down here bothering us all the time."

But I think maybe they *are* down here all the time, we just can't see them. I think maybe they are hanging around all the time making you hate your brother. Making you steal perfume samples from your Mom and bury baby birds that aren't even dead yet and eat lamb on Fridays. Lying and cheating and yelling and dropping bombs and raining radar-active fallout and poisoning the whole world. "Laurie?"

She doesn't answer. I turn on my back and with both my ears can hear the whoosh of her breathing that proves she has fallen asleep without me. I close my eyes and force myself to think Joan of Arc thoughts. Then I think about the good cloud people. In my mind I can see their icehouses, so blue, and see-through, they seem carved out of smoke. I can see them lying on their beds in their sleeping bags. Light and shy as wisps of moonlight, shadowy eyes flickering. I think about the good cloud people for a long, long time. And I think about this: Laurie will never get into heaven to partake of God's grace no matter what she does or doesn't do. She won't even have a chance to make her first confession and communion. Her life is headed nowhere really; she deserves to have a sign.

After a long time I get up out of bed, pausing after every creek and rustle so as not to wake Laurie. I tiptoe over to her bed. She is curled up on her side, one arm draped over the full moon of her face, her yellow hair spilled across the pillow. Her body rises and falls. Her deep, slow breath hums like the ocean you can hear inside a seashell. I slip my hand under her pillow until I feel it. I pull out the perfume-filled letter and close my fingers around it. Then I tiptoe over to my suitcase on the floor and shove it down under my clothes—all the way to the bottom. I climb back up in bed.

"Oh my God, I am *heartily* sorry," I whisper. Sorry for everything, really. I repeat those words a couple more times in my head to make them stick. I fall asleep before I can even remember the rest of the prayer, which is just typical.

Can You Tell Me Where He's Gone?

Today I am in trouble again for the look on my face. I walk into the kitchen to grab a cup of coffee Mom will only allow me to have exactly three spoonfuls of in my milk. Even though I am almost fourteen and have grown an entire seven inches since September—from five-foot-nothing-to-five-foot-seven—and am hoping to God I have finally achieved my full adult height. So I walk into the kitchen and pour a little milk in this teacup a friend of my parents brought me back all the way from England. This teacup etched with blue bells so delicate you can almost see straight through its curved sides to the bones in your hand, which could be why they call it bone china. I start pouring coffee *over* the milk and Mom creeps over and peers around my shoulder (she can no longer peer over it) until the coffee, of course, spills all over like she has jinxed it or something. So I turn around and almost immediately, she says, "Wipe that look off your face, young lady," before, honest to God, I have even had a chance to fire *the look*. "Wipe up that mess and finish getting ready for church."

I open my mouth to tell her I am ready, but she cuts me off. "Now, Colleen." she says. "That skirt won't do."

Looking at my feet, clutching my tea cup and my hatred for her like a canister of tear gas, I return to my room, my eyes skidding along the hall walls past a collage of pictures of Timmy as a baby, his cheeks painted on and his eyes dusted turquoise by some photographer who maybe never heard of color film or something. In my room, I stand before the full length mirror on my closet door admiring my perfectly beautiful mini skirt, a field of gold sprinkled with tiny pink and orange flowers, just right with pink ribbed tights and a matching poor boy shirt. This perfectly mod outfit my mother has suddenly decided is simply too alluring for me to wear.

I can't believe my mother, I really can't. Anytime I manage to look halfway decent—which is no easy feat, having grown from the smallest to one of the tallest girls in my class so that I am all bones these days without a breast in sight—my mother makes me change. It drives me insane. She only allows me to wear jumpers and, now that it has gotten warm, empire-waisted sundresses that poof out around my flat chest and make me look like one of those hideous dolls people inexplicably crochet to cover toilet paper rolls. Now I climb into one of these, a white eyelet abomination over a purple underskirt complete with—I swear to God—purple streamers. Making eye contact with no one, I grab my black patent leather purse and head for the car like something that has sprung to life and wandered off the top of some giant Easter bonnet or maybe some old person's birthday cake.

In church, I sit watching Father Welch—who has some kind of facial tick and tends to keep sermons short on account of forgetting what he wants to say next—derail once more midway through a convoluted speech about Mary Magdalene. My father says they send priests here to our sleepy little parish for rehabilitation and Father Welch definitely fits the bill. Now he cocks his head and stares off into space for a few minutes. People clear their throats and shuffle in the pews. Someone behind me coughs, as if hoping to rouse him. Father Welch's right eye twitches. Above him the light streams through a stained glass of the Virgin Mary squashing a snake with her bare feet. Her blue eyes sparkle, looking down at him, amused, ruthless. The entire congregation leans forward in their seats, breathless, wondering if somebody should phone in a psychiatrist or the fire department or the Vatican or something. Finally, he smacks himself on the side of the head and folds his hands. "Let us pray," he mumbles. And we know the sermon and his little mental vacation; are over for now.

Waiting in line for communion, I try to keep my eyes off Angela Green's impossibly long and glossy hair. Off her straight back in her navy blue mini skirt and matching vest, her shapely legs in pink tights, her small feet turned out like a duck in ballet position. Her lacy black lashes cast down over her folded hands. Angela Green, a year older than me, is everything I can never possibly hope to become: graceful, sexy, mysterious, and petite. Ensconced like a princess in a fairy tale in her family's enormous white house with black shutters on the green hill beside Riley's Funeral Parlor. She attends the expensive country day school where the kids wear black leotards and blue jeans; write music and poetry, roll their own cigarettes and study dance, the noun variety. Even in line for communion, people leave a little space around her, as though sensing royalty. You half expect them to curtsey, or reach for their instamatic cameras.

My father nudges me from behind, because I have drifted away watching Angela and, mesmerized, forgotten to move up in line. Lurching forward on my new stilt-like legs, I stumble toward the altar, startling Father Welch into a kind of elongated spasm. Angela glides away, oblivious, pausing between each step like a person in a wedding party. My cheeks burn as I stand before Father Welch, waiting, waiting, the eyes of the parishioners scorching the petals of my horrible dress. Waiting, waiting, as he unsuccessfully weeds through the hosts in the chalice for his missing contact lens, pausing now and then to smack himself upside his semi-bald head.

After church, I change immediately into cut-offs and a T-shirt, consider refusing breakfast just to spite them, but, in the end, am too starving to pull it off. I set the table, leveling the look at the linoleum beneath my feet to avoid inciting anyone before I can wolf down a couple of eggs.

Beside me, Timmy splits open his jelly donut and squeezes grape goo directly into his cavernous mouth. "Hey, Colleen," he says, elbowing me. "See-food."

"That's enough," Dad snaps. "Have another egg, Colleen. I can't believe you made Father Welch lose his contact lens like that. Like the poor guy doesn't have enough trouble. I really can't believe it."

"*I* didn't do anything." I struggle to suppress the look, slapping another fried egg on my plate. I pierce the yolk with my fork and let it run all over the white just the way I like it; mop it all up with a piece of toast.

"Isn't there something sacrilegious about a contact lens in the hosts?" Mom asks. "Not to mention unsanitary."

"What if somebody ate it?" asks Timmy. "Maybe Colleen ate it. And now she will grow Father Welch's eyes in her stomach."

"Mom," I say.

"Really, Timmy."

"Well, it's true, though," says Dad. "I mean, it had to go somewhere, right? What if Colleen or someone else *did* swallow it?" He shakes his head like this is one of the saddest thoughts he has ever had to contemplate in his entire life. "Maybe we should take you in for an X-Ray, kiddo."

"I'm sure it's OK," says Mom, taking the tiniest bites of egg white in the world so that it will, as usual, take her a half hour longer than anyone else to finish her breakfast while we all have to sit around watching. "I mean, they're so small, aren't they? I doubt it could do any harm."

"But they're made out of *glass*," says Timmy. "Aren't they made out of glass like glasses?"

"They're awfully expensive." Dad spears another piece of fried ham with his fork. "Maybe Father Welch should offer a reward in the parish bulletin."

"Yeah," says Timmy. "Then, if somebody poops it out, they can at least get some money for it."

Dad laughs like he thinks Timmy has turned into George Carlin or somebody.

Even Mom laughs in her silent way; lips pursed, shoulders heaving.

And I swear to God it takes every inch of self-control I can muster to keep my stone face from dissolving, to keep the look from leveling all of them once and for all.

I am lying under the huge peony bush beside our house, reading a book I stole from my mother called *The Group*, this really scary story about all these very smart women who graduate from college and end up spending all their time having sex with really bad men. I have just gotten to the part where this one woman shows up at this guy's room in New York City ready to have sex. I never knew having sex was this planned. I always figured love would just kind of ambush you and you wouldn't even have to think about whether or not it was the right person or the right time. For once in your life, you wouldn't have to think at all. But, according to this book, it doesn't always happen that way. Not by a long shot.

Now this guy is seducing her right there in his bed in his seedy hotel room in New York City that doesn't even have its own bathroom. And she is getting all excited. Panting and writhing around beneath his fingers. She is ...

"Colleeeeen!"

Does my mother have some kind of holy radar, or what? I slam the book shut and roll over on top of it, my heart racing. The peony petals press their sticky velvet against my cheek. I am suddenly dizzy, intoxicated by their powerful fragrance, enchanted by their dense white petals and hot pink centers.

"Colleen!" comes my mother's voice again from the side screen door, loud enough to wake the revolutionary war soldiers snoozing in their graves in the town cemetery down the street. Loud enough to rock the heavy blossoms on the lilac bush beside the fence. Loud enough to make sure God himself hasn't missed the exact nature of my reading material.

"Coming!" I jump up and stuff the paperback into the front of my shorts and pull my T-shirt down over it. Brushing off the grass I stare at the peonies a moment, squeeze my eyes shut and murmur a silent prayer. I pray that someone, someday, somewhere, will want me like that. Then I cross myself for thinking such thoughts and take off running to help Mom set the table. Before she starts yelling again and all those soldiers leap out of their graves to their feet, grabbing their muskets and going for what's left of their own heads.

In Mr. Chatham's social studies class the next morning the shit really hits the fan, as my father likes to say. Two boys—Kenny Bradford and Jamie Monroe—somehow snuck into school really early and moved his desk and chair out to the middle of the parking lot. Right between Mr. Abram's MG and Mrs. Gillespie's Dodge Dart; which was a pretty crummy thing to do considering Mr. Chatham's like one of the nicest teachers in the whole school, besides Mrs. Jamison, my English teacher.

Anyway, so there we all are waiting for the bell to ring and trying to pretend we don't notice the missing desk and can't see it through the window.

"You think he'll have a nervous breakdown or something?" Laurie leans over and whispers in my ear.

I shake my head no, even though it is not particularly uncommon for teachers at our junior high to have nervous breakdowns. Last year they had to take a substitute science teacher away in a straight jacket when—during a lesson on aero-dynamics—the boys wouldn't quit pelting her with enormous, elaborate, and excessively aero-dynamic paper airplanes. Just last month, Mr. Barnes, the vocal music teacher, locked himself in the bathroom with his metronome and refused to come out. The next day the principal announced over the loud speaker that he'd taken an indefinite sabbatical. "You're an indefinite sabbatical," Kenny Bradford whispered, and got sent to the principal's office.

"Well, what do you think he'll do to them?" Laurie asks.

I shake my head again. I don't like to admit but, really; I have no idea. I only hope it's violent.

"Well, you're not allowed to hit kids anymore, I know that," says Laurie. "They'll throw you in jail."

Too bad, I think, as the bell rings and Mr. Chatham marches in swinging his briefcase. He is exceptionally tall, with dark hair and circles under his eyes and this kind of caved-in, defeated hound dog face. He marches up to the clean rectangle of linoleum where his desk used to be and finds it missing.

Everyone holds their breath. Mr. Chatham paces slowly around the perimeter of the rectangle, studying it, as though hoping the desk will somehow re-materialize out of thin air like in a magic trick. A wave of nervous laughter rises and falls harder. Mr. Chatham sighs and turns toward us, raising his hound dog eyes. "Where is it?" His voice is flat.

The room has never, ever been so still.

I look up at him and he catches my eyes for a moment and I feel like maybe he thinks I did this. Like maybe he expects me to be the one to speak up. Like maybe I should have stopped this from happening somehow. Like maybe he's right. A sound starts to form in my throat but I swallow hard before even I can really hear it and stare at my folded hands.

Then Jamie Monroe can't help himself and starts to crack up and so does Kenny Bradford. Just about everyone in the class joins in, even Laurie. Annie Peters, laughing so hard she has to cover her mouth to hide her braces, points to the window through which you can see the desk plain as day perfectly parked in its space.

Mr. Chatham walks toward the window transfixed and stares at it for a long time. At last he turns back toward us and slumps down on the cinder-block window ledge and folds his arms. For a long time he says nothing. We sit in excruciating silence. When he opens his mouth, the stillness quickly becomes preferable to what he has to say.

"You are the luckiest group of kids ever to live in this country, ever to live in this world. You are healthier, richer, better educated than any generation before you. You are coming of age at a time when we have put a man on the moon, when we are learning to communicate instantly around the world by satellite, when medical technology can eradicate diseases that once decimated entire civilizations. At a time when the perils of our nuclear age have never been more threatening, a time when our whole culture, our whole world is demanding rapid change. And you, each of you, have the brains and the education and the opportunity to alter the very course of history for the better." He looks over his shoulder at the desk and shrugs. "Or, not. Anyone want to tell me who's responsible?"

I am careful not to look up this time.

"Fine, you're all on detention indefinitely until those responsible come clean."

"But Mr. Chatham," several students begin to protest.

He throws up his hands. "You all have things you're involved in after school, I realize that. When we find out who did this, you can resume your activities. For now, I want you to sit here and begin writing a 3,000-word essay on the topic of 'what I plan to contribute to this planet and why.' You can finish it after school in detention. Now get started."

"Dwayne, Rick, come with me. Let's go bring that desk back in here." The boys trail him out the door.

You could hear a pin drop. I know for a fact because that doofus Kenny Bradford drops one. Doofus. The word forms in my throat; stillborn.

It is Wednesday night. I am sitting beside my father watching the California Democratic primary returns in Los Angeles. It is almost ten o'clock and I can barely keep my eyes open but I really want to make sure Bobbie Kennedy gets the nomination. That's what I wrote about in my essay for Mr. Chatham. How I wanted to be like Bobbie Kennedy and stop the war and feed hungry children and save the world. Well, I love Bobbie Kennedy and I don't care who knows it. Sometimes I imagine myself a part of his family; playing touch football with all those kids on that endless green lawn in front of their mansion in Virginia. Bobbie Kennedy is the best person I have ever met in my entire life. Well, I actually did meet him once, I am not kidding, at this rally with my Dad in New York City. My Dad introduced me and Bobbie Kennedy leaned way over, looked smack into my eyes, and shook my hand. He was so tall it seemed like he was standing on his own private stage; so handsome he just kind of shone, as if some invisible stagehand was pointing lights down on him.

My whole family loves the Kennedys. In fact, I guess you would call my parents Kennedy groupies—first with John and then with Bobbie. They are the kind of democrats who wear those white plastic top hats with candidate's names on them and sashes of red-white-and-blue across their chests. My mother and father have both had their pictures taken first with John, and then with Bobbie. One wall of our family room, right behind the wet bar, has been converted into a kind of family shrine—for the Kennedy family, not our own. Because except for the ones that lame photographer took of Timmy, we hardly have any pictures of our own family. No one ever thinks to take them and—the few times anyone has tried—all they seem to get is someone's feet or the blur of someone making a run for it.

I only remember a couple of things about John Kennedy's campaign: singing the campaign theme song *High Hopes* with my parents at the top of our lungs with the windows rolled down in our car so all the Nixon supporters could hear and driving folk singers who looked like Peter, Paul, and Mary with an extra Mary thrown in with my Dad to some fundraiser. But with Bobbie's campaign, I haven't missed a beat. In spite of the fact that almost everyone in my school is a Republican or else, couldn't give a flying you know what. In spite of the fact that when we debated the Vietnam War in our sixth grade social studies class I was the only one who volunteered to speak against the war and all the boys made these cooing dove sounds throughout my talk. In spite of the fact that my classmates had already named me Saint Colleen when I tried to get our class to adopt this starving kid from Ethiopia back in fifth grade.

"Go to bed, Colleen," my father says, now. "Tomorrow's a school day."

"But I want to see if he gets it."

"He's going to. I really think we're looking at a win. But this is a big state. It could be very late before they know. It's almost ten o'clock; go to sleep."

"But, Dad."

"I'll wake you when they announce it, alright, already?"

"Promise?"

He holds out his pinkie for me to wrap mine around like I'm five years old again or something.

"Goodnight Dad."

"'Night Colleen."

I can barely make it up the stairs my legs feel so heavy—like my feet have turned into cinderblocks which they might just as well have; they're so big. I pull the covers over my head and listen to the sounds of insects rustling outside the screen in their secret starlit world. A cat cries; sounding so much like a baby it nearly breaks my heart. He'll wake me up when they hear, I tell myself, and drift off, believing.

Only he doesn't. The next morning, I wake up to the crackle of the TV downstairs; wander down in my nightgown, yawning in the blue-grey light. "Don't they know yet?"

Dad looks up at me from his barcalounger. His eyes are bloodshot which makes them look, in contrast, even greener than usual. He shakes his head and stubs out a cigarette. He hasn't shaved and—for the first time in my life—I can imagine what he will look like as an old man. He shakes his head.

"We are standing outside Good Samaritan Hospital here in Los Angeles waiting for another report on the medical condition of Robert Kennedy," comes the voice of a newscaster on TV. "Shot in the head last night seconds after finishing his victory statement at the California primary."

"Colleen," Dad says.

I don't understand. I look down at my father. "Shot?"

My father nods.

I find it hard to breathe. I don't really remember what happens next except that my knees kind of buckle and I sag down on the couch, my eyes glued to the TV screen just like Dad's. We listen as the morning newsmen tell the same story over and over again, flashing pictures of Ethel and Ted and Jackie and all of Bobbie's children in a pyramid on that great lawn in Virginia. And I know exactly where this is heading. We have been here before.

At some point my Mom and Timmy wander in and snuggle up together on the couch. Dad gets up to make us some breakfast which I refuse to eat.

"You still have to go to school, Colleen," he says. "Go take a shower."

I shake my head. "No way. They all hate him. I'm not going to that school where they all just can't wait for him to die."

"Just get moving," my father says. "You're already late. I'll give you a ride."

I squeeze my eyes shut to keep back the tears.

"You have to go to school, Colleen," my mother says. "Staying here won't help. Anyway, school will take your mind off it for a while."

Like I could possibly think about anything else but that poor man dying? Sometimes I feel like my mother and I haven't even met, if you know what I mean.

It is the longest day of my life. Mr. Chatham cancels detention and hands back our essays on how we could contribute to the world if we weren't such a-holes. When he hands me mine, he touches me on the shoulder. "I'm sorry, Colleen," he says. And I have to bite down on my hand to keep from crying. On the top of my paper he has written, "You're idealism is impressive. Keep it up!" Ha!

He puts on a film about the Depression so he won't have to talk to us. Then he puts on a pair of headphones and plugs them into his transistor radio and listens to the news.

Laurie shares her lunch cookies with me out of sympathy, which means she is really sorry because she hardly ever shares one single morsel of food. Mrs. Jamison makes us write about where we were when President Kennedy was shot—everything we can remember. I fill up four pages before the bell rings and it feels like I haven't even gotten started. I already made a scrapbook of when they killed John Kennedy but the scrapbook in my head—filled with pictures of Jackie and Caroline and John John and the eternal flame burning—is so much heftier than the real one.

I get home early—all extracurricular activities have been canceled not that we were allowed to go to them anyway—and resume my position on the couch in front of the television. We eat in front of the TV that night, deli sandwiches on hard rolls and sour pickles and cans of root beer from Girard's. Mom sends Timmy up to his room to play with his GI Joe so we won't have to miss a single minute of this long wait for Bobbie to die.

It takes 20 hours—the longest hours of my life so far. The next day at school, the flag flies at half-mast and for a while it seems like everyone—except for Laurie, thank God—has decided to leave me alone. And then, of course, there's Kenny Bradford and Jamie Wright who cover their eyes and make loud boo-hooing noises whenever I pass. What is the plural of the word doofus, I wonder? I will have to ask Mrs. Jamison. That afternoon, as I take my seat in her class, Kenny makes a pretend gun of his hand, points it to his forehead, pulls the trigger, falls out of his chair, and begins writhing on the floor, moaning. "Why couldn't you save me Saint Colleen? How could you let this happen?"

Mrs. Jamison walks into the room, finds him like that, and sends him to the principal's office. And I am this close, I swear to God, to marching into Mr. Chatham's office and telling him exactly who moved his car.

At the end of the day, they announce on the loud speaker that they're letting us out of school the next day at noon in honor of Bobbie dying. When I get home, Dad has come home from work early again and I hear him talking on the phone to Father Banner, this really cool priest. He used to be our parish priest but got transferred to some prison across the river for growing sideburns and wearing a black armband against the war. Dad and Father Banner have decided to go into New York City the next day to see Bobbie's wake at St. Patrick's Cathedral.

"I want to go with you, Dad," I say, pouring myself a glass of milk.

"Forget about it."

"I'm going with you, Dad." I fold my hands in my lap, prepared, if pushed, to summon the look.

"You're not missing school."

I tell him we only have a half-day and besides, no one's doing anything."I really need to see him one more time." Tears well up in my eyes to prove it. I look away.

Dad sighs. "Alright. Now go do your homework."

"I don't have any homework."

"Yeah, well go do it anyway."

We are standing in line outside St. Patrick's Cathedral. It is only eleven-thirty in the morning but it must be like 90 degrees already. There are so many people and everything smells like tar and smoke and sweat and something else too; possibly pee. We can't see the beginning of the line. We go up one street and down another with no cathedral entrance in sight. People with carts pass by selling pictures of Bobbie on key chains and T-shirts and coffee mugs. It's hard to believe they could make up this many tacky items so quickly. The worst part is; lots of people buy them. I can't tell if that's what makes me feel sick or if it is only the sun, pressing down on my shoulders like two hot, heavy Neanderthal hands.

Dad and Father Banner aren't talking much, except to shake their heads at the vendors. Dad asks me if I would like him to buy me a key chain and we all laugh, as though this is a really good joke. Every now and then, Father Banner asks me how I'm doing and I say, "Fine, just fine." Because I am going to get in there to see Bobbie, that's all there is to it. No matter how long it takes. No matter how bad it smells. No matter how hot it gets. No matter how sick this whole thing makes me feel.

It is really hard to stand this long in the sun. Every few minutes, people sort of collapse on the sidewalk, sitting and cradling their chins in their hands and staring into space. A group of Puerto Rican women has set up a stand with water. One of them runs back and forth carrying a dipper full to old people and pregnant women and so forth, the types who look like they're maybe just about to croak. Dad disappears for a while and comes back carrying three Orange Julius drinks for each of us and even though I normally can't stand it, I slurp down every drop. Still, I feel like one of those characters in a cartoon desert—stumbling around toward the mirage of a syrupy horizon. We have been in this line now for nine hours. My pink sundress clings drenched to my chest and I am actually grateful for the puffs of hot air wafting up at my bare legs as we step over the sewer grates.

Dad and Father Banner discuss our position in line endlessly, now and then pausing to tell jokes involving priests and ministers and rabbis. I tune them out. I listen instead to the drone of humanity around me. A round of accents and laughter and prayers and wiry men calling, "Get your Bobbie Kennedy souvenirs now, right here, while they last, ladies and gentlemen, while they last …" as though we are outside Yankee Stadium or something. And I feel the sadness of it all seeping into the pores of my skin. Sadness and something else too, something hollow and cavernous growing inside me. Something like hunger, only much worse; something that might never get filled.

We never do get in to see him. By eight o'clock that night, the sun is slipping away and, although we have reached the cathedral entrance, they're re-directing us around the block again. Making us re-circle the block like some kind of giant funeral conga line. I don't even argue when Dad and Father Banner say we have to give up. My mouth is too dry to speak.

"Let's get something to eat," Dad says, taking my arm.

"You alright, Colleen?" asks Father Banner.

Because I stumble, I feel light-headed. "Fine," I tell them, looking back over my shoulder at the people still standing in line. Their faces tipped toward the sun setting behind the cathedral, eyes wide with a mixture of pooling hope and dread; mouths open and expectant as people in some old science fiction movie waiting for a UFO to touch down.

At home I take a shower, soaping myself up really good, as if I could wash it all off me. I towel off, slip on my nightgown, and climb into bed. The air in the house is heavy and thick, turned almost solid by heat. I shut off the light and keep the door open, hoping to catch a draft from the living room fan. A heat-deranged

June Bug thuds aimlessly against my window screen. My pillow burns and I keep turning it over hoping to cool it down.

"Colleen, you still awake?" Dad calls from the doorway.

"Unhuh."

He sighs and steps into the room and stands beside my bed, arms folded over his chest. "Sorry we didn't get in to see him. But we tried, it's important that we tried."

"I know."

"You going to be OK?"

"Sure."

He sighs. "Goodnight, then."

"Goodnight, Dad."

He leaves and I can hear their voices—my mother and father's—running in fits and starts in their bedroom like water in a faulty pipe. After a few minutes my mother wanders in. "You still awake?"

"Too hot to sleep."

She sits down on the side of my bed.

I sigh. She is going to try to talk to me—I can feel it. The odds of our getting into a huge fight are heavily stacked against us.

"I'm sorry this is so hard for you," she begins.

"You know what—I want to move."

"Why?" she asks.

"At least in the city, there were all these people who cared. Not like here. We must be the only ones in this whole damn town who even tried to see him."

"Oh, Colleen," my mother says. Her brow is furrowed with the pain of the news she is about to deliver. "Not everyone feels things so deeply, you know?" She begins to reach toward me.

I concentrate with all the inner strength I can muster to keep her from touching my hair.

Her hand falls back in her lap.

I have not lost my powers.

"Not even all those people in line feel things as deeply as you do. Not everyone is like you, Colleen." She is leaning away from me now; ever so slightly.

And I can see by her face that she is perfectly serious, even though it must be one of the biggest understatements in the history of humankind. I imagine God himself looking down on us and cracking up; rolling his holy eyes.

She looks at me like she expects some kind of answer but I have no idea what she wants me to say. Even if I knew; the sad truth is I'm not sure I could bring myself to say it, not even to make the expression on my mother's face go away. I only know this: I don't think I really want to live in this town anymore. I don't even want to live in this country anymore to tell you the truth. There has to be a better place than this. Maybe I should run away to France and take up painting or drinking or something. Maybe—I don't know—the freaking moon.

Rose

You Might As Well Live

The bedding had begun to stink, no question about it.

Rose buried her face further down in the pillow, trying to calculate how long she had lain here like this, the hours stitching themselves together around her one upon another until she found herself enveloped in a kind of cocoon. Now and then she struggled to lift her head, a limb, her pinkie finger free from the sticky cotton swaddling to no avail. She remained hemmed in, muscles seemingly atrophied, once involuntary movements rendered elusively voluntary—paralyzed by her loss.

It had been weeks, she supposed, weeks bleeding into weeks. Each morning the sun sliced earlier through the inch or two separating the bedroom shade from the window's warped molding. She no longer needed both quilts but did not have the strength to remove them. And so she lay sweating in the gauzy world half way between wakefulness and sleep, trying to figure out how mother had risen from the covers each day after enduring the worst a woman could bear; not once, but on four separate occasions.

Stillborn.

The doctor's word still reverberated in her mind. Filling it completely and leaving no room for thoughts of God despite Victor's frequent attempts to bring in Father LaCroix to talk some sense into her. The priest had not been able to say why God had taken their first-born child, Loretta, after nine months, eleven days, and twenty-three hours of labor. A big baby—seven pounds and two ounces—with a mass of Victor's dark hair, symmetrical features, and the right number of fingers and toes—perfect in every way save for an inability to draw her first breath.

The doctor whisked her body away, refusing to let Rose hold her as she lay keening against the bloody sheets. An ashen-faced Victor intervened, grabbing their child and laying her gently on Rose's chest. Rose dragged her hand to her daughter's face, stroked her blue-tinged skin, the color of the milk left in the can after she'd scooped off the cream to churn into butter or ladle on a pie. Loretta. They'd named her after Victor's grandmother. He had always fancied the name. Had it been a boy, she had planned to name him Allen.

She must have passed out then. By the time she awoke, the sheets had been changed, the doctor's tools confiscated; all evidence of Loretta scrubbed from their lives. Buried in the ground in the family plot, Victor said, right beside his father. They had tried to rouse her for the funeral—didn't she remember?

"You need to get up now, Rose," Victor would say, setting her tray of tea and toast on the bed table when he came in from milking each morning.

"Won't you get up now, Rose," her brother Joseph and his wife Marta would periodically be summoned to plead, kneading their helpless hands in the semi-darkness.

"Time to get up now, Rosette," Mother Trambeaux would chant each evening as she set down the supper she'd prepared.

But not even Annette's fragrant ragouts could rouse her. Rose ate sparingly, mechanically, without tasting, her body taking only the scant nourishment necessary to prolong its suffering. Because hell might not prove punishment enough for the likes of her, she had decided. She would make her own hell right here in this bedroom in Lauraville, as close as she could get to the scene of the crime. Because in her heart of hearts—in her very *soul*—she knew perfectly well why God had taken Loretta. The night she had conceived her daughter—every night she lay down with her husband before and since—it was not Victor who held her in his arms but her first love, her only love, Allen. She had not been able to banish him, could not banish him still, even after all that had transpired. Father had tricked her into marrying Victor but he could not trick her into forgetting Allen. Her daughter had paid the price.

The door creaked open.

"Rosette?" Annette trilled. Her mother in-law's horse-like frame at odds with the delicate songbird lodged in her throat.

Rose tried not to balk at the affectionate nickname but could no longer picture herself however figuratively anyone's "little rose." She had aged in this bed, she felt; grown old, somehow, without ever growing up.

Annette blinked, inching closer and towering over her, abundant hair still without a trace of gray piled on top of her head. Staring down a nose long and flat as a clothespin, she tucked her plump hands into the sleeves of her worn, crepe dress.

Rose tried to smile but, honestly, could not tell whether or not her numb lips had actually cooperated.

"Rosette," Annette repeated, inching the bulk of her hip onto the bed and lifting her daughter-in-law's hand.

"I almost bled to death when I had Victor," she said. "They had to take my womb and I was so weak, I couldn't even hold him. Even after my strength returned I lay in bed and cried all day long, knowing I could never have another child, ignoring the one God had given me."

Rose lay still, rapt, peering up at Annette and wondering if she might be dreaming. Annette had never talked about her life.

"It has been almost a month, child." Annette ran her index finger along Rose's ragged nails. "I have made you a bath. I am going to bathe you now and dress you in clean clothes. Then we will take the carriage to church. Father LaCroix will hear your confession."

Lying on her side, Rose caught her breath, drew her knees and arms to her chest as if to conceal the stain of guilt she could almost feel seeping across her nightclothes. How did Annette know she needed to make her confession?

"The chickens are calling your name every morning, can't you hear them? They need you, mon cher. My Victor needs you."

Dizzy and weak, Rose sat erect beside Annette, hands clasping her dead mother's rosary, the pads of her fingers worrying the translucent white beads, pleading with the Blessed Mother for courage to utter the truth to Father LaCroix that she might be saved. Not absolutely sure which commandment she had broken but certain she had mortally sinned, if only inside her head. Another wave of grief shuddered through her. They were so unpredictable. She grabbed her stomach, brought her chest to her knees.

The horses reared as Mother Trambeaux yanked on the reins. "What is it, cherie?"

Rose shook her head.

Annette tied the horses outside the new clapboard church, ushered her inside and settled her down in an oak pew before disappearing to fetch Father LaCroix.

Rose's eyes fixed themselves on the awkward statue of Christ crucified above the altar, his bony arms and ankles dripping globs of red paint, his ribs prominent as the newborn lambs' she and Allen had once fed with baby bottles in his father's barn. Through a tall window the noonday sun illuminated a stained glass Virgin Mary, her pearly white toes squashing a scaled and slithering Lucifer.

Father LaCroix emerged from his office and ducked into the confessional against the wall.

Annette nodded and patted Rose on the shoulder.

Rose shuffled up the aisle, dragging her feet. Her heart fluttered between her shrunken breasts. She smoothed the polka-dotted dress Annette had made her down around the knobs of her pelvis. It felt good to be clean.

Kneeling, she bowed her head and, when Father LaCroix slid open the confessional screen, heard her own voice riding the gloomy stillness.

"Bless me father for I have sinned ..." she began. Always a good beginning.

When the time came to accuse herself her throat started to close and she half rose; the urge to bolt so strong in her limbs it took all her strength to resist it.

"Go on my child," Father LaCroix whispered.

He had lived a long time, 50 years maybe. She supposed he had heard all there was to hear. Her cheeks burned. "I have been unfaithful in my heart," she said. "I married a good man but there was another man before him, not a Catholic."

The silhouette of the priest's oversized gray head bobbed up and down.

Her folded hands started to tremble.

"Father, when I am with my husband, I can't get the other man out of my mind. I think God took our baby, Loretta, to punish me for it."

She felt a lifting then in her solar plexus. A physical sensation of relief not unlike the way a person felt after vomiting.

But the priest was silent a long time, and her fear returned.

"Do you see this man?" he said, at last.

"No, father. He's not from here. I don't even know where he lives anymore."

"You know you have committed a mortal sin?"

"Yes, father."

"And that God in his grace has given us the sacrament of confession to wipe away our sins that our souls might be saved from the flames of hell? That his only son Jesus spent thirty-three years on this earth in poverty and suffering to establish his church and leave us the sacraments to help us get rid of mortal sin?"

"Yes."

"Your penance in this case needs to be ongoing. Every time the devil whispers this man's name in your ear, every time an impure thought rises in your mind you must say these words child, over and over again: 'Jesus, Mary, and Joseph, help me not to do this sin.' Do you understand?"

"Yes, father."

"Repeat it back to me, please."

She did.

"You also must make this up to your husband. He works hard to keep food on your table. You have forsaken him these past weeks, thinking only of yourself. When you took the sacrament of marriage you vowed to be his partner in life did you not? You need to bring him another child as soon as possible. He needs help with the farm. 'Be fruitful and multiply,' God said. You need to put aside your grief and do your part. The Blessed Mother will help you. Pray to her constantly. Do you understand?"

Loretta had kicked against her taut belly for hours the night before Rose went into labor. How could so active a baby be gone? What if it happened again?

"Do you understand?" the priest repeated.

"Yes."

"Have you any questions?"

Rose hesitated. A question loomed in her mind but she still wasn't sure she could abide the answer. "Father, you baptized my baby, did you not?"

He sighed. "She was gone before I got there," he said.

An image of her daughter condemned to Limbo—rocking in the maple cradle Victor had slept in as a baby and denied God's grace for all eternity—momentarily knocked the wind out of her. She leaned her forehead against her knuckles and struggled for breath.

"So there is no chance ..."

"You need to think about the future, Rose," Father LaCroix said. "God will help you, if you remember to ask. And I will help you. Every time you feel temptation you can come to me. Use the sacrament God has given you, child. Your soul's salvation depends on it."

She nodded.

"Please go say the rosary now," he said, before lapsing into the Latin blessing.

"What got you out of bed?" she asked Annette on the way home.

"Pardon?"

"When you had Victor. What brought you out of it?"

"I was hungry," Annette said.

Rose smiled. Mother Trambeaux's revelation about the birth of Victor seemed to have forged a whole new connection. Rose pictured an invisible telephone wire—like those pictures she had seen in a magazine at the train station in Albany—stretching between them.

Annette shook the reins and tossed back her head. "I decided to live," she said. "Again and again, from moment to moment; I decided to live."

She could decide to live, too, Rose told herself, over and over, those first days after what she had come to consider her "ascension" from the bed. But it was not as easy as you might think. She eased back into the rhythms of life on the farm, tending her beloved chickens, cooking and cleaning and mending; boiling their soiled clothes, helping with the evening milking. Victor said nothing about their daughter's passing or the weeks that followed and the longer the subject remained untouched, the harder it seemed to broach. They had buried it, she supposed, just like Loretta, in the Limbo of their marriage. She had yet to find the courage to visit that tiny grave.

They shared chores, supper, and a feather pallet, but they spoke even less than before. The priest's words echoed in Rose's mind and still she could not figure a way to invite her husband into the impenetrable bubble that seemed to have inflated itself around her. She prayed to Mary, perhaps not constantly but whenever she thought of it. Often, watching her husband silently shovel potatoes into his mouth, a rivulet of gravy trickling down across his prickly chin; visions of Allen's broad shoulders and merry eyes undulating in her peripheral vision; she repeated the phrase Father LaCroix had taught her: "Jesus, Mary, and Joseph, help me not to do this sin."

One unseasonably warm, humid night in early June, the air in their upstairs bedroom still suffocating from the afternoon heat, Rose sat in the elongated twilight rocking on the front porch, staring off into the meadow at the wildflowers struggling to soak up a final shaft of nearly vanished sun. Victor came in from the barn, climbed the steps, and sat down beside her. He crouched over to unlace his boots, took off his socks, wiggled his long toes, and stretched his arms over his head. His neck and jaw were raw and creased from the sun, his sleeveless undershirt yellow with sweat. He pulled something out of the baggy pocket of his overalls.

"Won't you read to me, Rose?" He handed her a book of poetry: *Sonnets from the Portuguese.*

She turned it over and over in her hands, unable to reconcile its presence here in her lap on this dairy farm in Lauraville. Miss Williams had told them the story of Elizabeth Barrett and Robert Browning's extraordinary love, the boys whistling and hooting and swooning as their teacher recited the frail poet's words. Allen had never laughed, though. Allen had listened.

Rose raised her eyebrows. It seemed a completely improbable gift. Victor could barely read, after all. As the only one to help his father with the cows his appearances in the one-room school had been, at best, infrequent cameos. When his father died, he dropped out all together.

"Mother gave it to me," Victor said. "She thought you might enjoy it." He frowned, rubbed his forehead, and cleared his throat.

"Won't you read to me, Rose?" His voice was hoarse, the voice of a beggar.

The stain of a blush crept up her neck as she thumbed through the pages.

Victor leaned back in the rocker and shut his eyes.

Rose read until the light leached back into the fields and she could no longer make out the type.

"The Grady's were to host the Saturday square-dance but Marianne's new baby has come down with the croup," Victor said, the next day at dinner, as Rose lifted a tray of puffy white rolls from the oven. She was not much of a cook but had inherited mother's gift for baking and, in her better moments, liked to believe her tender rolls and crusts made up for tough roasts and rubbery chicken.

Rose wrapped the rolls in a clean tea towel, carried them to the table, and sat down beside her husband.

Victor did not look up from the table. "I thought maybe we could have people here instead. It's more than our turn, Rose."

"We need to say grace," Rose said.

Victor dropped the roll he had plucked onto his plate and bowed his head.

"Bless us, oh Lord …" Rose began.

They passed the plates around in silence. Rose turned her husband's proposition over in her mind like a found stone, weighing its value. Trying to decide if she could possibly endure the sympathetic faces of a dozen neighbors, the strains of fiddles and stomping feet, and this husband whirling her around the living room floor in the gay abandon only dancing seemed to wheedle out of him.

"I decided to live," came Mother Trambeaux's voice in her head.

"Rose?" Victor had not touched his food.

She would make Marta's pinwheel cookies and her deceased mother's spice cake with the boiled frosting, she decided.

Looking on their babies was the hardest part. Flossie Hogan and Maureen Dubois had brought the latest of their broods, too young for their eldest to tend, a boy and a girl, respectively, with flushed cheeks and the gaping eyes of the newly baptized that seemed to shed excess grace wherever they fell. Rose kept her distance but could not draw her eyes away from the baby girl, especially—born but a week before Loretta—who studied her, too, as if she resembled someone she had once known quite well.

Rose threw herself into the reels with a sense of deep relief, her mind blank save for the regimented steps and twirls, spinning in her husband's strong hands, laughing even when his head grazed the gas ceiling lamp in passing. Turning it off and on and off again to the rollicking amusement of everyone concerned.

She slept heavily that night for the first time she could remember since the early days of her pregnancy, blissfully dreamless, unruffled by the booming thunder all around them. Until Victor shook her awake, eyes wide with terror. "It's the old hay barn, Rose—fire!"

Still in her nightclothes she pulled on her shoes and charged after him down the stairs. The lightening had passed and the rain had dwindled to a misty drizzle. The cows in the main barn bellowed in fear. Victor stood beating at the flames with a woolen blanket. Rose grabbed a milk bucket beside the rainwater trough, filled it, and raced toward the fire, hurling water. The flames had already enveloped the east side of the building, devoured the dried-out wood, and consumed towers of baled hay within. Still they stood side by side, Victor wielding his blanket and Rose her bucket. Until the smoking structure let out a sickening groan and Victor grabbed his wife, threw her over his shoulder like a sack of potatoes, and dashed away. The barn collapsed, spitting and creaking, right before their eyes. When it had settled, Victor and Rose took off after the sparks to keep them from taking the milk barn, aided, at last, by the return of heavy rain.

After the morning's milking, Victor collapsed in the kitchen chair and laid his sooty head in his hands. Rose poured coffee, buttered toast, placed bacon on a plate and set it in front of him.

"What do you think God has against us, Rose?" he asked, after a while. As if she had some inside information.

It shocked her to hear her question spoken out loud—her husband's deep voice rendered it somehow ridiculous. A thought popped into her head, a blasphemous thought: What if it wasn't God at all, only lightening; only a nature as random and frightened as their own.

"Jesus, Mary, and Joseph, help me not to *think* this sin," she chanted in her head.

She stood up straight. "We will rebuild, that's all. The neighbors will help us rebuild."

He studied her, head tilted; eyes blank—as if they had only just met—before picking up his fork.

For several Sundays following mass the men and boys in the parish met to rebuild the barn while Rose and Annette prepared gigantic meals to reward them for their efforts, Annette sneaking wine into stews; Rose baking to beat the band. Each night, Rose bent her head over Elizabeth Barrett Browning's sonnets without looking up as Victor rocked on the front porch sipping cold tea. If he tired of them, he never let on. As the corn ripened in the fields and the hay grew tall, the poet's words stopped conjuring memories of Allen and Rose's need to have Victor drive her to Father LaCroix to make her confession grew less and less frequent. Still, she prayed a lot, mostly for God to help her understand why he would prevent an innocent child from entering his kingdom simply because of a mother's sin? Then she prayed for forgiveness for posing profane questions like these that would surely hasten her journey to hell.

One night, for no reason at all, Victor surprised her with a tub of ice cream flecked with peaches from Mother Trambeaux's trees.

He had cranked it himself in the barn between chores, hid it in the icebox. They carried bowls out onto the porch and fell on it like children, giddy and gluttonous, before settling down to read.

"When we first met and loved, I did not build

Upon the event with marble ..."

Rose thanked the failing light that prevented her from going on. Victor took her hand, twisting the loose wedding band on her finger round and round, round and round, unlocking something.

Later, after finishing their dishes, she climbed upstairs and washed her face in the basin, let down her braids, and brushed out her hair. Still thick and sleek from her pregnancy, it hung almost to her waist now.

"Blessed Mother, help me," she whispered, climbing in bed beside her husband and placing his palm on her breast.

Colleen

I Am a Rock

A short film about Mount Rushmore flickered across the screen; gigantic presidents' heads for no good reason carved into the side of this mountain—the world's largest coin.

"Who's that guy two rows back?" asked Laurie.

I turned my head in the dark movie theater but couldn't tell who she meant. "What guy?"

"Shhhhh!" yelled Carrie Adams. Carrie Adams thought she was *the* coolest thing, ever since she showed up back at school last September with boobs. Everyone said she stuffed, but she always got undressed *inside* her gym suit so you could never be sure.

"The one with the eyes on sidesaddle like Paul McCartney," said Laurie.

I craned my neck, hoping to catch a glimpse of the guy with the Paul McCartney eyes. At last the thick dusty beam of the movie projector flooded his face. Shaggy brown hair, thick, sculpted lips, and a nose that looked as if it might have once been broken. And Paul McCartney eyes that also reminded me of the eyes on that mask that means drama in the theater, vacant, tragic eyes designed to break someone's heart.

"Jeez," I whispered. "He's so, so *mature*."

"He's a *man*," Laurie breathed. "I think I'm in love."

To prove it she threw herself back in her seat, spilling half her popcorn on my lap. We both started laughing until Carrie Adams just about had a cow shushing us and I had to give her half my Chunky bar to shut her up.

I looked back over my shoulder one more time before the real movie started and it seemed like those eyes beamed right through me, I swear to God! Drilled all the way inside to where the real me normally hides. And it felt like Paul McCartney's eyes had seen me just step out of the shower or something. And here's the worst part about the whole thing: it felt *really* good.

Laurie lay on her stomach on her twin bed, head propped in the hammock of her hands, gnawing on the last brick of the giant Hershey's almond chocolate bar we bought on the way out of the movies. I lay on her ottoman pullout staring up at the gold ceiling and feeling like a piece of chocolate myself, nestled in a giant Valentine box. Last year, Laurie's mother decorated the entire house—wallpaper, carpets, drapes, upholstery, and ceilings—in shades of gold to cheer herself up. It worked for about three months. Then she turned back into her same sad self, prowling the kitchen for hidden Babe Ruth bars and poring through giant paint and fabric catalogues.

"Tomorrow, I'm starting a diet," Laurie said.

To tell the truth, she could use one. If she weren't careful, she would end up with wubs on the backs of her legs just like her Mom and big sister, Ellen; dents of lard that never even tanned.

"All I'm gonna eat from now on is water and bran muffins," said Laurie.

"With raisins and applesauce in them?"

"Right. Let's make some in the morning."

I loved those damn muffins—Laurie really knew how to throw a diet. "OK," I said. "I'll go on a diet too."

"Yeah; I'll do anything for Matthew Baker."

"Who said anything about Matthew Baker?"

That was his name. We found out from Carrie of all people on the way out the theatre door.

"How can we find out who he is?" Laurie had asked.

"He's Matthew Baker," said Carrie, rolling her eyes.

It was that simple. Thank God some people just couldn't mind their own beeswax.

"He goes away to school," she said, combing bleached hair out of her eyes with her fingers. "Everybody knows him, though, *everybody*," she repeated, just in case the fact that Laurie and I did not qualify hadn't sunk in the first time around.

"He just started as lifeguard at the swim club." She tossed her perfectly straight hair over her shoulder with a little flick of her head.

I had never hated her more in my life. "Been swimming lately?" I asked. I pressed my face right up against her hair. You couldn't help but notice how chlorine turned Carrie's hair green. It was her only fault so we always tried to make the most of it.

She flicked her head again. Her hair whipped across her other shoulder like a horse's tail, baring her back above her halter-top. "It's been raining," she snarled. "Where have you been?"

But we'd gotten what we needed. Matthew Baker, I thought now; such a romantic name. Matthew Baker, Matthew Baker, *Colleen Baker.* Suddenly I *had* to know where he lived!

"Go get the phone book."

"What am I some kind of untouchable slave from India?" Laurie said. But she hoisted herself up anyway and disappeared down the hall. She came back carrying a gold wicker tray. It held a phone book, a gold glass plate of Oreos, and two waffled gold glasses of milk.

"I thought you were going on a diet?"

She unscrewed an Oreo and plowed off the white cream with her teeth. "I said *tomorrow*, Colleen."

Outside the open window, the rain started hammering the pavement again. I grabbed an Oreo and dipped it in the milk. Laurie flipped on the radio.

"... I've been waiting so long ... To be where I'm going ... In the sunshine of your love ..."

The warm strains of Cream's song nearly dried up the rain.

I grabbed the phone book and turned to Baker—about 35 names. It could be a very long night.

"That's his car," said Laurie, "let's get out of here!"

She grabbed my elbow, charged down the road, and dove into a thicket of maples. We lay on our stomachs like turtles, peeking out from underneath the shells of our crossed arms. Hearts thumping, we watched the old white Mercedes coast to the bottom of the hill. At the stop sign, Matthew Baker looked over his shoulders from side to side, moving his big head slowly, like a bull.

The car disappeared over the hill and Laurie sat up and pulled out a rope of red licorice. "Jeez, he almost saw us," she said. She started chewing, groped inside the candy store of her shorts pockets, pulled out another rope, and handed it to me.

"No thanks." I felt a little sick from the sight of Matthew Baker's Mercedes—definitely the coolest car I had ever seen. Also from the four apple-raisin bran muffins with butter I'd eaten for breakfast. I craned my neck up toward his house. In the dull light it crept down over the hill like something alive, a creeping vine of white and grey shingles and fir-green shutters and windows cut into tiny, fairy-tale squares.

Matthew Baker's father was some kind of famous doctor. After we called 19 Bakers we found the right one—Dr. Morris T. Baker, 15 Cherry Hill Lane. Laurie's father said he was a heart surgeon in New York City. Turned out Matthew Baker was just about everything I secretly hoped to be: grown-up, beautiful, cool, rich, driving a car with leather upholstery the color of caramels.

"Wanna go to the pool?" Laurie asked. She squinted up at the morning sun.

"Oh, yeah. Most definitely."

We stood by the diving pool window. Little kids swam up, plunged themselves underwater, pressed their lips to the thick glass, and blew bubbles like kissing fish. The waves sucked back their legs and hips like an invisible vacuum. My brother Timmy somersaulted in front of us like the little showoff he has always been since the day he was born. He folded his index finger and pressed it to his nose so that it looked like an entire finger stuck all the way up to where most people have brains.

Above us, leaning against the giant diving board, Matthew Baker puffed on his silver whistle.

"Move it out guys!" he yelled, whistle still clamped between his teeth.

"Man!" breathed Laurie.

"… Come on baby, light my fire, try to set the night on fire," sang Jim Morrison from the radio resting on Matthew Baker's towel under the high board's shade.

We watched the kids struggle up the metal ladders. Matthew Baker grinned. His Paul McCartney eyes drooped. He removed a wad of Teaberry gum from his mouth, stuck it back in its paper wrapper, and set it on the towel. He climbed up the ladder to the 10-meter springboard; and slowly heel-toed toward the edge.

The sun's thin rays ignited Matthew Baker's hair. With three long steps and a hop, he bounced straight up in the air; calf muscles bulging under matted brown hair.

"… You know that I would be untrue, you know that I would be a liar. If I were to say to you. Girl we couldn't get much higher …" sobbed Jim Morrison in the perfect stillness.

Into the air shot Matthew Baker, tucking and tumbling twice before slicing the water, his body a blade.

The water filled his Exeter T-shirt like a sail, exposing his tapered waist; lightly furred chest.

Laurie and I watched, transfixed, as he swam directly toward us.

Holding the railing, he plunged down to the window and opened his eyes. And then—I am not making this up—Matthew Baker blew us an actual kiss!

"Man," said Laurie. "I could use a snack."

We walked for a while down the sloping grass, the long way, avoiding the mosaic of blankets and lounges strewn closer to the big pool, dodging my father with his squirt guns and Groucho Marks glasses; his card tricks and teenager jokes. Escaping Laurie's mother, curled up on her gold blanket with her depression and the latest *Cosmopolitan* magazine.

Dodging them all we scanned the dense grass passing below our bare feet for lurking bees.

"I think someone likes you, Colleen," Laurie said, after a while.

"What?"

"Matthew Baker. I think he likes you is what. Why else would he blow *you* a kiss?"

For a moment, I pretended it was true. I tried on the fragile lace thought of Matthew Baker actually liking me but it just didn't fit.

"Yeah right," I said. "Maybe he was blowing you a kiss did you ever think of that?"

Laurie looked thoughtful. "I don't think so," she said, after a while. "I'm fat."

I'm fat, she said, just like that. It was enough to make me burst into tears; like I needed another reason.

"You are *not* fat," I lied. "Besides, I'm straight as a board. I'm *flat*, remember? Remember last spring when Charlie Shafer put that 'Flatsy' doll in my locker? 'She's flat and that's that,' remember?"

We walked for a while in silence, facing the terrible truths of our own bodies, until we reached the cement patio with its white, round, metal tables and striped umbrellas blooming like rusty flowers. Behind the counter stood Mrs. Larson, the owner's Swiss wife, a skinny brown cigarette lodged in the vise of her thin fingers. She had short blonde hair and eyes the color of those ice packs you put in a cooler to keep the potato salad from poisoning someone. Mrs. Larson stood smoking her cigarette, staring off into her private arctic space.

"Ggggg … earlsssssss?" she growled at last, rousing herself.

"I'll take an egg cream, please," I told her.

Laurie hesitated a moment, then sighed. "I'll just have a large Tab with lemon, Mrs. Larson," she said, suddenly dieting again.

A sharp yellow eyebrow shot up the rink of Mrs. Larson's forehead. She placed her cigarette in a glass ashtray and went to get our drinks.

"Hey girls, how you doing?" boomed a man's voice from behind us. "Find any boyfriends yet today?"

I rolled my eyes at Laurie and looked down at my bare feet. They seemed to have grown to adult size over the last year ahead of the rest of me; like a dog's. The voice belonged to my father; of course, flip flopping toward us with his grin the size of Madison Square Garden.

"Ha!" cried Timmy. "Like boys would want to catch their cooties!" He spat a big wad of spit out the side of his mouth, narrowly missing Laurie's foot.

"Gross!" I cried.

"Timmy!" Dad yelled.

Then he turned back on us. "What's a matter? Cat got your tongues?" He wedged himself in between us at the counter. "Hey Mrs. Larson; lovely day, huh?" My father couldn't stand her.

Mrs. Larson nodded like an enormous mechanical toy. She set two white-and-green waxed paper cups in front of us, draped herself over the counter again, picked up her cigarette, and looked beyond the sorry sight of us all.

"Look at that little flirt," said Laurie. "Can you even believe her?"

We stood in line for the three-meter board, watching Carrie Adams toy with Matthew Baker.

"Looks like you got a headache," she cooed, bulging out the top of her microscopic bikini.

She definitely didn't stuff.

"I know what to do for *that*," she said.

Matthew Baker sat between the boards, dangling his feet in the water. Carrie scooted up behind him and began circling his temples with her pink fingertips.

"Ahhhhhhhhh," Matthew moaned.

Seriously, it was enough to make you puke.

"*Colleen!*" called Laurie from behind me. "Come on!"

"Hey, move it will ya," yelled Matthew Baker.

It took me a minute to realize he was yelling at me.

"Hey, YEWWW, I said move it!" he shouted, untangling his head from the web of Carrie's fingers long enough to give his whistle a quick, sharp blast.

I dashed down the rough turquoise board, flipped once, and landed flat on my stomach with the world's loudest smack.

Underwater, I clutched my chest and held my breath. I absolutely could not allow myself to break the surface. I would just have to drown.

I swam to the window, groping the railing, still holding my breath. I would stay here forever. Dying couldn't be worse than this. But then—driven by some kind of primal, diabolical will to live completely beyond my conscious control—I suddenly shot up, sputtering and gasping for air.

"You OK?" someone whispered in the water behind me.

It was Laurie, of course, patting my back like a friendly seal.

I nodded, coughing.

"Hey kid? You OK?" yelled Matthew Baker.

But I didn't answer.

Kid? I mean, seriously?

"Yeah, kid?" Carrie chimed in with a little slutty smirk. "How you doing?"

"I can't believe he called me a kid," I said, for about the 25th time.

Laurie and I lay on a blanket we'd rescued from enemy family territory and dragged to the ruffle of woods bordering the swim club. I couldn't stop imagining using my magic powers to shrink Carrie Adams to the size of a Barbie doll so I could snap off her empty, little head. "I mean I'm the same age as Carrie F-ing Adams, for God's sake," I said. "Plus, I'm *much* more mature."

"Except in that one, little area."

"Shut *up*," I said.

"Sorry. Anyway, somebody should tell him we're going to high school year after next. Maybe I will just have to tell him myself."

"Don't you *dare*! Don't you dare say one word to Matthew Baker or I'll *die*. I swear to God, Laurie, I'll just die!"

For some reason Laurie started giggling uncontrollably.

I ignored her. "What if I never grow boobs?" I asked the sky. "What if I just keep getting taller and taller and never get my period and never grow boobs and have to wear baggy sweaters and plaid skirts and go to college for the rest of my life and do endless experiments on fruit flies because no one wants me?"

It seemed the direction my life was heading, after all.

With my thumb, I flipped on the wheel of my new transistor radio.

Surprise, surprise, Paul Simon was singing *I Am a Rock*. It seemed to say it all.

Laurie and I touched the tops of our heads together, lying side-by-side, clutching imaginary microphones; our own little island. "An island never cries," we sang.

We walked along the long, sizzling road wearing our fathers' T-shirts like mini-dresses over our bathing suits, beach towels slung over our shoulders, our Dr. Scholl's sandals smacking the blacktop. Every now and then, Laurie—who had never really mastered walking the Dr. Scholl way—slipped off her shoes and we had to stop while she rearranged her toes around the little hills of molded wood.

We were heading for my house, about three miles away. For a while, Dad and Timmy had stalked us in the Rambler, completely cracking themselves up until a guy behind them started blasting his horn and calling Dad names.

We passed the state hospital for the mentally ill that might be some old college with its ivy-covered stone buildings and slanty green golf course lawns. Now and then, we passed a house with an iron sign that read, "George Washington slept here." George Washington definitely got around. It was our town's only joke.

"God, it's hot!" said Laurie, tripping and sliding off her shoes again. She hobbled over to one of several boulders placed in the curve of the road to stop cars from taking the turn too fast and smashing into one of George Washington's former bedrooms. She collapsed on a boulder, grabbed one foot, and started rubbing.

"We're never going to get home if we keep stopping like this," I pointed out.

A horn beeped, and there was Matthew Baker. Matthew Baker hunched over the wheel of his white Mercedes, coasting to a stop beside us; driving right off some movie screen and smack into our lives.

"Hey, girls," he said, fondling a cigarette. "Wanna lift?"

I froze. Up close he looked like … like a Kennedy, for Christ sake, like Bobby F-ing Kennedy! Like half Paul McCartney and half Bobby F-ing Kennedy. Really, it was too much. I felt like I might pass out or something.

"We'd love one," said Laurie, elbowing me in the ribs.

Still, neither of us moved.

"So, like, get in," he said, shaking his head.

Laurie opened the back seat door and shoved me in first. I crawled over the hot leather and there was Carrie Adams in the front, smiling that fake smile of hers but absolutely fuming underneath, you could tell.

"Carrie, how you doing?" I asked, as if we were long lost friends. Little rodent.

Laurie shut the door and Matthew drove off, humming to himself. "I don't want a pickle, I just want to ride on my motor sickle," he hummed.

He turned up the hill to his house.

Carrie flipped her horse hair over her shoulder and yawned, like it was no big deal.

Laurie pressed her knee against me hard.

I pressed back.

He turned into a driveway that wound up behind the house and ended in a clearing of weeping willows.

"Got to change," he said, climbing out of the car. "Then I'll take you home."

He disappeared into the house.

Carrie got out and stretched her arms over her head. "You coming in or what?" she asked.

We climbed out, too, and followed her onto the screened porch and into the house. Inside, there were hardwood floors, white-washed walls, and beamed ceilings. On the walls hung strange masks and oil paintings of African people that looked like they'd escaped from a small museum in New York City we visited on a field trip in the fourth grade. The living room's roof rose in a V over an enormous rock fireplace. A wall had been knocked out and replaced with glass so you could see straight through to a wooden deck and all the way down to the river.

On the glass-topped coffee table sat a pile of *New Yorker* magazines and this other one I never saw before called *Gourmet*.

"Where *are* you, Matthew?" Carrie whined.

"In here," he called.

We watched Carrie follow the trail of his voice and vanish down a long hall. This house seemed to just go on and on and on; like the Macy's in Newark.

I plopped myself down on the white leather couch. The backs of my legs felt sticky. I picked up the *New Yorker* and flipped to a story by a guy named John Updike. But before I could get anywhere at all, Laurie started moaning.

"Will you just look at this," she moaned. "Lobster Bisque!" She waved a *Gourmet* centerfold under my nose. In the foreground sat a table set with pewter bowls, slim green bottles of wine, a bucket of clams, and a tureen of pink lobster floating in cream. In the background, tall windows, an open glass door, and a grey wooden porch towered over the ocean. The picture cast a spell. It sucked at your ankles like a rip tide. There was no use fighting it. But before I could surrender to the current and claim the life I'd had coming all along, we heard a sound like a muffled scream.

Laurie raised her eyebrows at me, frowning. I shook my head and shrugged. It came again, louder this time. There was no question about it being a scream. A girl's scream to be precise: Carrie F-ing Adam's scream.

Laurie and I jumped up and just stood there a moment—the "fight or flight" response in action—just like I learned in biology class. And then a rush of energy surged up the back of my legs. I felt like Clark Kent, I really did; about to dash into a phone booth and change into Superman. I sprinted down the hall toward the scream and kicked open the partly closed door.

"What are you *doing*?" I demanded, in my most mature voice, the kind I usually reserve for humiliating Timmy.

The blinds were drawn. A hot pink and yellow psychedelic poster from the Jimi Hendrix album, "Are You Experienced?" swirled in the dim light. I could see Matthew Baker sprawled on the twin bed, pinning Carrie Adams down with one arm, his other hand invisible under the film of her shirt.

"What do you think you're doing?" I repeated.

Behind me, Laurie flipped on the light switch.

"Unhand that girl!" I cried.

Matthew Baker blinked up at us a moment in the sudden light. Then he started laughing. "Unhand that girl," he repeated to himself, and sat partway up.

Carrie wiggled out from under him, swiping away a tear with the back of her hand.

"It's alright, let's go," I said.

She rose slowly and backed away, smoothing her shirt and shorts with her palms.

"Hey," said Matthew Baker. "We were just having some fun. You don't have to get so pee-ohed. Mellow out, would you. How about a smoke?" He picked up a half-smoked marijuana cigarette from an ashtray on the night stand and lit it with a flick of a yellow lighter. I had never seen a marijuana cigarette. All of a sudden, I wished I was somewhere else like in church or baking cookies or watching *I Dream of Jeannie* re-runs with Timmy. The room smelled sickly sweet, like the incense they shake around in mass that always made me want to puke.

"Let me just have a smoke," he said. "Then I'll drive you home. Really, man."

I pushed Carrie and Laurie out the door behind me. "No thank you. We've got to leave *now.*" I closed the door all the way. Behind it, I could hear Matthew Baker squeak up off the bed. "What the fuck?" he said.

I dashed down the hall into the living room to where Carrie and Laurie stood looking lifeless as clothes on a hanger.

"Run!" I mouthed; shoving to get them started.

We raced out the door and down the long driveway as fast as we could on our Dr. Scholl's, not slowing down until we reached the main road.

"Can we stop a *minute*?" asked Laurie, once we were out of sight of the house. She shuffled over to a boulder and leaned against it, panting.

Carrie Adams raked the hair off her face with her fingers. She crossed her arms over her chest and stared at her feet.

"So what happened?" I asked.

"Yeah, did he try to …?" Laurie began.

Carrie sighed. "He was smoking a jay," she said. "Then we were … like French kissing, you know?"

We had no idea.

"Then he just got, like out of control, you know?"

Laurie looked completely absorbed, like someone watching a really good movie.

Carrie shrugged. "It happens."

We nodded some more.

"But, are you really OK?" I asked.

And I know it's hard to believe it, but Carrie F-ing Adams started to cry. She knelt down holding her stomach and just started balling her head off. I leaned over and patted her on the back. Laurie came around her other side and patted, too.

"It's OK," I said. Even though, to tell you the truth, I had no idea if it was.

"No it's not," she wailed. "Everyone hates me. *Everyone!*"

"Guys don't hate you," Laurie pointed out with her usual tact.

I made a face at her.

"Yeah, right," Carrie cried. "Guys just want one thing and you know it! And everyone else hates me. I don't have any friends."

"What do guys want?" asked Laurie, in a pleading voice. "*What?* I do *not* know—*what?*"

"People don't *hate* you," I said, still trying to calm her down. "Maybe they're just jealous."

"Jealous of what?" she asked, lifting up her head, her hair matted and clinging to the side of her tear-streaked face.

"Your hair," Laurie said. "You have beautiful hair."

"The chlorine turns it green!" She pressed her face back into her hands and started sobbing all over again.

Laurie and I exchanged quick glances. I stared down at my watch. 5:30, already. Deep, dog doodoo; no doubt about it.

"Look Carrie," I said. "People think you're stuck up. That's why you don't have any friends. But maybe you're not stuck up. If you're not, we can certainly be friends, OK?"

She lifted her purple face.

I handed her my towel.

She started dabbing at her eyes. All that streaked black mascara made her look like a prom queen in a horror movie. "You mean it?" she asked. "You're not just saying that because I'm crying?"

Laurie rolled her eyes.

"Nope," I said. "Let's give it a try. How about we all go to the movies tomorrow night?"

"Well ... OK, then."

We helped her to her feet and smoothed back her beautiful green hair.

"You still coming for dinner?" I asked Laurie.

"Lasagna, right?" she said, stepping back on her shoes.

"So I guess you're safe now," I told Carrie.

"Oh, sure," she said. "Please don't say anything about this," she added, grabbing my hands.

"Of course, not."

"Thanks. Tomorrow night, then?"

"Right."

We turned down Pinewood Street toward my house. Carrie headed over the other side of Route 9W. For a while we walked in silence, letting the day's strange events filter down through us, letting the embers of Matthew Baker's pedestal sift down around us like ash from a marijuana cigarette. Letting the summer scents—the climbing roses and peonies, the honeysuckle and creeping jasmine—coax us back to ourselves. Drawing comfort from the familiar signs about George Washington and Mad Anthony Wayne and that horrible traitor, Benedict Arnold; shuffling down this old path of betrayal and falling out of love with Matthew Baker.

As soon as we reached my driveway, I knew the jig was up. Sure enough, we stepped through the screen door to find Mom standing there with her arms crossed over her chest. Dad and

Timmy sat waiting at the set table. It looked like they'd just sat down, though, which meant we were only on the edge of trouble, not yet all the way over the cliff.

"Where have you two been?" Mom asked.

"It's my fault, Mrs. Shea," Laurie said. "My feet got really sore. I'm just no good walking in these shoes."

Mom's eyes darted from Laurie's face to her feet, then to my face—which I had conveniently turned into stone—and back to Laurie's face again.

"Well, poor thing," she said. "Sit down and eat. We'll take a look at them after dinner. You want iced tea girls?"

I hung our towels in the bathroom and sat down between Laurie and Timmy. Under the table, she squeezed my hand.

"We have a little surprise for you, folks," said Dad.

"Oh, *no*," we whined.

"That's right. Time once again for this brief message from our fearless leader."

From under the table, Timmy produced an enormous white cowboy hat and placed it on his head. He folded his hands in front of him like someone praying. From under the hat, his mouth moved slowly, as though made of clay.

"My fellow Amer-a-cuns," Timmy drawled, imitating President Johnson who everyone hated for one reason or another. Either for not getting us *out* of the war, like my family, or for not winning it; like Laurie's. President Johnson made Carrie Adams look popular.

"I come here today with a heavy head, I means heart," slurred Timmy, imitating President Johnson.

Dad started laughing hysterically and so did Laurie, choking on her iced tea and spitting some in Dad's face, which only made them both laugh harder.

"I am *not*, I repeat *not*, sending no Texas boys to VEE-ETTE-NUM. I means, NOM, I means NAM. No siree-Bob!" cried the hat.

I reached over and pulled the hat all the way down over Timmy's head and pretended to strangle him.

"Unhand that boy!" shouted Laurie.

And we both looked at each other and busted out laughing so hard we practically fell off our chairs.

Our raised voices spread through the kitchen and all through the house like chants at an anti-war rally. Until pretty soon everyone was laughing and holding their stomachs. Even—I swear to God—Mom.

Annette

One Small Step

"Mom, Colleen is pinching me again!" shrieked Timmy, launching Annette upright with a worried glance at the nightstand clock. 7:30—she had overslept again; she really must get a better alarm. She shot out of bed, yanked on her robe, and tore down the hall of their Cape Cod home where her 14-year-old daughter and ten-year-old son stood locked in combat again outside the bathroom door.

"Mom, make her *stop*, she's giving me an Indian burn," her son wailed. "I was just trying to get into the bathroom to take a pee for Christ sake."

"Knock it off, both of you!" she shouted, despite last week's vow to refrain from losing control in front of them as Monsignor McGowan recommended. It only fueled a power struggle you could not win, he suggested, without any prompting at all from his seat behind the confessional screen. Leaving her to ponder how a 50-year-old man from whose loins no seed had ever sprouted could have gleaned such wisdom.

"Shut up you little maggot," Colleen fired back. "Mom, he swiped my curling iron. I'll die if I have to go to school looking like this. I mean look at me, without the curling iron it just goes all spastic."

"You got that right!" Timmy yelped.

"Knock it off, I said, both of you." She had them by the neck now, like cats; exerting all her strength against their centrifugal force. At last, panting, she pried them apart.

"You," she snapped, poking her son's bony chest. "Go get the curling iron."

"But I didn't."

She made a little stop sign with her palm and narrowed her eyes the way she had been practicing in front of the mirror—scary, evil, psycho Mom.

"Thanks Mom, I can't believe him sometimes, I ..."

"And you," she spat, whirling around to face her daughter. "Take off that handkerchief of a skirt you're wearing and put on some real clothes."

Colleen rolled her eyes, hugged herself, and swayed back and forth on her colt-like legs before stomping away in her Doctor Scholl's sandals.

"And both of you get yourselves in the kitchen," she yelled over dueling slamming doors. "Breakfast's in five minutes."

Breakfast, she thought, dropping Pop Tarts in the toaster and pouring orange juice and milk. She filled the percolator, spread mayonnaise on squishy white bread and topped it with shards of Velveeta cheese, the same sandwich she'd been making her son since kindergarten. She wrapped it in wax paper and added the requisite cheese crackers, a lunch full of no real food that conformed to his white and yellow culinary palette. As usual, she added a banana she knew he would not eat to ease her worries that he would never grow thanks to her inept mothering.

She had no aptitude whatsoever for this job. She realized that now that she had actually ventured out into the real world. Granted the town library might not constitute the real world but she was earning a weekly salary, contributing to the family, and holding down a job she was actually good at. A job for which she felt far better equipped than this one she had stumbled into refereeing between these two warring creatures. She, who considered herself above all else a peaceful person, a civilized, educated person, despite the odds stacked against her.

She glanced at the clock on the wall, a wedding present, its hands shaped like human hands with real fingers, adjectives replacing numbers, a running barometer of her shifting moods.

Seven-forty-five, it read; half way between "exasperated" and "ambivalent."

Timmy thrashed through the kitchen first, propeller-like arms churning, upsetting the box of Frosted Flakes and, in a pathetic attempt at damage control, knocking over a glass of juice.

Her shoulders shot up to her ears. "Sit," she hissed, and her son backed off, a look of terror in his saucer-shaped eyes. He caught his foot on the chair behind him and tumbled backwards head over heels in a smooth, cartoon-like movement, as if he'd been secretly studying the opening of the *Dick Van Dyke Show* for tips. She bit her hand to keep from bursting out laughing and giving the little bugger exactly what he wanted.

"Sit," she repeated. She held out the chair, steering her son into the seat, and plunking Pop Tarts and a Flintstones vitamin down in front of him.

"For Christ sake, Mom," he began.

She pressed a finger to her lips. "Since when did you start taking God's name in vain?" she asked.

"It's not God," he said. "It's his son. And everybody says it."

"You mean Billy? Did you get that from Billy? I told you I don't want you playing with that kid."

"Mom, can I borrow your belt," Colleen demanded, planting a kiss on her mother's forehead.

"What's wrong with Billy?" asked Timmy, rhetorically, as if they had not had this conversation about the new boy down the street at least a dozen times. As if she had never mentioned his friend's suspension from school for threatening a kid with a Swiss Army knife, the incident involving Mrs. Grant's prized tomato patch, and his interrogation by the police following the recent arson of the former—now vacant—elementary school at the bottom of the hill.

"I have nothing to hold these jeans up with," continued Colleen. "They're enormous on me. I mean since you won't let me wear anything that *fits*."

"I'm not getting into Billy right now," said Annette, pouring coffee. "Just watch your mouth."

"*Mom*, what about the *belt*?"

"Take the belt, Colleen," said Annette. "And sit down and eat."

"Thanks Mom, I don't have time, I'll take it with me." Colleen wrapped a Pop Tart in a paper towel. "See you Mom, see you rodent." She seized a pile of books and dashed out the door.

"Christ!" Timmy shouted.

"That's it." Annette picked up his plate and tossed it in the sink with a flick of her wrist. She handed him his knapsack.

"Go," she said, with a tap on his bottom.

"But, Mom."

"If you miss the bus again, you'll just have to walk," she said, trying her best to sound like she really meant it. "Two whole miles, Timmy. It'll probably shave off half your body weight."

He glowered up at her.

"Have a good day," she said.

With a sigh that would have made his sister proud he turned on his Keds and fled, smacking the screen door behind him.

Annette lifted the cup to her mouth but the coffee was cold.

"Christ," she said.

There were certain things Annette actually loved about this town and they were almost entirely horticultural. She adored walking down their hill to Main Street to work, plucking at the holly hedges and running the waxy leaves between her fingers. Now and then stopping to shove her whole dark head into a cluster of lilacs and inhaling until the heady fragrance left her almost undone. She loved the forsythia and peony bushes hugging the squat white colonial homes; the minty lawns and orderly flagstone paths dripping tulips, irises, lilies and asters; week after week, some new life exploding.

She loved the porch swings and National Landmark signs boasting sleepovers by George Washington and the museum on the hill above the river filled with Revolutionary War memorabilia where ancestors of the town's noble founders each year performed their inebriated reenactment of the Battle of Mad Anthony Wayne. She loved the idea of celebrating a renegade general's death wish but had not much use for the present town's old-guard residents, who still looked down their blue-veined noses on her family and their carpetbagger kind. She had spent twelve long years under the figurative microscope of Rocky Ledges' inbred daughters; she lately doubted she could survive a dozen more.

Trotting down the manicured brick path on her heeled sandals toward the gray stone building she slipped her key into the lock of the arched wooden door that reminded her of an illustration from *The Seven Dwarfs*; seduced anew into efficiency by the tidy surroundings.

"Here again?" she said.

The young man who stood beside her had showed up all week but she hadn't paid him much mind. Now she studied him, taking in his wide shoulders at odds with an otherwise slight build, the worn jeans and pressed, button-down shirt, a mane of shaggy, mousy-brown hair, and deep-set, startling turquoise eyes that had her squinting for evidence of tinted contacts to no avail.

He rubbed his jaw with a startled look, as if amazed to find hair sprouting there. "Robin," he said, extending his hand.

She took it, admiring the long, tapered fingers and pale, bald knuckles so at odds with her freckled, ragged-nailed digits. "Robin," she found herself repeating. "As in Christopher?" Because he looked the part, an over-sized, aging, fairy tale of a boy.

He smiled and shook his head, cheeks erupting in crows-feet that sent a little shiver of relief through her. "No, *first* name. *Robin*, as in Hood."

"Annette Shea," she said.

He followed her inside and set his satchel down at a table as she made her way around the large, high-ceilinged room, flipping on lights, standing on tiptoe, and brandishing a long stick looped on one end to open the tall Tudor-style windows and let in the breeze.

Old man Hurley shuffled in and headed for the row of magazines on the wall, settling into the worn, leather sofa with the same issue of *Life* he had perused for hours the day before. Funny in the head already his daughter claimed, although he had only just retired from the Gypsum plant last year. Still, he had lost his wife but months after buying a used motor home in which to see the world. It sat in his driveway, grimy from the long winter's dousing of salt and sand.

Not far behind him charged "Racin' Raymond," the retarded man so named for his habit of peeling down the streets on foot clutching the dismembered steering wheel of his mother's old Pontiac. He skidded to a screeching halt, acknowledged Annette with a sideways flick of his permanently tilted head, flipped off an imaginary ignition, parked his steering wheel against the wall, and jerked toward the young children's area. Extracting a copy of *Mike Mulligan's Steam Shovel* from the stacks and squeezing into a miniature plastic chair.

Annette hurried around restacking books and straightening magazine racks, answering a couple of phone calls, and sneaking looks at Robin Hood wildly scribbling away on a yellow legal pad. A couple of generic looking senior citizens hobbled in and out—what accounted for the morning rush.

After a while, aware that hardly anyone else would show up until the onslaught of mothers and young children who came for Story Hour at 2 p.m., she pulled up a chair beside Racin' Raymond in what had become a daily ritual, gently wrestled the book from his hands, and began to read in a sing-song voice. Her angelic reading-to-children's voice you'd think might have had some positive affect on her own wayward spawn. Racin' Raymond eyed her in profile, bird-like, unable or unwilling to bend his neck to face her, a beatific smile gracing his crooked beak. By the time she finished, Old Man Hurley and even Robin Hood had fixed their eyes on her, silently cheering for Mike Mulligan and his trusty steam shovel, Mary Ann. A feeling she had not had since childhood scampering through the field high with hay, a feeling of absolute oneness with this earth and everyone in it, sifted down on her. Racin' Raymond rose, grabbed his steering wheel, shifted, and throttled away.

"Where'd you learn to read like that to children?" asked Robin Hood, stepping out from behind the ancient maple as she rushed down the steps at 4 p.m., having turned over her shift to the community college intern who covered the last three hours of the day.

She caught her breath.

"I'm sorry, didn't mean to startle you."

"It's OK. Actually, I don't scare that easily."

It was true. After losing her father and brother, giving birth, raising kids, finding her neighbor, Alice, in a tub of water pink with blood, watching helicopters lifting kids into body bags, John and Martin and Bobbie gunned down, Nixon elected in excruciating Technicolor on their new Zenith, what edge could fear possibly claim?

"So?"

He was saying something, had *said* something, she was doing that more and more lately, favoring inner dialogue over outer; disappearing into her head.

"You read so well to children," he said.

"I've had practice. I read to my children all the time."

"Past tense; they're grown, I take it?"

"Fourteen and ten. My reading days are over."

"Not even the ten-year-old?"

"Going on twenty. 'Christ, Mom, that would be *mortifying*,'" she said, in a seamless imitation of her son. She had always been a gifted mimic. Perhaps it was time to begin cashing in on her true talent. Tease up her hair, start smoking again, and sacrifice her family to a career as a standup comedienne a la Phyllis Diller.

He smiled, the fine lines shooting out from the corners of his eyes somehow integrating the haphazard features—large nose, wide mouth, narrow chin—like a connect-the-dot drawing.

"Buy you a quick soda?" he asked.

"I have a family," she blurted. "I need to get home, make dinner, and help with homework." She felt as if she'd been reciting something without even knowing it—Timmy's Cub Scout pledge or the Ten Commandments, for example.

"Just ten minutes?" He smiled down at her, a boy again, just another kid. "I'm new in town. Don't think I've talked to anyone in two weeks. I'm afraid my voice is about to start rusting."

"McCoy's has a fountain," she found herself saying, thinking of that clock radio she'd had her eye on.

They sat side by side at the granite counter nursing egg creams like high school kids in a time warp. His last name was Manet, he told her, like the painter, no relation, French on his father's side, just like her.

"What brings you here?" she asked, swiping at a head of light brown foam with the tip of her long silver spoon.

"My uncle owned a cottage in Tompkins Cove. He died right after Christmas."

"I'm sorry. Were you close?"

"Very. He never married; left me the house. He was a painter—never famous or anything but made a living of it. My father was an accountant in Westchester, for God's sake; my mother was June Cleaver. First Catholics in the Country Club. Tennis and Daiquiris and the whole nine yards. My uncle just said screw it all, and followed his bliss. I needed a break and I guess I had this idea of trying to see if I could find the person I started out to be."

She nodded. She knew that fantasy, had penciled it in on her imaginary "to do" list right under "find God, work on marriage, and develop parenting skills."

"A break from what?" she asked.

"I'm a professor at Hunter." He rolled the paper from his straw into a tight ball. "American literature. Taught an elective called the Language of Revolution that catapulted me to campus fame and nearly got me fired."

"Revolution," she said. "As in American? Not the most distinguished time in our literary history but you've come to the right place."

He shook his head. "Revolution in the broader sense. Emerson and Thoreau. Ginsberg, Hunter Thompson, William Burrows. Women, too—Dorothy Parker, Joan Didion, Sylvia Plath—people stepping out of the box of traditional mores, political and/or literary."

His eyes glittered.

The teenaged soda jerk behind the counter looked vaguely familiar, too old for one of Colleen's friends and too clean cut for someone she'd met at an anti-war rally. Still, she felt suddenly exposed sitting here with this boy-man, this *revolutionary.*

"So what are you writing?" she asked, flustered.

"I've been trying to write a novel for years. I decided to take a sabbatical the end of last semester, a year off to see if I could make it work, finally. I don't know, my uncle's death, watching kids get blown up on TV, it got me thinking. If not now, *when?*"

He came off earnest, she admired that. Earnest and lonely and harmless and also terribly brave for upping and walking away from his life in the city, committing to face a blank page day after day, believing he might actually have something to say—the delicious audacity of it.

"Anyway, I was burning out. I got thrown in jail twice last year when the kids took over the administration building. I mean, I'm on their side but I take an awful lot of heat. I guess I'm tired of getting tear-gassed and listening to rhetoric that is really just empty slogans for most of them, I suspect. I just want to string words together for a while. Look at the stars. My uncle's house is in the woods. There's this great little clearing. I bought a telescope last week. You should come have a look some time."

He had his elbows on the counter, sleeves rolled up to reveal the down on his forearms; hands folded, as if in prayer. Those startling, otherworldly eyes bored into her as he rattled on about the Milky Way. She could not remember the last time anyone in her family had actually *met* her eyes. She thought of her mother and father seated across the claw-footed dinner table at the farm, inspecting their plates as if searching for clues to meaningful life in the universe. Eyes—even when raised to one another—forever slightly out of sync, as if focused on a stunt double seated several inches away.

She didn't flirt, as a rule, might just as well have been voted least likely to flirt in her high school class instead of her actual claim to fame: "most punctual." Still. She suddenly spun around on her stool, almost giddy, before coming to her senses.

He laughed. "What?"

She glanced at her watch. "Oh God, I need to go." She rose and slid a couple quarters toward him.

He slid them back, but she ignored the gesture.

"See you tomorrow, then," he said.

"Tomorrow, and tomorrow, and tomorrow." She had once studied Shakespeare. Where had that girl gotten to? She hurried away, all at once tired of tear gas and hollow rhetoric, too, and was halfway home before she realized she'd forgotten all about the clock radio.

"So Leigh wants me to go with her to her uncle's place in Jones Beach for the long weekend," said Colleen. "We'll leave right after school on Friday."

"We *would*," Annette said.

"What?" asked Colleen.

"We would leave right after school on Friday," Annette said. "We have not given you permission yet."

"Pass the chicken," said Gerry, through a mouthful of potatoes.

"Mrs. Twardowsky would drive us and her uncle has this cottage right across from the beach. I've never even been to Jones Beach, for Christ sake, Mother, who knows when an opportunity like this will present itself again."

"No fair," said Timmy, punting a pea across his untouched plate with his fork. "I've never been to Jones Beach either. Plus, Jesus, Mom, she said Christ. I thought we weren't allowed to say Christ."

"Or, *Jesus*," Annette said, raising her brows. She turned to Colleen. "The pool opens this weekend. I thought you wanted to be there."

"It's because it's Leigh, isn't it? You can't stand her, Mom, admit it."

"This is exactly the kind of thing that makes me sick," muttered Timmy.

"I like her just fine," Annette lied. Leigh, with whom Colleen had been joined at the hip since she showed up in her class last year, reminded Annette of a female Eddie Haskell from the *Leave It to Beaver* show, toadying to your face and ever scheming behind your back. Still, she couldn't put her finger on anything Leigh had actually done, and pitied her for losing her father in Vietnam.

"*Dad*," Colleen said, on the verge of a whine.

Gerry's fork clattered against his plate. "It's up to your mother. I just pay the bills around here, remember? Anyway, Don Segal invited the whole department up to his cabin on Lake George for the weekend to knock out a new Ovaltine campaign."

"I told you Frank and the kids are coming for a barbecue and staying Sunday night?" Annette said.

"I know; the guy's a jerk. But I really don't have any say in the matter."

She stared at the recent addition of his fair, sparse sideburns. They gave his ruddy face a grimy quality that made her long to take a washcloth to him. And that crack about the bills.

"Please, *Mom*," Colleen pleaded. "This is the chance of a *lifetime*."

"No one ever listens to me in this house has anyone ever noticed that?" said Timmy.

Annette sighed. She could not believe Gerry was abandoning her to entertain Frank and Myra and their five obnoxious children. Nephews and nieces who made Colleen and Timmy seem destined for sainthood. Nor could she keep track of the number of *lifetime* chances she had recently granted her daughter. And when the hell was Gerry planning to break the news of his impending absence? They were not done with this conversation.

"All right," she said. "But I need you to clean the house and change all the sheets before you leave."

"You are the best!" Colleen bolted out of her chair. "I need to go call Leigh."

"You have not been excused," said Annette.

"Well, this just sucks," said Timmy.

"Go to your room," Gerry said.

"Christ." Timmy shot out of his chair and caught his belt on the tablecloth, launching his plate Frisbee-like across the linoleum floor, peas ricocheting against the wall.

There was good news and bad news that weekend. The good news? Three of Frank's children had strep throat, causing them to cancel their visit. The bad? Timmy had worked himself into a major snit and stopped speaking to his mother altogether, which, the more Annette thought about it, might turn out to be good news after all.

She stood up to her elbows in suds as her son huffed past her in his theatrical way, stomping and sighing as if auditioning to understudy for his older sister. Really, where had these children gotten their dramatic talents, she wondered; certainly not from her side of the family. And Gerry's reserved their histrionics for wakes and funerals, although members of his sprawling Irish clan did tend to perish with astonishing regularity.

When Timmy trudged through the room for the umpteenth time, humming a little funeral dirge through his clamped teeth, she asked him what his problem was.

"Why can't we go to the parade like other normal people for once in our lives?"

"I don't support this war. You know that. I can't go out there and act all patriotic. It would be hypocritical."

"Hippa what?" Timmy said. "People are dying, Mom. You don't even care about them."

"I care." She bit her lip and turned away. It was his body she pictured, after all, in every single TV frame; his body, grown and maimed. She drew a deep breath. "Why do you think I've been protesting the war?"

"People are dying," he repeated, enigmatically.

"Fine, we'll go to the parade," she snapped. "Go put on your swimsuit. We'll head over to the pool right after."

He sprinted out of the room, grinning and triumphant.

"I wouldn't have expected to find you here."

The voice was familiar. Annette's head snapped around to find Robin pressed in behind her. In the street, humpbacked World War I veterans in full uniform hobbled behind the Rocky Ledges marching band. Relatives in civilian clothing pushed several paraplegics nodding off in wheelchairs.

"I might say the same of you," she smiled, hand caressing the waves she had set that morning, vowing to wean herself from the lacquered beauty parlor do she had favored. Longing to grow out the lustrous mane of her youth like the Breck girls on TV, to feel the slap of it against her bare shoulders one more time before it turned gray and frizzled as her mother's.

Beside her, Timmy glared up at the stranger.

"Robin; my son, Timmy. Timmy, this is Robin Manet. He comes to the library sometimes."

"Man, those guys have muskets," Timmy said, waving a tiny American flag.

The Rocky Ledges Historical Society marched by in full regalia, rifles smacking their backs, swords clanging at their waists, flushed and glazed in the already summer-like heat. No anti-war protestors heckled. It did not even occur to anyone here to do so. A person had to drive twenty miles south or across the river to find a decent rally.

"This is a total trip," Robin said.

Annette nodded, embarrassed, as if responsible for her neighbors' spectacular apathy. They didn't see anyone returned from Vietnam in the ranks marching and wheeling by, as if the war had not touched this place, had not robbed a half-dozen of its sons.

"Buy you guys a pizza?" Robin asked, after the last of the uniformed brigades had headed for the cemetery.

"Actually, we were going to the pool," Annette said.

"Sure," said Timmy.

"I love pizza, cheese pizza," said Timmy, strings of mozzarella suspended whisker-like from his upper lip.

Annette could not quite put her finger on the reason for her acute self-consciousness sitting here at *Angelo's* with Robin and her son. Of course there was the matter of her marital status versus his lack of one, but, with Timmy between them, an unwitting albeit solid chaperone, even Monsignor McGowan couldn't fault her—could he?

"This is not half bad for the burbs," Robin said.

"Yeah," Timmy agreed. "They have better pizza in the city. I always stop at this one place with my Dad on the way to Shea Stadium. They have real root beer, too, the kind that comes out of a kegger with the foam on top. We have the same last name as Shea Stadium but I always tell people that actually there is no relation."

Kegger? Annette had to smile at the way Timmy had begun reinventing his life for this stranger, implying that excursions to Shea Stadium were regular rather than once-or-twice-a-season affairs spurred by free tickets from Gerry's boss.

"I am so glad to hear you are a Mets fan," said Robin. "I don't know what is worse, Yankees or Republicans."

"Republicans," said Annette.

"Hey, you want to come to the pool with us?" Timmy asked.

"I'm sure Robin has better things to do with his time," Annette said, in a growing panic.

"Thought you would never ask." Robin reached out and tousled Timmy's hair.

As if sitting next to Robin on a lounge chair in last season's worn black bathing suit was not bad enough, Leigh's Mom, Edie Twardowsky, having dropped their daughters at her brother's place the night before, immediately decided to join them complete with her lifetime supply of Bain de Soleil and the requisite San Tropez tan.

"I needed some time to myself, if you know what I'm saying," she explained. "It is just so trying to be the responsible one all the time, day in and day out. A person needs a break."

Annette had never considered what it would feel like to be a widow, a single parent, even though, more often than not, she thought of Gerry as another child rather than a real participating partner.

Robin chatted politely, widening his eyes now and again as Edie described her freewheeling life in Texas (vague allusions to a dance career with carnival overtones) before she'd married Leigh's father and hit the road as an Army wife. "I thought I wanted to travel," she said, long, manicured fingers undulating in the air like an aquarium flower. "We hadn't counted on this war."

Her moth-like eyes fluttered away the tears standing there.

Annette squeezed her hand. Her grief seemed real enough. Maybe that's why she found herself a couple hours later as Timmy's fingers began to shrivel from chlorine inviting Edie and Robin back for dinner. She had all that meat thawed from Frank's cancelled visit, after all; it would be sinful to waste it.

Now she carried a tray of marinated London Broil and potatoes wrapped in foil to the charcoal grill Robin had managed to get going. She did not grill, that was Gerry's domain; even cooking day in and day out taxed her. She had never warmed to Julia Child's antics like her former neighbor, Alice, before her breakdown; relied instead on Peg Bracken's *The I Hate to Cook Book*.

Edie, who had spent a good half hour mixing and tasting a pitcher of Whiskey Sours, topped off their glasses and raised her own. "To summer."

Annette sipped her drink and smacked a mosquito on her sunburned arm. "Are these bugs bothering anyone else?"

"Bugs don't go for me," Edie said, scraping a maraschino cherry off its stem with her pearly whites. "I guess I'm just not sweet enough," she added, in a new, baby-like voice Annette had never heard her use before. "How about you, Robin?" She had slipped off her high-heeled plastic sandals. She reached out a blood red manicured toe and—Annette could not believe her eyes—jabbed the back of his bare knee.

Robin spun away from the grill as if seared, lifting his drink. "They like me, too," he said, staring straight at Annette, as if the revelation set them apart as some kind of united, exalted prey. You could almost see a bond knitting itself tight-rope-like across the air between them. Edie's eyes followed it, too, her candied mouth relaxing into a disappointed stick of limp, red licorice.

By the time they finished eating it was nearly dark and the whiskey sours had clearly worked their magic on Edie.

"What is that you put on the ice cream, again?" she asked, leaning over the citronella candle, its plastic netting casting a latticework of shadows across her cheek.

"Just a splash of coffee," Annette said. Chalk another one up to Peg Bracken.

"Speaking of coffee, I'll take some more." Robin held up his mug. "Can I get you some, Edie?"

She waved him away. "I best get going."

"Sure you're OK to drive?" Annette asked.

Edie frowned. "It's only six freaking blocks."

"I could walk you," Robin said.

Edie rose unsteadily, leaned over, and pecked at Annette's cheek. "This was really nice of you." She straightened up in slow motion. "Have fun, you two," she called over her shoulder, shocking Annette into remembering exactly what it must look like, leaving the two of them there to their own devices; in Edie's mind; anyway. She should tell him to leave, but how did one do that without sounding rude?

Robin whisked the tray out of her hands and headed for the screen door.

Inside, Annette relaxed again as she washed and he dried, chatting about Rocky Ledges' finest assembled at the parade, the pool edged with prone, flabby bodies greased to the gills—*Edie*—as if they'd been playing house like this for decades. The way she and Gerry used to talk when they'd come back from parties after they first married. All at once she missed her husband. *That husband*; anyway; or maybe, too; *that wife.*

She found Timmy asleep on the couch in the rec room with the TV on as if standing in for his father. She turned it off, covered him with a blanket, and dimmed the light.

"I poured you more coffee," Robin said, as she came up the stairs. "I thought we could sit outside for a few minutes more. It's a full moon."

"Moon River," she thought, the lyrics floating by in her head, letter by letter, like Alphabet soup. She had always wanted to dance to that song but Gerry, unlike her father, had never really taken to dancing. Little beads of sweat erupted between her breasts under the loose linen shift. Robin reached up and tucked a loose tendril of hair behind her ear. It seemed so caring a gesture, almost paternal and yet.

She followed him outside like one of those enchanted girls on *Dark Shadows*, the Gothic soap Colleen and her friends were so addicted to. Like an ingénue bitten in the neck by a vampire; condemned to an eternity of longing.

They sat side by side all silvery on lawn chairs sipping coffee and gazing up at the sky.

"When I was little, I used to climb up in my window when the moon was full and pray to my people to come and get me," Robin confided. "I never thought I was from here, you know? I always had this sense of being far away from home."

"I did that, too," Annette blurted. She had never told anyone. She smacked at a mosquito on her leg, and he laughed, a choking laugh that might have been a moan.

And then they were all tangled up together, his tongue in her mouth, the sweet chlorine sent of him, his beard prickly on her neck. A kiss like no other that went on and on until one or both of them, (she could not say who, had lost all consciousness of where she stopped and he began) wrenched free.

"Jesus," he said.

"You'd better go." She was on her feet; hugging herself.

He turned and headed down the driveway.

I must be insane, she thought, lying on her back. Moonlight spilled through the window liquefying her limbs. She replayed the scene leading up to the kiss over and over, searching for clues to what might have triggered it: the shared childhood suspicion that they both hailed from another planet; the ability to attract more than their fair share of mosquitoes? Seriously?

She had allowed herself to be kissed by another man, unleashing a torrent of un-tapped desire. And now, genie out of the bottle, she could not get him out of her head, despite the reality of Timmy breathing in and out right down the hall, despite the reality of Gerry who had called almost as soon as Robin's tires crunched out of the driveway.

"Miss me?" he'd asked, as he was wont to do whenever he called from a business trip. It had not occurred to her before that he never said he missed *her*, simply demanded the requisite pledge of allegiance.

She was being unfair, she knew, hoping to somehow justify throwing herself into the arms of another man like that in her own backyard. She ran her fingers through her hair, tucked an errant wave behind her ear as Robin had done, imagining his fingers on her neck, tracing the smile at the base of her throat. The phone rang.

"I have to see you," he said, his voice like a knife to her back. "Tomorrow?"

"We're going to the pool again." She pulled the white sheet up to her chin as if to cover her body's offensive urges, replaying that kiss like a song.

It was almost morning before she fell asleep.

Sleep evaded her entirely those giddy weeks of their affair yet she remained supercharged, able to juggle work and home with complete efficiency, easily chiseling out time for Robin. They had spent the next day together at the pool, arriving separately this time, making a grand show of it being oh so coincidental for Timmy and Edie, and arranged to meet later that week at his house. She told Gerry she was going to an antiwar rally in New City. The lie popped out of her mouth fully formed as a gum ball, the first in a seemingly endless supply of brightly colored orbs that Gerry swallowed whole.

Driving the winding road to Robin's place that first night she tried half-heartedly to convince herself they could keep it platonic. She would simply explain the kiss had been an aberration, the result of an overdose of whiskey sours and a full moon. But when she tried to open her mouth, sitting on his uncle's chipped and creaking metal porch swing set out on a triangle of lawn overlooking the river, Robin lifted her face in his hands as if unearthing buried treasure and she forgot the lines she'd rehearsed. No one had ever touched her like that. It was such a relief. Tears streamed down her cheeks as they rolled off the swing groping like teenagers and did it right there in the grass as the sun bled into the horizon. The ghost of Ichabod Crane, that kindred headless spirit, stampeded through the woods in the gathering dark. Later, as stars flared like sparklers, Robin dragged his telescope out and they huddled together swatting mosquitoes and searching for home. They fixed their eyes on Orion's belt, the middle star where the buckle would be, winking a little brighter than the rest.

"That's it," he said.

She laughed. She felt like a kid again, rushing through the fields, a whole alternate future unraveling in front of her like a runner at a church wedding.

"Do you ever think they're watching us out there?" she asked. "Watching us; with telescopes of their own?"

"Absolutely. Only they're much more advanced. They can actually see us on a giant screen. They watch us like a movie."

"That's comforting," she said, tucking the sheet around her bare breasts. "So you think they're beyond all this earthly violence?"

He nodded. "Why not?"

It was a nice thought. She settled into it for a moment before her busy mind jerked her away.

"Why are we here?" she asked. "I mean, how could we leave a place like that?"

He pulled her onto his lap, lifted her hair, and nibbled at the nape of her neck, sending little shivers down her spine.

She shut her eyes as he pressed her back down into the sweet clover; easing down into her like the piece she'd been missing all her life.

They met once a week at first so as not to arouse suspicion but she soon started making up other excuses to dash out at night. Running errands she couldn't squeeze in during the day—a lecture on the Dewey Decimal System, or a speech at the community college. Gerry never questioned her but when he ironically started showing an interest in sex again she begged off, citing female troubles, an excuse he seemed to buy. Then one night she came home from Robin's later than planned to find her husband sitting outside on the patio; his cigarette a tiny torch in his hand.

"How was the rally?" he asked.

"Pretty tame," she said, wondering if another lie even mattered at this point. She was going to hell. She had no illusions about her final destination.

"What's going on, Annette?"

Shit, she thought, sinking down beside him.

"Are the kids asleep?" she asked, stalling, waiting to hear what he knew.

"There wasn't any rally tonight, was there?"

And still, *still*, she could not bring herself to speak the truth. This was her husband, after all, the man who announced that first day they met playing volleyball at Waynesburg State that he intended to marry her. He had worn away her resistance with a dogged determination so unlike her father. Eventually his overwhelming confidence in them as a couple had infected her, too, coaxing her into believing that his rapt attention might make up for the adoration she had never gotten from her parents, who seemed to have used it all up on their firstborn girl, the infant that got away.

She waited, her thighs glued together by the incriminating stickiness of Robin's sperm.

"I checked in the paper," he said. "There wasn't any rally."

"I got it mixed up," she said. "I drove out there and when the field was empty I drove over to the Nanuet mall."

"And what did you buy," he asked.

"Just window shopping." She rose, grateful for the darkness that hid her burning cheeks. She stooped over and pressed her lips to the orb of thinning hair on his crown, swallowing an unexpected wave of affection and the almost immediate sickness that followed it.

He said nothing as she turned her back on him; her father all over again, no matter how he had started out.

Sometimes, stretched out on Robin's lawn, they talked about running away together, walking out on the lives they had made, and heading west. He could get a teaching position at Berkeley. She could wear flowers in her hair and take a job in a Montessori School like she'd planned before she got pregnant with Colleen. She was never really serious about it but the fantasy—suckled by their words—fattened until she could almost see Rocky Ledges disappearing in the rearview mirror of Robin's dilapidated Volvo. The miles erasing the features from her husband and children's shocked faces, leaving them blank as those mannequins used to test a car's safety in head-on collisions.

It began to worry her, how little she seemed to care about abandoning the people she loved. The lack of sleep eventually took its toll and she stumbled around in a daze, coming to her senses all at once while standing in front of the card catalogue struggling to decipher numbers and letters that might have been hieroglyphics. Dozing off while reading to Racin' Raymond; forcing him to rouse her with an escalating set of steam-shovel soundeffects. Once she misplaced her keys for days only to discover them nestled in an egg carton in the refrigerator. Finally, feeling as if she might be losing her mind, she drove twenty miles to a church she had never attended before to make her confession.

"Bless me father, for I have sinned," she whispered. She had covered her face with a black lace mantilla, as if she could hide.

Behind the screen a priest who, in silhouette, resembled Spencer Tracy—who everyone knew had carried on scandalously with Katherine Hepburn—had the audacity to ask if she was planning to end the relationship.

"I can't bear the thought of hurting my family," she replied. A more palatable version of the truth than the actual one: that she could not shoulder the burden of guilt any longer.

"Then you must sever your ties with this man immediately," Spencer Tracy said.

After she'd finished the penance the priest gave her, she pressed the pearly white rosary beads to her lips, asking to hear God's voice. She had a fleeting vision of herself, posing Mary-like in blue robes, but no clear directives.

When she pulled up in front of the house, Edie Twardowsky was sitting in her gold Cutlass in the driveway with the windows rolled down, *It's the Time of the Season* by the Zombies (Colleen's current favorite) blasting from the radio and riding the muggy air. Annette—reluctant to start soiling her newly cleansed soul—resisted the urge to continue down the street.

Edie cut the music. "I've been waiting for you," she said.

In the kitchen, Edie removed her oversized, Jackie Onassis-style sunglasses. She'd been crying.

"Are the girls OK?" Annette asked, suddenly alarmed.

"Fine. Look, I'm sorry but I didn't know who else to go to. I don't really have any friends here."

Annette waited, her mind running through the speech she would have to make to Robin as soon as Edie left, her scant resolve already wavering.

"I'm pregnant," Edie said. She drew a ragged breath.

"I'm so sorry," said Annette, because obviously it was not a happy condition. "I didn't know you were seeing someone."

"That's the thing. I'm not really seeing anyone." Edie sighed. "I ran into Robin a few weeks ago at the pool and invited him home. We had a few drinks. One thing led to another, you know, and … I used a diaphragm but I hadn't used it in years and who knows if it had a hole in it or something. I'm sorry. It was just a one-night thing. He was all freaked out about it afterwards. I know he has feelings for you."

Annette grabbed her stomach, as if kicked. She pictured Robin and Edie rolling around on that horrid shag carpet. "Why are you telling me this?" she asked, all at once oddly detached, as if watching Edie hawking her sad story on TV like the women on that pathetic TV show *Queen For A Day*, competing in tragedy for a new washing machine.

"I can't have this child," Edie said, "I know what the church says but I can't do this to my daughter and I *won't* do this to myself. I was hoping you might drive into the city with me next week. I'm afraid to go alone."

God works in mysterious ways, her mother used to say. Not an hour ago she had prayed for guidance and here was Edie bent over the kitchen table sniveling into her iced tea. For a moment, Annette found herself marveling at the symmetry of God's plan for her redemption. She did not believe in abortion, but she could see how Edie might believe it a more humane act than bringing another child she could not seem to handle into this world. Besides, it would not be the first time Annette had gone against the church. Pregnant with Timmy, she had developed a blood clot in her leg and, when their Catholic doctor announced he would save the baby over its mother if necessary, she and Gerry had found themselves a Jewish doctor bound by no such Papal edicts. She went on birth control pills after miscarrying during her final pregnancy. The grief had paralyzed her for weeks. She did not want to end up like her neighbor, Alice, roaming the halls of some mental hospital, brain cells shocked out of her, and children in foster care. The living had claims upon a person, too. Wasn't that why she had already decided to end it with Robin? Robin. He said he wanted to spend the rest of his life with her. Right.

"Of course I'll go with you," Annette said.

He cried like a baby when she confronted him in his driveway without getting out of the car. He was drunk, he said; and had smoked a joint he'd been saving to reward himself for finishing the first five chapters of his book. (She had not known he smoked pot—had she known him at all?) Besides, Edie had thrown herself at him, he said.

Annette held her palms to her ears until he talked himself out, staring straight at the windshield.

"Annette, please, we're the same, you and me, I'm your missing rib, remember, I ..."

She turned on the ignition and started to back away, his hands still gripping the car door.

"Annette, please. It was just sex. It didn't mean anything. It wasn't like what *we* had. Jesus, this is nineteen-sixty-nine."

She hit the gas.

Neil Armstrong and Buzz Aldrin had landed on the moon a couple hours earlier. Annette had made meatloaf and mashed potatoes and corn on the cob—Gerry's favorite meal—and set their supper out on TV trays when Gerry came home from driving Colleen and Leigh to see *Romeo and Juliet*.

"What's all this?" he asked, on the verge of a smile.

"I thought we could watch the moon walk. It's supposed to happen sometime in the next couple hours." She and Robin had planned to be together for this. *Moon River*, and all that jazz. She pushed her thoughts away.

Gerry collapsed in a chair beside her. His sideburns had filled in and he had grown a mustache that balanced his long face and brought out the dimple on his right cheek she'd thought had disappeared.

"Timmy, come and eat with us," she said.

Her son blinked up at her from the rug, surrounded by small plastic green army men, as if blinded by the sudden flash-lit beam of a Vietcong.

They ate in silence, watching photos of the Apollo 11 launch days earlier and the Eagle landing a few hours ago. After a while, Timmy scrambled back down on the floor and Gerry rose, returned with two bottles of Budweiser, and handed her one. He studied her as he clinked his bottle against hers, brows raised, as if asking a question. He had not asked her again about her whereabouts that night or any other. She beamed back at him with as much reassurance as she could muster.

Gerry hoisted his bare feet up on the coffee table, placed her hand on his thigh, and lit a cigarette.

They would be OK, wouldn't they, the crew of Apollo 11, and the Shea family, too?

She awoke to find Colleen inching in beside her, her cheeks tear-glazed, Timmy passed out face down on the floor among his battalion, bottom in the air, as if awaiting execution.

Gerry snored. Walter Cronkite rattled on.

"What is it?" Annette whispered.

"Nothing," said Colleen. She sighed, Juliet-like.

Annette cupped her daughter's chin in her hands the way she had when she was little.

Colleen had stopped confiding in her last year but she knew from finding her diary that she had a crush on that new lifeguard Drew Peters, a high school senior at some prep school for Christ sake about to draw the draft.

Colleen nestled into her mother's ribs and Annette held her breath, afraid any movement might sever the gossamer bond between them. She thought about that book by Betty Friedan that had pushed Alice over the edge with its empty promises. She thought about Edie in her Jackie-O glasses, a scarf tied over her hair, slipping into that doctor's mildewed walkup like some kind of Russian spy. She thought about the way she herself had interpreted the loneliness that lived inside her as something to be solved *outside*, by a man. For a moment, she could almost see a world in which her daughter would not follow in her tracks. She had wanted to step out of the *role* she found herself in, not her whole life; she knew that now. She loved her children, still loved her husband, really. He was just as trapped as she was. She would go back to school, she vowed, not just resume the interrupted life she had started, but start all over again. Who did she want to be?

"Look," breathed Colleen.

On the screen, Neal Armstrong climbed down the Eagle ladder in slow motion and placed his stubby boot on the surface of the moon, followed by a crackly audio transmission they could not understand.

"Wake up!" said Annette, shaking Gerry's shoulder.

"That's one small step for a man, one giant leap for mankind," Neal Armstrong said, clear as day, all the way from the moon.

"Christ," said Colleen. She squeezed Annette's hand.

Gerry rubbed his eyes.

"What happened?" Timmy slurred.

"They just walked on the moon, you little maggot," Colleen said.

"And nobody woke me? Jesus, this is just the kind of thing that makes me sick."

Colleen

We Shall Never Pass This Way Again

Colleen scowled into the mirror plucking at tufts of undeniably green hair.

"Jesus, Leigh," she said. "I thought it was supposed to give me highlights, not some alien head. My mother will have a veritable cow."

"I'm sorry," Leigh said. "But, really, I'm telling you, it's not that bad. It's just the light in here, my mother's stupid color scheme. It distorts things."

"Maybe we could go down to the drugstore and find my old color and just turn it back?"

Leigh shook her head. "I tried that once on my hair and it kind of turned it into this strange substance." She sighed. "You're just going to have to wait a few weeks."

A few weeks? Even before the calamity of the hair Colleen didn't know how she could possibly survive the next few hours. They were about to head down to McGovern campaign headquarters to watch the returns; her mother had offered to give them a ride. Her mother had at least voted for McGovern, unlike the rest of her friends' parents including Leigh's Mom, what with Leigh's father being a Vietnam Vet and all. As though voting Republican would bring him back. Colleen fastened her St. Patrick's Day hair in a ponytail and bit back tears.

"How about a hat?" Leigh said. "Remember that big floppy hat I bought? Very cool; like Sly wears."

Colleen tried it on. She thought it made her look insane—like the Mad Hatter tripping—but, really; what choice did she have? She pulled the crushed velvet folds down over her eyes and sighed. Think cool, she told herself, as though she had ever spent a single cool moment on the planet. This is the first day of your cool, new life, she chanted in her head, tucking the ponytail under her raincoat and climbing into her mother's Impala.

Annette looked her up and down in that way of hers. "Nice hat."

Colleen cringed, grateful to have temporarily avoided the inevitable showdown. They drove in silence for a while, a cold rain beating intermittently against the windshield. Seals & Crofts were singing their song *We Shall Never Pass This Way Again* and Colleen prayed to God it might be so as she spied on Leigh through the rear-view mirror.

Leigh sat with her hands folded, scrutinizing the naked silhouettes of oaks and maples. She had recently replaced her wire-rim glasses with hard, emerald-tinted contact lenses. Puberty seemed to have temporarily squelched her tendency to run off at the mouth all the time. It also had divided them. Leigh had traded the space in her heart Colleen once occupied for a revolving door of boys she sampled and discarded like candies in one of those Whitman samplers she loved so well. Watching her now, Colleen thought she might have been considering the effect of Republican wire tapping on the outcome of the campaign. But she also might have been weighing how her new orange bell-bottoms hugged the swell of her thighs. Like Colleen, she had campaigned hard, but unlike Colleen, she didn't seem all that concerned about the outcome or its highly suspect causes. Colleen continued to study her, hurt and baffled, emotions she refused to get used to. Even in the waning light Leigh's blonde hair illuminated her shoulders and Colleen found herself reflexively sucked in, as if for sustenance; plant to sun.

"Do you think he has a chance, Mom?" Colleen asked, after a while.

Annette sighed. She seemed to be sighing a lot more than usual lately. Colleen couldn't tell if it was because her father rarely came home for dinner anymore or because he occasionally did.

"I don't know, honey," her mother said. "Elections are tricky business. Sometimes there are upsets, though."

"But it would be a long shot. I mean, in your opinion?"

"A *very* long shot."

It was Colleen's turn to sigh. Why even go, she wondered. What's wrong with this country, anyway? Why would people rather vote for a crook than someone who wanted to end the war for good? Because Eagleton had once had shock treatments when half the country needed them? An enormous sense of not getting it settled over her, a condition she had struggled with all her life. A sense that seemed only to be growing these days, developing a life of its own; a gaping rift inside her; a fault in the earth she had no clue how to bridge.

At headquarters beneath the harsh fluorescent tubes even Leigh's hair took on a greenish tinge and Colleen fingered the brown velvet hat for comfort as she had once stroked the satin edge of her blanket, lying awake waiting for the Commies to drop the bomb. People stood in small, grim clots rocking back and forth and drinking beer out of bottles. Patty Wilkes, the new eleventh-grade English teacher—the kind who liked to dress exactly like their students—fingered her crocheted vest and smiled. She turned and poured beer into two Styrofoam cups so people would think it was Coke, Colleen supposed. "Bottoms up, girls," she whispered. "I think it's going to be a long night."

"I don't," said Pete Carney. Their social studies teacher had crept up on them in that stealth way of his. He had a wrestler's body—broad-shouldered, slightly stooped over, and always in motion. His abnormally large hands worked in the air when he talked—stacking and building—until he plunged them back into his sports jacket pockets with an apologetic shrug. He had this way of looking up from under his brows at you that—at least for a moment—hypnotized you into thinking you really mattered. Even when he laughed he seemed sad, as though he didn't get it either; Colleen liked to think. "The returns are already coming in," he added. He launched the tragic look. "They're predicting a landslide."

Colleen sipped her beer and tried to drag her eyes off Mr. Carney's mouth; to wrap her fat green head around what he was saying.

Leigh twirled a strand of hair around her finger, her default gesture. "They're all idiots," she said. "I mean, we knew that, didn't we?"

Mr. Carney kept his eyes on her.

The contact lenses had transformed her into a beauty, the kind that made grown men stop in passing, wheel around, and suck in their breath. Colleen wondered if she could somehow talk her mother into buying her a pair; even though she didn't need glasses.

"That's the spirit," said Ms. Wilkes. "That's the American way." She raised her beer bottle in a toast, not nearly her first, Colleen suspected. The people milling about them seemed all at once defeated, shoulders slumping as they sidled up to the TV mounted overhead in the corner.

"Why?" asked Colleen, unaware she had even spoken, thinking about the weeks and months of canvassing they'd done—ringing doorbells, dropping literature on asphalt stoops. Considering the bumper stickers and buttons she kept in her locker and distributed despite her classmates' lack of enthusiasm or, more often, downright disdain. Thinking about the possibility of her brainless brother being called for the draft as the war trudged on, ending up crouched in some rice paddy in Vietnam or Cambodia when he couldn't even pour a glass of milk for himself or part his hair in a straight line. She shuddered.

It turned out Mr. Carney could read her mind, just as she had always suspected.

"I think you have to look at the bigger picture," he said, softly, to prove it, running his giant hand through a tangle of tweedy hair. He touched her on the back lightly with his hammerhead fingertips. "People voted for Nixon because he opened up China. They ignored the Watergate story because they believe in the presidency. They refuse to see it eroded."

"But they want to continue this war," Colleen said.

Leigh shifted in her clogs, combing the crowd with her eyes, clearly bored with their ideological banter. They had lost a battle, so, on to the next. She believed in issues but only as end products, Colleen realized; commodities you could purchase through smart investing; a string of hotels on a Monopoly game boardwalk. Not a Democrat at all, when you came right down to it. Why hadn't she noticed it before?

"The people want things to stay the same," said Mr. Carney. "They always begin with denial. They can't take it in yet. It's a kind of ..." His hand swayed in front of his chest, conductor-like. "Educational curve. This country has gotten so polarized over civil rights, the war; the whole women's thing. But this campaign shifted everything further to the center. We'll be able to look back and see that. Mark my words."

The center, Colleen thought with scorn. I do not plan to spend the best years of my life in the Goddamn center.

"My, my, my," Ms. Wilkes said. "Just listen to all those mixed metaphors." She shook her streaked-blonde head. "You're really losing me, here, Peter. Anyway, if anything, I think this demonstrates just how far to the right this country has swung, despite the whole—how did you put that again—'women's thing'?"

Mr. Carney opened his mouth and clamped it shut again. He threw his hands in the air and caught them. "History will tell," he said, with a little bow of his head.

Colleen caught the charge between them—a volley of toxic smiles—and wondered if they had once been lovers.

"Come on, let's go watch the returns," Ms. Wilkes said, suddenly cheerful again. "I want to see Nixon stand up there and lie some more. I want to remember this clearly and be able to say I told you so when that crook finally meets his maker."

Someone turned up the volume on the TV and Colleen drifted toward it. Whispers died as David Brinkley reported McGovern had scheduled a press conference in 45 minutes. Colleen sipped her beer. Graham Culver, in his third year at New Paltz, nodded toward her. He hardly ever communicated verbally. How could someone so quiet major in theater?

"How are you doing?" she asked, rushing to take the emotional temperature of everyone around her.

He shrugged.

"Mr. Carney says it's because of China," she said. "Nixon winning, I mean. But I don't know. I think it's because people in this country are so afraid of any kind of change that ..." She raised her hand to run it back through her hair and found the hat instead. She patted it. She had no idea what she thought, really. She finished the beer in her cup. "You know?" she said, for lack of something better, once more barely skirting the black hole that had already sucked up her words and apparently a good portion of her brain.

Graham cocked his head and stared.

The hat had slipped back on her forehead, exposing her frizzy green hairline. She slapped her hand over it and yanked it down over her ears.

"Twenty minutes," Ms. Wilkes, said, back at her side. "Have you heard he's going to concede in twenty minutes?"

"Concede?" asked Colleen. "You've got to be kidding." She was talking too loud, she knew, but couldn't seem to stop herself.

Several campaign workers' heads whipped around. They glanced at each other and smiled, nodding, as if to say, "Ah, but she's so young."

"Anyway, that's the word," said Ms. Wilkes. "Why don't you take your hat off, Colleen? You look warm."

She was warm, as it turned out; in fact, almost dizzy. She slipped off her cardigan and tied it around her waist. She peered down at her own body as if from a low-flying plane. What had she been thinking to dress all in brown? With the hat, she resembled an elongated acorn or some kind of overgrown fungus. "Did he *say* he was going to concede?" she asked, struggling to steady her voice. "Did anyone actually hear him say that?"

Ms. Wilkes' eyes swept over Colleen's gnome-like facade. "What else would he have to say?" she asked, rhetorically. But her eyes were kind.

Graham Culver's lips twitched from the pressure, Colleen supposed, of trying to seal themselves shut long enough to keep from busting out laughing.

A necklace of sweat that had formed under the hat began migrating outward bead-by-bead across Colleen's forehead. Her knees swayed. Images around her began decomposing into tiny black-and-white dots, grainy as the newspaper photos she'd buried in her underwear drawer of Bobby Kennedy dropping to the floor at the Ambassador Hotel in a pool of dark gray blood. She knew what that meant. She had passed out before from the heat of her own unmet expectations. "Excuse me," she mumbled, shuffling sideways away from them, crab-like.

Somehow she made it across the whole room like that, drawn toward the cold air seeping through the glass door someone had propped open with a cinderblock. She stepped over it and out into the frigid night, her breath sending little white clouds into the still air. She walked down to the next storefront, Murphy's toy store. At six years old she'd had to return a bag full of toys she'd bought there with a ten-dollar-bill she found on her mother's carpet. She could still see Mrs. Murphy's face looming down at her from behind the counter, as though studying some kind of shoplifting insect.

Now she sunk down on the steps and yanked off the hat, running her fingers through her hair and allowing the hurt and confusion to steam off her until her teeth began to chatter and she pulled the sweater back over her arms. After a while, she rummaged in her shoulder bag, grabbed a cigarette out of its little cardboard box, and sat striking matches against a book until one flared. She inhaled deeply, shivering.

A bark of a laugh, a laugh she knew only too well, cut the stillness. Leigh? She glanced up over the deserted street, the parallel-parked cars; eyes searching a street lamp as though half expecting to find her best friend buzzing it like a moth. She heard the laugh again, followed by a muffled, "Shhhhhhhh."

"Leigh?" she said, bombarded by more noises now—muted, crackling, shuffling sounds--emanating from a bright green Volkswagen; Mr. Carney's car, parked two spaces down. A small bright firefly flickered inside it. Stubbing out her cigarette, Colleen stuffed her hair back in the hat and headed for the car. She peered in the window and found Leigh in the back seat draped between Mr. Carney's bent legs, lounging against his chest clasping a joint in her ribbon-like fingers. Grinning, she offered it to Colleen. Mr. Carney beamed up at her from under droopy lids, no sadder than usual.

Colleen spun around and headed back inside.

The crowd had knit several new rows to the semi-circle around the TV. McGovern had already begun his short speech, face shiny as wax under the cameras' glare. Colleen inched in beside Ms. Wilkes, half expecting to see it melt. McGovern read from a sheet of paper and began thanking a long list of people. Beside him his wife gazed out at nothing in particular. The light had gone out behind her eyes.

Ms. Wilkes grabbed Colleen's hand and squeezed, as though they were friends. When McGovern finished, some people turned and headed for the door while the true masochists waited around to hear Nixon.

"Well, I guess I really don't have the stomach for this after all," Ms. Wilkes said. "I think I'll take the rest of my six-pack and head on home. I'd be happy to give you a ride; Leigh, too, if you can track her down in the next five minutes."

Colleen wanted more than anything to take her up on it, Leigh or no Leigh, preferably no. "I'll just take a quick look," she said.

Ms. Wilkes nodded. "I bet she could find her own ride home," she said, leaving Colleen to wonder if she knew about Leigh and Mr. Carney. If maybe Colleen, once again, was the only one who didn't get it.

She started for the door, mentally debating her next move, but Leigh and Mr. Carney intercepted her. Smiling, relaxed— well, *stoned*, when you came right down to it. Colleen found she could not even begin to meet their glassy eyes. "McGovern just conceded," she mumbled. "Ms. Wilkes said she'd give me a ride home. You, too; if you want."

"Hmmmmmmmm," Leigh stretched her bare arms up over her head, arching her back.

"I'll take you home," said Mr. Carney. He didn't seem the least bit embarrassed, as though he considered it entirely normal; making out with a student in his car.

"No, I better go with you," Leigh said. "You look kind of down."

"I'm fine," Colleen snapped. She gripped her hands together tightly to prevent them from slapping her, scanned the room for Ms. Wilkes; spotted her, and bounded away.

"Hey," Leigh said, catching up with her. "Come on, now; there'll be other elections. They'll catch him, I'm telling you. He won't finish out this term. He'll get impeached."

Colleen rolled her eyes.

"*What?*"

"Jesus, Leigh. You know what."

"Pete? Come on, Colleen. We didn't *do* anything, if that's what you mean. Jesus, we were just fooling around."

"Ready girls?" asked Ms. Wilkes. She wore a gold leather jacket that hugged her body and belted around her narrow waist. From one arm a six-pack of Michelob--minus three bottles—dangled. She lit a Tarreyton, somehow, with one hand, and blew smoke rings over her shoulder. Colleen began to really like her.

They piled into her beat-up Mustang, Colleen in front and Leigh in back. Ms. Wilkes flipped on the radio. "*We shall never pass this way again*," sang Seals & Crofts, once more, a kind of anthem for the whole evening. Colleen wished she could get it in writing.

Ms. Wilkes dropped Colleen off first. "Don't take it too hard," she advised, patting her on the shoulder. Her eye makeup had smeared, Colleen noticed, as though she had been crying. She was nice, actually, once you got past the hipper-than-thou fashions.

"See you tomorrow," called Leigh. Colleen pretended not to hear her.

Inside, Mrs. Shea lay asleep on the couch, a puddle of vanilla ice cream congealing in a bowl on the table beside her. On the TV, a group of newscasters in gray clothes debated the significance of the landslide. Colleen shook her mother's arm.

"Hey, sweetie," Annette said, blinking up at her. "You OK?"

She wished people would quit asking her that. She must look like some kind of walking wound. "Fine," she said. She shifted her face into neutral like one of those blonde newscasters who managed to smile even as they read cue cards describing mayhem in a steaming little country on the other side of the world. "Dad still out?"

Annette nodded blankly; a newscaster in training. She sat up and stretched. "I think I'll turn in soon, too, right after I hear the rest of the precinct results. Would you check Timmy for me?"

Colleen nodded. "Night, Mom," she whispered. But the television had already re-absorbed her mother's brain.

She opened the door to her brother's room. A ladder of cloudy light sifted through the Venetian blind slats onto the carpet and bed. Timmy lay on his side in his pajamas clutching the GI Joe doll the little mutant ought to have outgrown years ago. He had kicked off all his covers. Colleen lifted them off the floor and tucked him in again. He was still her little brother, after all. She slipped the doll out of his hands, resisting the urge to snap the head off its stubby neck.

In bed she lay on her back, her body leaden: visions of snickering classmates swirling in her head. How could she ever leave the house again? How could she live in a country that would let this election happen? Then there was the matter of Leigh and Mr. Carney. She lay awake all night searching the ceiling for answers, signs of any possible benevolence in the sky beyond the shingled roof.

The next morning, Annette sat at the kitchen table in her bathrobe reading the paper through red-rimmed eyes. In passing by her parents' room Colleen couldn't help but notice the undisturbed side of their bed. She bee-lined for the aluminum coffeepot.

Her mother glanced up. "What's with the hair?"

Colleen sighed. "It was just supposed to be highlights."

"One of Leigh's ideas?"

Colleen nodded. She really couldn't take a lecture right now, and, summoning all her telepathic powers, willed her mother to drop it. "I know it looks bad, Mom. Believe me; I hate it, too." Her voice caught and for once the spell she cast on her mother took.

Annette folded the paper and slapped it on the table. "It will grow out," she said. "I'll see if we can get some kind of rinse to tone it down until then."

Colleen carried a cup of coffee to the table and sat down. "What about Dad? He's going to kill me."

Her mother shook her head. "Let me worry about that." Her eyes reminded Colleen of Mrs. McGovern's on the TV screen last night. Colleen wondered if she had stumbled into a science fiction movie in which they had stolen the women's souls and replaced them with low-voltage light bulbs.

Her mother reached over and touched her shoulder. "You can stay home today if you want. It's OK with me."

Colleen wiped her eyes and blew her nose with her paper napkin, considering the offer. But her mother's pain—the badge of betrayal she wore on her chest these days—seemed more dangerous a proposition than the snake pit awaiting her at school.

"That's OK," Colleen said. "I'm bound to catch a lot of grief about the election. I might as well throw the hair in, too, and get it all over with in one fell swoop." Mr. Carney first period; for God's sake.

"That's my girl." Annette kissed the top of her daughter's head and wandered away down the hall.

At school, Colleen didn't wait for Leigh's bus but headed straight inside to her locker.

"Joan," cried Kirby Nicholson, an enormous, neckless linebacker whose head seemed abnormally small and flat on his body, well suited to housing his scant gray matter. "Is that our very own Joan, I mean, Colleen of Arc? Could we have a word with you?" he fawned, shoving a pretend microphone in her face. "We'd just like to get your thoughts about McGovern's race. We were just debating here over whether he lost by the biggest landslide in the history of the world, or simply the history of these benighted states of America?"

Colleen hugged her books to her chest and tried to step around him.

"Curb it, Clowny," said Mr. Carney, striding up beside them.

Kirby threw up his hands. "Just trying to talk politics, Mr. Carney; on this historic morning after."

"Don't you have somewhere else to be?"

Yeah, like the moon, thought Colleen. Funny, she'd been so worried about her hair and no one even seemed to notice. Maybe the years of willing herself invisible had finally paid off. She shifted her eyes into soft focus transforming the tunnel of students into a blur of faceless mannequins and scooted past them, avoiding further contact with Mr. Carney. "Full-of-Blarney

Carney," the boys called him. Jealous, she had once thought; and, as it turned out, with good reason.

"Colleen," a familiar voice called, but she refused to turn around.

Leigh charged up in front of her. "Come here," she said, yanking her wrist.

Colleen wiggled free. "No thanks."

"Yeah, well you have to. You're my best friend, remember?"

"Give it a rest, Leigh." Colleen headed for Mr. Carney's empty classroom, but Leigh followed, of course, damn it all to hell.

"Look," said Leigh. She plopped herself down at the desk beside her and lowered her voice. "Are you pissed because I made out with Mr. Carney? I mean, did *you* want to date him?"

Date him? In spite of herself, Colleen had to laugh. It was just like Leigh to ask such a completely irrelevant, ridiculous question. But honestly she didn't know why she felt so betrayed. Because she disapproved, or because she wished Mr. Carney had slipped his hand under her blouse instead? What exactly was bugging her? Colleen pressed her index fingers to the insides of her eyes. "I don't know. I guess this election just has me really kind of freaked."

"You listen to me," Leigh said. "I know it seems like people just reek right now but this is going to turn around, I'm telling you. Hell, things are even changing for women. And you know what? By the time we're old enough, we could run for office ourselves!"

Leigh's face shimmered, newly gilded. Colleen saw she meant it, and smiled. "Why on earth would anyone in her right mind want to actually run for office?" she asked.

Leigh tossed her head. "Well they won't crucify me. I'll run for president one day, you'll see. And if you won't be my vice-president, you can be Secretary of State or something."

"Chief of Staff," said Colleen.

Leigh nodded. "What's that again?"

"Shut up," Colleen said, smiling. "You are such an idiot."

"True enough but here's the thing. You have got to stop caring so much or you'll end up getting shock treatments and it'll be curtains for both of us."

The bell rang and students shuffled toward their desks examining their feet.

"We have each other, remember?" Leigh mouthed.

Colleen studied Leigh through a haze of exhaustion: the glowing fake irises, the dimples that never went away even when her face was slack. Colleen thought of Mr. Carney's juggler's hands toying with the buttons on Leigh's blouse. He was losing his hair, why hadn't she noticed that before?

She thought of Ms. Wilkes with her fringed skirts and iridescent eye shadow and bitter smiles, her mother huddled over her students' composition books, the unruffled sheets on her father's side of the bed, George McGovern swaying at the podium reading from the prompter in his deadpan voice; the sun setting in his wife's eyes. No matter where she turned, she couldn't find anyone she really wanted to be like—not even Leigh.

"I really am starting to like your hair," Leigh whispered.

Conjugating Sleep

The cooks are yelling again for no apparent reason in a language I have no real desire to understand, a language that grates on my ears and nerves, at times resembling a growl, at others the distinct phlegmy gurgle of spitting. A customer at table eight, some John Travolta impersonator, an unruly ascot of black hair embellishing his open collar, has his hand in the air again, clamoring for my attention, as if I have any control over the whims of these Aegean refugees. Cursing me and my colleagues for the demands we make upon them merely by slipping our tiny lined order sheets over the aluminum barrier between us, behind which skewered lamb smokes and spits on open grills and a bald, meatball-shaped man named Peter coughs into a giant vat of hummus.

Across the vast, warehouse-like space studded with wooden tables of various shapes and sizes and vintages, John Travolta writhes away in his chair, index finger stabbing at the air, and I am about to risk a verbal thrashing by asking Peter if he has the spanakopita and gyros plate I ordered 20 minutes ago when the Gods—in a most uncharacteristic move—venture down from Olympus on my behalf in the form of my boss, Anastasia.

"Colleen, I want you to switch sections with Debra," she says. She pats me on the shoulder. "I'm moving you up front with the family. Alicia didn't show up again, we have no choice."

Overwhelmed by her obvious confidence in me I nonetheless wipe my hands on my apron, throw back my shoulders (I was a dancer growing up, I have the posture to prove it) and glance fleetingly at Peter and his meatball brigade, nonplused by the insolent way he stares straight at my chest with a little smirk I have never encountered on that bulbous-nosed, ill-shaved, surly-lipped mug of his before, deciding I would prefer the usual evil-eyed tirade. Still, Anastasia is finally allowing me to wait on the *family* after seven whole weeks of serving tight-fisted students, T.A.s, and professors who left me counting their meager dimes and quarters and occasional dollar bills in the wee hours in the vain hope of making enough profit to cover my rent and maybe even cut back on my shifts, the vain hope of one day snagging more than a few hours of sleep before dashing off to another lecture on the lurid Freudian aspects of *Wuthering Heights* and *Jane Eyre* or the latent feminist consciousness lurking in the work of Jane Austen.

"Hey, honey," mutters a hunch-backed man in a black suit, a starched white shirt, and a skinny navy blue tie. A field of sparsely seeded gray hair plagues his pebbled scalp as he peers up at me through a pair of black, rectangular-shaped glasses behind which roam a rheumy set of asphalt-colored eyes. He clenches a cigarette between gnarled, liver-spotted knuckles and I watch its Slinky ash grow, defying gravity, holding my breath against the moment when it will collapse on the long, rough-hewn table where he sits at the head, seemingly unaware of the glass ashtray not a foot away. I slide it toward him.

"Bring me a cup of coffee, will ya, honey, and an ouzo and a glass of retsina for the lady here," he mumbles in a Greek accent that seems deeper and flatter than Anastasia's boss and distant cousin, Andros, the thirty-something, manic-depressive, here today, gone tomorrow owner of the *Athenian Kitchen*. Beside him, a girl about my age stretches her arms over her head like a cat, tossing a mane of dark hair over her shoulder with a flick of her head (a technique I have never truly mastered and so have come to despise) before folding and resting both pale hands on the man's shoulder with a sigh, heavily made up eyes fluttering like trapped moths. I cannot help but ogle the pea-sized sapphire on her finger.

"Give Papa a kiss," the man grumbles and the girl obediently pecks at one of many deeply grooved furrows that seem to have accumulated decades of ash.

I glance at my watch: 1:55. I will have to get the liquor order in right away before they shut the bar, I think, scurrying away actually touched by the thought that the obvious elder of the family has taken his granddaughter out for a nightcap. Even criminals have their soft sides, I think, because the term *family* is code for Mafia, mob, machine, whatever; Greek, in this case, and pretty much in charge of the entire restaurant and club scene in Kenmore Square and God only knows what the hell else. Even gangsters have their soft sides, an argument I ventured in writing workshop just the other day in an unsuccessful effort to convince yet another male Hemingway wannabe that no one is ever wholly good or bad, not in life and not in fiction. We all hold our share of light and darkness (regardless of what the nuns tried to drum into me). I order the ouzo and wine and dash off to grab the coffee.

By the time I return, the table has completely filled with what one might at first mistake for a convention of funeral directors, men in black suits ranging in age from 30 to 80, many with young girls (even younger than moth-eyes or moi) draped on their shoulders, girls who appear ever so wide awake despite the obvious fact that they have long surpassed their bedtimes. Amidst a haze of smoke and a cacophony of raised voices, people fire orders at me and I scribble away, beaming; more coffees and ouzos and retsinas; Saganaki and hummus and avgolemono and platters of Kalamari. I start to explain the bar is closed but a hush falls over the table and Grandpa massages the pocket of his jacket. I imagine a weapon concealed there and back away, deciding to allow Anastasia—who after all has grown up with this *family*; is likely related to these people—to break the bad news.

Rushing toward the kitchen, legs churning (sometimes I *love* my job, after two in the morning when a second wind kicks in, adrenaline suddenly infusing my limbs, the juice of revived efficiency a welcome sting in my veins), I deal the orders out to Peter who actually smiles an almost normal smile, picking them up and turning them over one by one like lucky cards at a black jack table, maybe. I have graduated, I congratulate myself. I'm working the *family* now.

"How's it going?" breathes Anastasia, smacking a stack of menus against her black crepe pants. She has such a dulcet voice for such a tall, large-framed woman. An odd voice for a Greek of any stature, really. (They are, as a group—and I do not mean to stereotype—the loudest human beings I have every encountered save for the Puerto Rican family that moved in down the street my senior year and started blasting salsa music and grilling goats in their front yard, and my Uncle Lester; related only by marriage and unilaterally shunned by both the Irish and French sides of my family.) Short flaps of gleaming black hair obscured her ears; a Kewpie-Doll mouth worked at odds with her oversized eyes and nose as if transplanted from someone else's face. A second-generation immigrant, she anchored the adrift kitchen and wayfaring front of the house, balancing Andros' proclamations of doom and torpedo-like rages with a hand to an apoplectic shoulder, a whispered reversal of yet another of her cousin's ill-founded edicts. In short, she ran the joint; the wait staff would not have endured without her intervention and homicide certainly would have claimed the kitchen.

"Great," I tell her. "They want ouzo, though. I tried to tell them the bar was closed, but."

She shrugs. "I'll take care of it. I should have told you, I'll handle the liquor orders. It can get pretty hectic down there, Colleen—call if you need a hand."

I nod, trying to ignore the reference to "down there," evocative of a viper pit. "Really; it's fine, so far. They're not hitting on me, if that's what you mean," I cannot help but add, invigorated by the sight of Peter pressing a plate of dolmades into my hand. (Being hit on—along with sorry tips that required ridiculously high volume to counterbalance—was a reality I had nearly accepted as my chosen lot for opting to make up to my parents the additional tuition required by choosing a private over a state school.) "Anyway it's so cute, I mean, the way they bring their daughters and granddaughters with them."

Anastasia starts to laugh, quietly, of course, shoulders soundlessly heaving. Peter lobs a torrent of Greek and she murmurs a response. A volley soon overcomes the kitchen, whizzing back and forth over my head among the feckless battalions stooped over sinks and grills, punctuated by guttural chortles and guffaws that leave my cheeks burning. I stack plates of salad up my forearm as I have learned to do, still watching Anastasia, who suddenly swivels to face me again, seeming to register the confusion in my eyes.

"Sweetie, those are *not* their daughters and granddaughters."

"Ah." And the light dawns on my own naiveté like another tequila sunrise, illuminating the wicked truth of these mistaken alliances.

"Hookers?" I mouth.

She nods and I scurry off to a score of Peter and company cracking themselves up at my expense to get a better look at these women my age and younger, searching their faces in the neon lights spilling through the storefront glass from Commonwealth Avenue for whatever I have missed, a window into their world, a peek at a road not taken. Hoping to flee the grim reality of the weighty innocence I have been unsuccessfully trying to chuck for the past several years, a brief sexual encounter with my high school boyfriend, Scott—that may or may not have technically constituted intercourse—not withstanding.

My legs ache and I know I should go home but Peter has filled a sundae glass with wine the color of prune juice he claims to make himself and I sit at the employee table outside the kitchen enthroned between Anastasia and Mary Ann, a forty-year-old

Southie with three grown kids and a slew of ex-husbands who has worked here for a decade, ever since Andros' dad sent him to America to run the place, or, more likely, to get him out of the country before he got himself killed. Peter pulls up a chair and gestures toward my wine glass. He has suddenly, inexplicably taken a shine to me and I don't dare risk reversing my good fortune.

"Good," I say. I raise my glass in the air. "Bien, bueno," I add, resorting to my high school French and Spanish, even though it actually tastes exactly like it looks. Still, it is beginning to work on my over-amped system and, before I know it, my glass has miraculously refilled itself and I find that the taste grows on you rather quickly.

"You did great tonight, Colleen," Anastasia is saying, which is not entirely true. To say I survived is perhaps a more accurate description of my family initiation, a point of view I try half-heartedly to advance before the women flanking me cut me off at the pass.

"Nonsense, Colleen, you were superb, they all told me so, *honestly*," Anastasia insists.

"They are very good at feedback," Mary Ann says. She rubs her eyes, the irises a bull's eye in a dartboard of concentric dark circles. "I'll grant you that."

"The thing is, they are *so*, I don't know, normal-seeming," I say.

"Real family men," says Mary Ann. "I mean the way they take their daughters and granddaughters out on the town."

Anastasia's fig-shaded eyes crinkle in amusement. "That was good, Colleen, you have to admit. That was classic."

"Right." (Is there *anyone* in Kenmore Square who has not yet heard this story?) "But I mean, I thought they would look more dangerous, you know? It kind of freaks me out that a possible murderer could resemble your best friend's father."

"You were expecting eye patches, maybe?" Mary Ann says.

"I know what you mean," says Anastasia. "One of them *is* my best friend's father."

Mary Ann throws back her head and laughs.

I sip my wine, basking in the warmth of my new insider status. The other girls have long since fled. Peter rises and returns with a plate of Galactobouriko, my favorite dessert on the planet, and shoves it toward me, mumbling something to Anastasia who cocks her head, studies me, and nods. "You're too skinny, he thinks, we need to put some meat on those bird bones."

"Merci, Gracias," I say. I plunge my spoon into the custardy, syrupy confection. Wondering if I fell asleep on my feet during my last shift as I have been known to do (even though falling asleep in my own bed these days eludes me), if my exhaustion has finally toppled me and I have lapsed into some kind of dream-infused, pastry-laden, Greek Dickens-scripted coma.

"Not many of our girls make it through a single night with the family," muses Anastasia, train of thought unimpeded by Peter's shocking generosity. She holds a Kalamata olive between thumb and forefinger and expertly pops out its pit before depositing it on her tongue. She has beautiful hands, I have never noticed before, long-fingered and satiny and dimpled, with squared off, pink-tinged nails.

"Remember Janine?" barks Mary Ann, throwing back her tousled, bottled-red head and firing a missile of smoke toward the ceiling fan. "Remember when she locked herself in the freezer and refused to come out and you had to talk her out of there?"

"She tried to use a butter knife on Peter here," Anastasia says. "Poor mixed up kid."

Mary Ann erupts in another spasm of laughter culminating in a coughing fit of mammoth proportions that prompts me to stub out the Tarreyton I bummed from Anastasia and beat her on the back until she spits delicately into her cloth napkin, leans back in her seat, and lights another Camel, raccoon eyes taking in something on the ceiling invisible to the rest of us.

Peter tops off my glass again and the world starts to spin. "I really need to call a cab," I slur, attempting to push up out of my chair.

"Mario!" barks Peter, and a boy I have never seen before materializes at his side, a boy in a double-breasted white chef's shirt and jeans and sandals, my age or older, wearing the face of Michelangelo's David.

Peter issues an indecipherable order, the boy disappears, and I collapse back into my chair.

"I mean it, Colleen, you're a natural," Anastasia is saying. "I could really use some help around here, I cannot count on Andros and I am seriously burning out. I haven't taken a vacation in five freaking years. We'd pay you well. I'd teach you everything I know. There might even be a partners' share down the road if you play your cards right."

I try to force my sleep-deprived, alcohol-riddled brain to veer with the drift this conversation has taken to no avail. "I'm a student," I protest. "I'm in school."

"You could take some time off," she says. "*Find* yourself. Isn't that what all the kids are doing these days? Weren't you just complaining you didn't know anymore why you were getting an English degree? Maybe you need some real-life experience. You could always cut back to part time. And you wouldn't have to worry about money anymore. Honey, working these hours and trying to do school, too; I'm telling you, it'll kill you." She rests one beautiful palm on my thigh and my whole body seems to dissolve under its silky weight.

"Cab," says Mario, sneaking up behind me. I pull on my trench coat and back away from the table smiling and waving goodbye. Silently he steers me out the back door and into the alley, past metal dumpsters bulging with plastic bags filled with rotting food and frozen flies. A rat the size of our family's cat darts between the idling Yellow Cab and me. I lunge toward Mario's chest and it takes me a moment to identify the source of the piercing yelp I hear as coming from my own throat.

I stand still a moment, shoulder to shoulder, studying him out of the corner of my eye. We are exactly the same height—boys my age are always taller or shorter but never my same size—I find it somehow soothing. He opens the door for me and I climb inside. The cab pulls away and I glance back out the window but my five-foot-seven Michelangelo's David appears to have transported himself back to Florence. Somewhere behind this tunnel of Brownstones we are racing through, a siren trills and the red neon line of dawn suddenly illuminates a heretofore unfathomable horizon.

She works hard for the money, so hard for the money, Donna Summers booms to the staccato slap of my roommate, Judith's, platform shoes across our apartment's bare hardwood floors.

She stomps around our three-bedroom, fourth-floor walkup in rapid circles like a small, over-fed dog before returning to the bathroom with which my bedroom shares a thin, dry wall and firing up her blow dryer again, a drone that eliminates once and for all the possibility of grabbing another half hour of sleep. I am sprawled on my stomach, face cemented to my pillow with drool, trying to invent a childhood that might account for a person behaving like this. Because Judith is the most self-centered and oblivious human being I have ever encountered in my nineteen years on this planet and I honestly don't know how much longer I can put up with this.

When my roommate, Carrie, and I first rented the flat two months ago we thought it would be a cinch to find a third roommate but you would not believe the number of complete losers who paraded through these walls before we settled on Judith just in time to make our first month's rent. Almost immediately, she astounded us with her stupidity and insensitivity, spraying insect repellent *inside* the refrigerator for example when she caught a wayward roach making a run on an ill-wrapped piece of cheese and then informing us that it had puddled in the egg container and needed a thorough defrosting and cleaning.

"Didn't she know this stuff is poison?" Carrie seethed.

"I know."

"What, does she think we're like the Irish maids?" Carrie's eyes frosted over, leaving me—a model of tolerance by comparison—to step forward and deal with it.

"We all need to take care of ourselves around here," I said, a regular Kissinger-in-training; over a pot of herbal tea I had brewed. "It seems like the person who made the mess should be responsible for cleaning up the mess."

Judith smiled (she never stopped smiling, a fake smile plastered on her face day and night; she was a TV major in the communication school, after all. Future anchorwomen could not afford frowny faces—you could get wrinkles!). She shook her head back and forth in that way of hers, a Parkinson's-like gesture designed to show off the glossy brown waves of her Farrah Fawcett do, her dangling, jeweled earrings. She was a BP, short for "beautiful person," the self-proclaimed nickname of the majority of B.U. students who hailed from Bronxville or Great Neck with more money than brains, brandishing their parents' credit cards and an eye-numbing cache of Disco paraphernalia.

She smiled before uttering the sentence that has been ringing through my ears like a bad song stuck in my head ever since: "Oh, but I wasn't brought up to clean refrigerators."

Shocked, enraged, flabbergasted, speechless, I retreated to my room and have not approached her since but decide, lying here listening for the sixth or seventh time to what passes among her people for music, watching the digital clock creep from 8:56 to 8:57, that the time has come, as they say, to talk of many things.

I wrap myself in my mangy chenille robe, push up off the old twin bed my father and I lugged from storage in my basement in Rocky Ledges, New York, all the way to Back Bay, and stumble into the hallway nearly blinded by the overhead bare-bulb light to find Judith reading the *Boston Globe* and innocently spooning Danon Yogurt into her rubied lips at the kitchen table Carrie and I bought from the boys who rented before us, along with a spring-shot couch covered in a mostly worn-off Brillo-like fabric and a black lacquer coffee table.

"Judith," I bark, over the music, but (surprise, surprise) she can't hear me.

I march into her room and turn off the stereo; march back into the dining room.

"Oh, Colleen," she says, glancing up, blinking behind her violet-tinted, oversized glasses. (Her nearsighted, artificially fringed eyes appear larger than life behind the thick lenses but I know from seeing her spectacle- and makeup-free they are actually quite beady.) "Didn't know you were up."

"Judith." I plop down across from her in one of our wobbly chairs, leaning my elbows on the pocked gray Formica. "I'm pretty sure you realize this but just in case it has somehow escaped you, I work four nights a week until four in the morning. I don't get home until dawn. I have eleven, sometimes ten o'clock classes the next day. I need to sleep in until the very last moment or I will eventually perish. Only that hasn't been happening."

"Insomnia?" she says. She twirls a chunk of hair around a manicured finger sporting the longest, reddest nail I have ever seen, a nail only a person not brought up to clean refrigerators could possibly maintain. "I have some sleeping pills my Mom gave me and a prescription for Valium. You can have some if you need them. I can always get a refill."

My head throbs from last night's infusion of wine and sugar. I rub my gritty eyes. OK, so irony doesn't work; ditto sarcasm. I will try to be literal. It is not my forte, but I will give it a shot.

"Judith, I can't be taking a sleeping pill and expect to wake up four hours later and be on my way." (I am pretty sure about this because my mother's best friend when I was little went through a sleeping pill phase during which she was difficult to rouse even after twelve hours and eventually had to be returned for reprogramming.) "Besides, that's not the point."

Judith glances at her watch and shoots up out of her chair. "Sorry, Colleen, but I got to get out of here. I'm meeting this really cute guy from my news-writing class to edit our story about that girl that got raped and killed last week in Cambridge? Did I tell you we got this fabulous footage yesterday of her parents just completely losing it when the police showed up to break the news. I am so going to ace this class."

She trots over, plucks a fitted denim jacket off the lopsided, tarnished brass coat rack Carrie and I found at a garage sale over the summer near her home in North Jersey, and slings her satchel over one shoulder.

"Judith, the thing is; you have got to quit blasting music and clomping around on those shoes of yours on mornings after I've worked. I can't go on like this. I'm wasted, I feel like I'm looking at the world through layers of gauze, I'm going to flunk out, I'm going to have a nervous breakdown, please—you've got to help me out here."

"*God*, Colleen," she says. She peers up at me with a disgusted, bulgy-lipped smile, as if I am that offending roach all grown up despite her best efforts. "All you had to do is ask."

I sigh, biting back tears of frustration.

"Oh, and Colleen," she calls back over her shoulder from the warped threshold: "The bathroom's a bit of a mess, in case you haven't noticed. The tub could really use some work."

I salute the closed door, mentally adding the phrase "cleaning bathrooms" to the long list of tasks Judith was not raised to do.

Je dors, tu dors, elle dort, nous dormons, vous dormez, elles dorment, I scribble in my lined notebook, sitting in Mr. Armor's Shakespeare Tragedies I class trying to tune out a discussion about the adolescent self-absorption at the base of Hamlet's ruin in favor of my own self-absorption which finds me conjugating the verb *to sleep* in French and Spanish in the wild hope that I might find it more accessible in a foreign language.

Je dormirai, tu dormiras, elle dormira, nous dormirons, vous dormirez, elles dormiront, I scribble, in the vain desire that conjugating the future tense may somehow win me a night's future rest. (As illogical an assumption as the obsessive practice of copying: *Mrs. Colleen Ryan, Mrs. Charles Ryan, Ms. Colleen Ryan,* over and over again into my Mead composition book in junior high, attempting to manifest a happily-ever-after ending to my futile crush on Charlie Ryan.)

I glance over to find Carrie quizzically staring at me out of eyes the color of a Giotto sky. I slip my notebook to the edge of my desk to allow her to read. She smiles, shakes her head, arranges her nearly waist-length golden brown hair behind her ears in her slow-motion way, and scribbles in her notebook: You are losing your mind.

What's your point? I scribble back.

She presses the back of her hand to her mouth to conceal a smile.

"Ms. Shea, Ms. Bailey, something you'd like to share with us?" warbles Mr. Armor, Adam's apple bobbing around in his Icabod Crane neck like a loose ball bearing. Before I took this class I didn't think it possible to destroy Shakespeare but Mr. Armor has done it handily with his pedestrian interpretations and barely concealed rage at the human race in general for a host of unknown transgressions. Really, this is the kind of thing I had to put up with in Catholic grade school but do not feel deserve from this particular university given the tuition my parents and I have been barely scraping together.

When I was about three years old my mother had once again tried to make me nap (which I fought valiantly and consistently day in and day out). Still, she forced me to go to my room every day at two o'clock and stay there for at least an hour to prevent herself, I suppose, from rushing across the street and downing a bottle of her friend Alice's sleeping pills. One afternoon, lying on my bed on my side, playing with wooden clothespins on which I'd crayoned faces, I accidentally drifted off, only to dream of another mother, another me, living another better life that did not involve naps. I awoke and raced into the kitchen where my mother and Alice (said pill popper who finally ended up in the loony bin) sat swilling coffee, demanding to know who was real: the mother in my dream or her? I have never quite accepted her answer. This is just another bad dream, I tell myself, now, watching a greenish blue, raised, worm-like vein on Mr. Armor's temple pulse. I really have been sleeping all along.

Carrie and I shake our heads in unison and before Mr. Armor can further patronize us, a shaggy headed kid in the front row unwittingly intervenes in our behalf by glancing at his watch.

Mr. Armor lunges forward on his Daddy Long legs, yanks off his own watch and dangles it in the guy's face. "It's eleven-fifty-five," he shrieks. "You only have to endure me for five more minutes, Mr. Chillelli."

Everyone stares at his or her desk which does not prevent our collective peripheral visions from registering the astonishing sight of Mr. Armor's hands flying up and down his scrawny limbs as if frisking himself in an unsuccessful effort to regain his self-composure.

Yo *duermo, tu duermes, el duerme, nosotros dormimos, vosostros dormis, ellos duermen*, I write, rubbing my bloodshot eyes.

If one more stiff with a hooker on his arm so much as asks me for a glass of water I swear to God I will run screaming out into freezing traffic and never look back.

Needless to say, my brief honeymoon with the family has come to a bitter end. I cannot believe the complete self-centeredness of these hoodlums who place their orders practically one olive at a time leaving me endlessly sprinting back and forth to the kitchen for a cup of soup, a plate of cheese, a burger, a baklava (which I have decided must be the first thing they offer you to eat on arrival in hell). I have lost so much weight my gold cotton uniform hangs sack-like on my flat chest and I am exhausted to the point that when the one who resembles Sonny in *The Godfather* decides to ignore me as I stand there trying to deliver a plate of hummus and a basket of pita, my eyes fall shut and do not open again until the hummus has completely slipped off the table of my forearm. I watch it arduously coat his jacket sleeve, reflexes shot; my brain unable to relay a message to my hands quickly enough to prevent a full-blown chickpea mudslide.

"This is exactly what I'm talking about sweetheart," Anastasia says, after we've closed, after I offered to have his jacket dry-cleaned and he gallantly refused (leaving me in the uncomfortable position of owing a hit man!).

I sit methodically filling red plastic ketchup bottles, attempting to restore some order to the hopeless chaos my life seems to have of its own accord become.

"An assistant manager does not have to run around like a banshee," she croons. "An assistant manager gets to work day shifts, too, sometimes, if you quit your classes that is, or at least cut back to half time."

"I've got to put these away," I tell her, too tired to argue. "Oh, and Anastasia, can you cash this check for me before you leave?"

"Shhhh, shhhh," she says, shaking her head, her own little version of "tisk, tisk," plucking the check out of my hands and heading for the cash register. (*The Athenian Kitchen* insists on cashing all employee checks in-house—a *family* thing, I'm told—wink, wink.)

"Buy you retsina?" Mario asks, as I close the supply closet door. I flinch. "You scared me. You always come out of nowhere, how do you do that?"

He shrugs. "I'll bring it over," he says.

I head for the employee table.

"I'm going home," says Anastasia, pressing a wad of cash into my hand. "Give you a ride?"

Mario sets two glasses of wine on the table and plunks down beside me.

"No thanks. I'm still pretty wound."

"Just think about it, Colleen," she says. "That's all I'm asking."

When she has gone, Mario raises his glass and clinks it against mine. His eyes are soft brown, a darker shade than mine, round and simple and dog-like. I have an overwhelming urge to rest my cheek against his neck.

"What's wrong?" he asks.

We have known each other less than three weeks and yet I already feel transparent around him, no, worse: undressed, naked, although not in an entirely bad or weird way. He seems to register my every mood. I see myself in all my agony reflected back from his perfectly chiseled face. I drag my eyes away, fearful of stumbling and drowning there, Narcissus-like.

"What makes you think something's wrong?" I ask, evasive. I don't know anything about him, I remind myself, except that he is supposedly Peter's nephew sent here by his parents to work, saving money to go to a U.S. school. He claims to have his eye on Amherst, wants to be a writer, a poet, maybe, ha! (He has absorbed my story, my emotions, my conflicts, sitting here staring back at me, my own Platonic twin. Sometimes I wonder if I have imagined him.) It is all a story, I remind myself, a cover; I cannot trust this boy, I know nothing of his real life, zero, zip, rien, nada.

I sip my wine.

He continues to stare, patient, my own Trojan horse.

The thing is—something *is* wrong. Last night, my first night off in four days, I awakened to Carrie shaking me out of a nearly sound sleep to a phone call from my fifteen-year-old brother, announcing my father had walked out on my mother for good;

my mother had taken to her bed. He wanted me home—*needed* me home—and if I didn't come home he was hopping the next train to Boston. (My family of origin, an ever-inflating grenade, had long lay waiting for someone to light its fuse and my father's secretary Janine had been only too happy to comply. BOOM! They had rented an apartment together, Timmy said. My mother had gone catatonic; someone had to do something; *I* had to do something.)

My parents, of course, had a much different take on the situation when I interrogated each of them at length by phone, a pointless intervention that cost me a night's tips. "Your brother is grieving," my mother said. Sounding pretty much like always, a tightly modulated voice piped out of airport speakers reminding you that unattended bags would be detonated.

"He said you couldn't get out of bed!" I countered.

"He's at a difficult age. Anyway, you know how he gets. Your father is having a mid-life crisis, that's all."

"Oh really; another one?" Because in truth, my father had already grown a beard, bought a hot rod, and tried to smoke pot with me, a humiliating turn of events even I, no stranger to humiliation, had failed to foresee.

"He'll come around," she said.

"Timmy said he moved in with that, that …"

"Really, Colleen, it's OK. He's making a fool of himself and everyone knows it."

My mother derived great comfort from her martyr-like role in this world and seemed convinced that the more public her persecution, the more points earned in heaven. "Would you put down that cross for fifteen seconds," my father used to say, back when they were on teasing terms; a decent line I had adopted as my own and still batted about now and then. Still, this was going too far.

"You don't even give a shit do you?" I said. "For God's sake, Mom, you've been married to this man for more than two decades. How can you let him do this to you?"

"This does not concern you, Colleen. "You have absolutely no idea what goes on in a marriage."

But I thought I did understand the way her rationality/rigidity, his flamboyance/recklessness—opposing traits that once created a kind of stable, parallel track—had, over the years, derailed.

"Jesus Christ, Mom," I said.

"Watch your language, Colleen."

"Your mother and I have not lived as man and wife for some time, Colleen," my father said, broaching territory into which I had no desire whatsoever to stray. "I should have taken matters into my own hands a long time ago."

"Leaving your wife for a woman half your age is taking matters into your own hands? Jesus, Dad, you are such a cliché."

"This is not about Janine. This is between me and your mother. Don't worry; I plan to be very fair about this. And I'll still pay for school, if that's what you're worried about."

"I don't care about school anymore," I cried. (A lie, of course, because Anastasia's persistent offers of an alternate reality had made me realize just how much I *did* care about school. I did not want to work at the *Athenian Kitchen* for a bunch of gangsters the rest of my life. I wanted to grow up, write the great American novel or maybe get appointed to the Supreme Court, pay off my loans, and get back at my parents once and for all through the undeniable perfection of my own marriage and stellar parenting abilities.)

As if suddenly channeling for my mother, my father issued a long-suffering sigh.

Tears stung my eyes. I had spent my whole life adoring my father and his childlike ways. Now I would have to hate him for them.

"It will all work out, Colleen," he said. "You'll see. I know it's painful right now but you'll get over it."

"And what about Timmy? Are you even aware he wants to move in with me?"

"He's at a difficult age," he said. "You know how he gets."

Mario watches, as if he can see straight through my forehead to the pathetic little documentary playing in there.

"How do you say to sleep in Greek?" I ask.

"To sleep?" He looks puzzled.

"Right."

A sound full of static—-like when you turn the volume up too high on a set of lousy speakers—issues from his throat.

"Write it." I reach into my purse and pull out the pad and pen I lug around in the unlikely event my muse should decide to start dictating.

His hand scratches across the page leaving a hieroglyphic trail in its wake and dashing all hopes of breaking another international code.

I sip my wine, unaware my eyes are falling shut, my head bobbing on my neck as if lulled to sleep on a train. Another vision swirls in my head, swimming in a soft pinkish light. I am dressed in street clothes, green corduroy pants and a matching jacket from the Anne Klein outlet down the street. I am happily zipping around greeting customers at the restaurant's front door, stopping to chat and joke with family members, smoothing Peter's rumpled feathers with a sing-song voice and a peck on a grizzled jaw, checking the accounting on the pastry orders, comforting a new employee whose first customer found the ragged top of a beer bottle inexplicably embedded in his yogurt and honey. It is 6:30; a reasonable hour for dinner and my brother sits alone eating at a table overlooking the glassed dessert counter, working on his homework. At eight o'clock, I'll be off and we'll head home to our apartment where he has taken Judith's bedroom (Carrie and I tossed her out on her privileged derriere) and I am making up the additional rent with salary from my new assistant manager's job, having finally taken matters into my own hands (as I should have done years ago), setting my parents free and smuggling my brother out of their neurotic web.

In slow motion my wine glass tips and rolls toward the table's edge, pale yellow nectar dripping onto my knees. I jolt awake as if slapped.

"Come lie down," Mario coaxes, dabbing with his napkin; pulling me to my feet by the wrist and then—I am not making this up—picking me up like a child in his strong arms.

He carries me into a cell-like room with cement walls and floors, a small aluminum sink, and a bunk bed, puts me down on the lower bunk; slips off my shoes. He lights a squat white candle on a low table beside the bed and switches off the overhead fluorescent light. The walls are bare, save for a poster of *Earth, Wind & Fire* and a wooden cross with a two-dimensional, expressionless Christ painted on front. Books are piled in neat little towers against the walls and a small black boom box rests on top of two pushed-together piles. I stretch out on my side, watching him crack open the barred window looking out on a sleet-slicked sidewalk and slip in a tape, something sweet and jazzy, Winston Marsalis, he tells me, a song called *The Wee Hours of the Morning*—ha! He kicks off his shoes and climbs in beside me fully clothed.

I turn to face the wall, my back fitting like a missing puzzle piece into the groove of his body. And really, oddly, there is nothing sexual about it, I notice, briefly wondering why that would be. Drifting in that all-too-familiar space between exhaustion and hyperactivity, the jetlag that has become my permanent state of being. Thinking about Anastasia's offer, rescuing Timmy, severing ties with my insane parents, the warmth of Mario's neck, the tangy herbal scent of him, the strange monk-like quality he exudes, saxophone sobbing and piano keys running like water in my ears. The derelict possibility that sleep—true, deep, uninterrupted sleep—might yet erode the thick ball of sentiment collecting in my throat.

Against my back, Mario's bellow-like lungs expand and contract rhythmically. He is already asleep; how do people do that?

I nestle deeper into him, thinking to absorb the elusive state by osmosis, wondering if what I have needed all along is simply a warm body with whom to share the dark.

Je dormirai, tu dormiras, elle dormira, nous dormirons, vous dormirez, elles dormiront, I murur, over and over, as a man I hardly know who might be a killer connected to a whole international network of killers momentarily stirs, stroking my hair, and I descend into stillness, assuring myself that it will all work out. That I, too, am simply at a difficult age; that I have, in fact, dreamt this entire thing—this restaurant and Judith and Carrie, the family and Peter and Mario and Anastasia, my parents and my brother and their ongoing drama—that I will awaken to the real world; the real parent I first glimpsed at three years old. If only I close my eyes, breathe deeply, and keep on conjugating sleep.

Rose

Infantile Paralysis

A soft mewing like that of a newborn calf stirred her.

Rose pushed hard to rouse herself from the depths of sleep—as if toeing against the muck at the bottom of a deep lake, before shooting to the surface—only to find herself still lying on a mattress that sagged so in the middle it took all her strength to lunge up and away from the deep well of Victor.

The sound coaxed her down the hall along a sequined trail of starlight sifting through the windows of the children's room where Franklin and Annette slept toe-to-toe against one wall. She meant to follow the noise—that might prove but the latest addition to Sassy's ever expanding brood of scrawny kittens—straight out to the barn. But it dawned on her, gliding past the closed door of the bedroom in which nine-year-old Joe lay stiff and prone these past months as she pressed cold cloths to his forehead, fed, and bathed him. As she read to him from the Bible or sometimes even from the comics Franklin had stashed beneath his mattress before the quarantine rendered such secret frivolity luxuries they could ill afford. It dawned on her, then, where the sound was really coming from.

In slow motion, as if lifting a can filled to the brim with milk still warm from the teat, her hand ascended from her side toward the doorknob, grasped the icy metal, and turned. She pushed and the door gave way, creaking on neglected hinges.

Joe stood in his nightclothes beaming up at her, palm pressed against the mattress, feet planted on the floor. His mahogany hair stood straight up, mashed flat against his skull from so long at the pillow. He was wearing his sliver-of-moon smile, despite the sound emanating from his throat, higher pitched and more melodic than she had realized, somewhere between a wail and a song. Without bending his knees, toddler-like, one leg swung forward. Its foot thumped against the floor, followed by the other.

"Mama." His cheeks were jeweled with tears.

"Allen," she whispered, pushing toward him through air grown suddenly thick and heavy as moss.

She awoke panting, as if she'd been chased. A hand to her mouth to silence the name she feared had escaped it. Her mind swirling with images of her child all mixed up with her long-lost love Allen. The memory of *his* leg, taken in another war, had somehow inserted itself into the jigsaw of memories she carried in her head; severed pictures of Joe's paralysis, miraculous recovery, and enlistment last spring. Her son was headed for Italy under General Patton, he last wrote. Not yet eighteen and already hunting Germans.

"Holy Christ, Rose, he's a survivor, if anyone is," Victor said, the day he'd signed the papers allowing their son to enlist without deeming it necessary to consult her. The day he'd lied—*lied*—about Joe's age. "He survived infantile paralysis, woman, for Christ's sake. Let him fulfill his destiny."

The taste and smell of her anger—sharp and metallic, earthy and blood-like as the saturated rags she used to absorb the near constant flow she had lately endured—engulfed her. She might have struck him, she later thought, had not Father LaCroix's advice come boomeranging back to her: "Jesus, Mary, and Joseph help me not to do this sin."

The priest's incantation had intervened in her behalf innumerable times in their marriage. Through the loss of two babies, the burning of their barn, the Great Depression, bouts of scarlet fever, her son's paralysis, their eight-month quarantine, and nearly losing the farm to the bank. But try as she might she could not form the words in her head that day last spring when her exuberant son twirled her around the kitchen before kissing her goodbye; giddy with the thought of striking out on his own, as if off to build a railroad.

Two seasons later, she still could not bring herself to utter Father LaCroix's incantation; the words she knew could coax from Heaven itself the gift of forgiveness. Instead she pressed through the long days washing and mending their clothes, tending her chickens and vegetable patch; putting up corn and beets; jam and pickles for the long winter; cooking, baking, and helping Honora and Annette with their lessons. All the while inching around her husband, eyes glued to her feet, as if avoiding a muddy puddle in her Sunday shoes. Carrying the sin of bitterness in her heart, pressed like a scapula between her sagging breasts. And now Allen had resurfaced in her dreams. You could not trick the Lord. He saw right through your shenanigans, his Superman vision illuminating all the earthly treasures you would covet over his love. He saw, and he delivered his verdict.

She pushed up out of bed for real now, the dream still sticky upon her, running her hands over her netted hair, her face, and neck; as if displacing persistent cobwebs. The only sound now the drone of her husband's snoring. At the window she pushed back the gingham curtain she made last month from cloth left over from the girls' back-to-school jumpers. The stars had faded, leaving a milky sky awaiting the first flush of dawn. On her fingers she counted the time difference between New York and Italy. Would her son be taking lunch—eating spaghetti in a vineyard out of his helmet, the fugue of mines and gunshot momentarily interrupted? She fell to her knees. "Jesus, Mary, and Joseph." She pressed her mouth against the steeple of her hands. But her renegade lips would take her no further.

She stood and relieved herself in the pot in the corner, walked over to the vanity, poured water into the bowl, and splashed it over her face again and again, shivering.

Honora stood at the stove stirring a pot of corn meal mush when Rose came in from the chicken house carrying a bowl full of eggs, dressed in a housedress shiny from so many launderings, a buffed look about her face from the scrubbing she had given it. Try as she might these days, she could never seem to feel clean.

"Where's Annette?" she asked.

"I sent her out for a pitcher of milk."

Rose studied her niece, her brother Raymond's child who had come from Braeburn to live with them when her mother died despite Victor's anguish about another mouth to feed. She had proven a good girl—helpful and hardworking and God-fearing— until the last year or so, when boys seized the territory that had once occupied her brain. Rose tried to remember herself at seventeen but found she could not. Even the memories of Allen's attentions had blurred to the point they seemed transformed into photographs from someone else's past.

The girl's auburn hair grazed her shoulders in loopy curls she had set with bobby pins the night before. She had grown again and her breasts and hips heaved against the cotton shirtwaist dotted with tiny bluebells. A real leather belt that once belonged to Mother Trambeaux bit into her narrow waist. She was beautiful. Curious, Rose had not noticed it before.

Annette exploded through the door, pounding her feet on the rug, beads of milk strafing the wall and stove from the overly full pitcher.

"Annette," Rose said. She pronounced the word like her deceased mother-in-law, the child's namesake: "An-ETTE," with a little chomping French poodle bite at the finish. At eleven, her daughter's gangly body served only to confound her, every movement fraught with hazard.

"Sorry, Mama." Annette placed the pitcher on the table and mopped her hands on her already spattered dress.

"Please cut up some bread for toast," Rose said.

"As I was saying," said Honora, spooning hot cereal into bowls. "There is a box dance Friday and I wondered if we could kill a chicken this time and I could fry it up and make biscuits. Cassie Hogan brought fried chicken and biscuits to the last dance and she had the whole school bidding on her. It had to be the food, Aunt Rose. You've seen her, she looks like a horse."

Annette threw back her head and whinnied in appreciation and the two girls got to cantering around the table, holding their sides in laughter, as if Jack Benny himself had spoken.

"Sit down, the two of you, right now," Rose said; her own voice, shrill, in her ears.

She did not like to speak to them like this, had never warmed to the role of disciplinarian, but someone had to keep them placing one foot in front of the other, mindful of the assaults lurking around every corner in this world. Worshipping God in every moment so that if, in his wisdom, he decided to pluck you from this earth you would be ready—with laundered undergarments, so to speak—to join him in Heaven.

She placed a bottle of molasses on the table to sweeten the girls' cereal, set to frying eggs in lard for Victor and her eldest, Franklin, due in from milking at any moment. If only she could have the house to herself. She craved news of Joe; longed to turn on the radio and hear what Edward R. Murrow had to say about the war in Europe. But it did the children no good, these stories that had seduced their brothers into combat. She wanted to shield them from the high cost of democracy. And for that, too, she supposed she would pay a price.

"So what do you think, Aunt Rose?" Honora was saying. "Can't we kill a chicken for the box dance?"

"We'll see."

"That means no," Annette mumbled.

"That means, we'll see," said Rose, voice rising in irritation. The children seemed to be gunning for her lately, the shrapnel of their demands ricocheted from all directions. Maybe it was just the change of life; Mother Trambeaux had had her moods, too, although she never mentioned the bleeding that could go on for weeks. The bleeding that caused Rose, at times, to keel over from the simple exertion of lifting a frying pan, the girls buzzing over her with wide frightened eyes; hot peas pinging across the floor.

Still, her father would have taken her to the barn and paddled her for such a tone in her voice. A vague feeling she had failed them washed over her. A wave of milky tea backed up in her throat. The eggs smoked on the griddle. She flipped them onto plates. Victor would not complain about their scorched, ruffled hems. But he would stare at them a long time before lifting his fork to make sure she knew he had noticed.

"Hey, Mamo." Franklin lurched up behind her and grabbed her by the shoulders. "You're looking glamorous as usual. Watch out, Rita Hayworth, eh?"

The girls chortled.

"Mercy," said Rose, swatting at his long limbs as if at a giant fly. Three years Joe's senior, Franklin defied the stereotype of an oldest child. Of course, he had not actually been first; their stillborn daughter Loretta had taken that honor with her to the grave. Rose sometimes couldn't help imagining her grown into the perfect, compliant child—pillar of responsibility, tireless listener, infinitely sensitive to her mother's complex feelings—the understanding friend and companion that had eluded Rose all her life.

Injured on a PT boat in England last year, Franklin had been discharged and shipped home to a rehab center in Albany. That's when Joe had gone to his father. The Trambeaux family needed representation, he argued. Franklin likely would have reenlisted had his brother not beaten him to it—Victor could not run the farm anymore without at least one of his boys. Now he walked with a hitch from the bullet in his hip they would not risk removing. To Rose's chagrin, he had taken up with Anna Wyatt, a fast, young Presbyterian woman with hennaed hair who worked in the mill outside Waynesburg.

Victor pushed through the door, nodded, and took a plate.

Franklin slid into a chair beside his sister. "Hey, Annie, hey curly," he said.

"Honora wants to kill a chicken and fry it up for the box dance so Gabe Dumont will buy her," said Annette.

"Shush." Honora elbowed her cousin in the ribs.

Victor carried his plate to the table.

"Tommy Dumont's little brother?" asked Franklin. "That little worm?"

"Clear your plates and grab your lunches, girls," said Rose.

"You just shut your trap if you want me to keep mine shut about you and Anna and …"

Franklin dove at his cousin as she passed.

"Stop it, all of you," shouted Victor.

The girls grabbed their sack lunches and scattered.

Franklin slathered more of the pasty white Oleo on his toast.

An overwhelming desire to swallow a whole lump of real butter—the kind she had churned every morning before the war—nearly took Rose's breath away.

Victor stared at the charred egg on his plate a while longer before lifting his fork and knife.

Rose stood at the counter crimping the edges of two apple pies. Her crusts were the county's tenderest—she took two blue ribbons last year at the fair, a victory that left her puffed up with pride no amount of Confessional penance could deflate. Through the open window, the unseasonably warm October air carried on top of the usual manure a whiff of smoke from the men burning remnants of corn stalks in the field, mingling with the aroma of cinnamon and vanilla into a pungent perfume she would not soon forget.

The doorbell rang.

"Mercy." She wiped her hands on a tea towel and smoothed her apron.

Her hand flew to her heart when she saw the Western Union man standing there.

She shut the door behind her and carried the telegram to her rocker beside the piano. It needed dusting, she noticed, she had not played since Joe took off. She sat down and studied the elaborately painted Asian vase Mother Trambeaux had left her, its pebbled, wanton surface swelling like a woman's hips from a tiny waist holding a clutch of Black-eyed Susans. The smell of pie and smoke stung her nostrils. She worked her thumb across the envelope, unfolded the message, and read:

The Secretary of War desires me to express his deepest regret that your son Private Joseph D. Trambeaux has been reported missing in action since ten October in Italy. If further details or other information are received you will be promptly notified.

Ten October, she thought. One day shy of his eighteenth birthday. They had celebrated in his absence with his favorite lemonade cake.

"Thank you, Father," she whispered, running her finger over the unevenly typed letters as if reading Braille and repeating the words out loud. *Missing*, they said. Missing did not mean dead.

She knew she should call Victor and Franklin in from the fields but to what end? Instead she sat in the rocker, for once indulging in the extravagance of complete inertia. After a while, she plucked the rosary from her pocket and began worrying the beads with her fingers, lips moving soundlessly, eyes riveted on the empty swing outside the front window. All the children had once favored that swing, fought each other for the right to it. Suspended from the sprawling oak, it moved back and forth, back and forth, as if all by itself through the still, Indian summer air.

Rose and Annette were out at the henhouse another Indian summer day when Joe, just home from school, came shuffling out in his overalls, rubbing his neck.

Annette charged his legs.

He grabbed her wrists and swung her around; her cotton dress ballooning in the wind.

"Your father would like you to go feed the horses," Annette said.

"OK, Mama," said Joe. "Want to come with me, Annette?"

The child panted like a dog in affirmation. Almost two, she still had little need to speak, what with her brothers constantly translating for her.

Resting on her knees, Rose had their old rooster, Charlemagne, by the neck. Time to show us what you're made of, she thought. He had been a good husband to the girls, a hearty sire. She would stew him for tomorrow's dinner with the green onions still poking their heads up in the kitchen garden, while he still had some meat on his bones, use his juices for soup.

Joe took his sister's hand. They'd been thick as thieves, those two, since Annette's birth. "Mama," he said, turning back over his shoulder.

She glanced up.

"My neck—it really hurts."

Of its own volition her hand relaxed around Charlemagne's gullet. The exonerated chicken hobbled away toward his favorite hiding spot under the back porch, wagering the cats were still in the fields.

"Come inside," she said. She yanked her son by the wrist with such force that Annette started to cry.

Rose smoothed a quilt across the kitchen table. Victor swung their undressed son up like a baby and placed him there.

"Mama." Joe's coppery eyes pleaded.

She took his hand. "It will only last a second."

He moaned.

"We have no other choice," she said. The Serum might save his legs—his *life*—the doctor said. It was their only hope. "Remember how brave you were when you had scarlet fever? They thought it would weaken your heart but it didn't, did it? You came through with flying colors. You were made for great things, Joseph. You'll come through this, too, you'll see. Now, pray to God. God is with us. Always with us," she lied. Because—honestly—she already had her doubts.

She made her voice as soothing as she could; hoping to drown out the sounds of the doctor's tools scraping in the sink behind them. Even though he was too old for lullabies, she longed to sing to Joe as she had when he was little, and might have, too, had Victor and the doctor not been standing there. Had Franklin not been pressed against the wall, clutching Annette to his chest. What if they got it, too?

"We're ready, Victor," the doctor said.

He had come from Waynesburg, been up all night, he told them. What with five new cases of infantile paralysis diagnosed in the county in just one week.

"Take your sister out of here," Rose said.

"But Mama," Franklin protested.

"Now."

"Turn over on your stomach, son," Victor said.

"Mama!"

"I'll be right here, sweet boy; I promise."

"Hold his legs, Victor," the doctor said. "Get his shoulders, Rose."

Rose had never seen so large a needle. She pressed down on her son's bare shoulders and squeezed her eyes shut; summoning Mary in her aquamarine robes—descending in an iridescent bubble like the good witch, Glynda, in *The Wizard of Oz*.

The sound her son made when the serum shot into the base of his spine was not of this earth. It didn't last long, though, thank God. He passed out from the pain.

Annette and Honora raced through the door and flung themselves at her, rousing her from the trance she had slipped into watching the swing.

"What are you doing home so early?" she asked.

"They announced it at school, Mama." Annette bounded into her mother's lap. "Joe, and Davy Donovan, and Harold McIntosh—what does that mean; 'missing in action?'"

Honora pressed a finger to her lips but Annette had eyes only for her mother.

Rose struggled for composure. "There was a battle I suppose," she said. "They could be hiding somewhere."

"Or captured," said Annette, eyes already leaking. "Captured by the Germans!"

"Come on, Annette." Honora yanked her cousin to her feet. "What can we do to help, Aunt Rose?"

Rose sighed. Of course he had been captured—captured or killed. She refused to think about it. God had spared her child twice before. Rose had prayed endlessly to Saint Catherine of Siena, her mother's namesake, an Italian saint who had intervened in Joe's behalf. She had named Annette's older sister after her as promised when Joe recovered from scarlet fever. Unlike her first child, Catherine at least lived long enough to receive the Last Rites. Later, Joe walked again at Saint Catherine's bidding; taught his little sister, Annette, to dance.

"Catherine," whispered Rose.

"Aunt Rose," Honora said, almost touching her hair. "What can we do?"

"Go get your Uncle."

Chalky as corpses Victor and Franklin stomped into the kitchen behind the girls. For once Annette did not remind them to remove their boots. She shot Honora a questioning glance but the girl shook her head. She had not told them. She didn't have to.

Annette held out the telegram. Franklin lunged for it; Victor could not read. But her husband shook his head. "Read to me, Rose," he said.

In the early days of their marriage, before the children came, reading poetry aloud—Elizabeth Barrett Browning in particular—had somehow helped bridge the jagged chasm between them. But she had long since stopped reading to him. Now she read without looking up, unable to meet his eyes.

It wasn't so much a cry as a howl, the sound detonating from Victor's throat that blasted the children—even grownup Franklin—from the room. Sent them pounding up the stairs, ears pressed against the grate above the kitchen stove to eavesdrop in safety. Her husband collapsed into her and did something she had never seen him do, not even when his mother died; Victor cried, great wracking sobs that reverberated in *her* solar plexus. She held him, stroking his face and neck, red and ridged as corduroy from his time in the fields. She could almost hear the children holding their collective breath upstairs. She might have forgiven him right then and there had his tears turned themselves into words. Instead he dried his eyes with the back of his hand and headed out to the barn without as much as a backward glance at his wife. In the morning his thick head of black hair had gone completely white.

The doctor said Franklin and Annette would be fine if they got through a day or two symptom-free. Victor and Rose pulled Franklin's bed out of their sons' shared room and converted the long hallway into a bedroom. They moved Annette—who really had grown too big for her cradle—onto a mattress on the floor near her big brother. By the time Rose knelt beside Joe's bed that first night he could not move at all and lay terrified, eyes roaming the ceiling and unable to sleep. She crawled in beside him and smoothed his damp hair. He drifted off at last to the rustling sound of her prayers but Rose lay awake hours longer, begging Saint Catherine to spare her son. She did not allow herself to think about the disease claiming anyone else in her family. She could not permit that thought to surface in her mind and hold on to her sanity.

In the morning, she woke before dawn, padded down the hall, and covered her other two children. Franklin lay all tangled up in his quilt, long limbs jutting out at impossible, reassuring angles. Annette squirmed under her mother's touch. Rose went to her own room, pulled on her robe, and descended the stairs.

Victor sat at the kitchen table still in his work clothes from the day before. He rubbed his face. "What will we do, Rosette?" he asked. "How will we live?"

The doctor had placed the farm under quarantine. They could not sell their milk; could not leave their property.

Touched by the use of his dead mother's pet name for her, Rose grabbed wood from the pile, went to the stove, and stoked the fire; bent over the sink and pumped water into the kettle, Victor's question echoing in her head. She didn't know how they would live. She hoped God might; Jesus, Mary, and Joseph, with a little help from Saint Catherine.

"I'd better get to the milking," Victor said.

"I'll go with you."

The cows still needed milking, even though they would have to spill their sweet, white livelihood back into the earth. It would break him. She could not let him do it alone.

A silence settled over Victor those weeks after that first telegram. He shuffled through the house like a sleepwalker, falling into their bed each night and rising in the morning, shoveling food into his mouth and heading out to turn the fields for winter all without speaking. After a while, the children replaced their strategy of trying to engage him with jokes and stories with the equally ineffective tactic of trying to avoid him all together. A maneuver Rose, who insisted on keeping up the normal rhythms of life, would have none of. They would all sit down to supper as always, thank you very much; partake of the sacraments of Confession and Holy Communion. Honora would go to her box dance; Rose even killed a chicken for her. Franklin would go out on the town in his questionable girlfriend's tasteless new car. Annette would read with her mother and work on her sums and play the piano when Rose saw fit.

Swept up in the self-concocted illusion of normality, the children took on their roles with gusto, converting their most mundane activities into a heightened, more idealized set of routines that in later years would gleam brighter than the rest in their arsenal of memories. Only Victor remained aloof, conspicuously absent from Saint Andrew's, wolfing down meals and leaving the table without even bothering to excuse himself.

Instead of sleeping, Rose prayed. When she wasn't praying, she wrote to the Adjutant General who had notified them, keeping her letters brief and avoiding overly emotional displays she sensed would do her no ultimate good, appealing instead to the Army's sense of justice.

"I would just like to know more about the circumstances of my son going missing," she wrote. "Has he been captured? What was he doing when he disappeared?"

Reasonable questions, she thought, questions that took her mind off possible answers.

In early November, another telegram confirmed their worst fears.

Through the longest winter of their lives Rose prayed. Every day after the morning's milking and disposal, she bundled the children, hitched the horses to the sleigh and drove a mile-and-a-half through tunnels of snow that threatened to collapse on their heads to where the road intersected with the road to Quebec. Every day, a different neighbor left them food: sacks of flour, slabs of bacon or stew meat, and jars of wax beans and stewed tomatoes. Rose and the children dug the box out of the snow—thanking God for their neighbors' generosity—and headed back home.

Franklin and Annette lived outdoors—digging out snow villages until their clothes soaked through and their teeth chattered. Then they headed for the barn, tormenting the cows and feral cats. Climbing the silo and hurling themselves into bales of hay. Rose worried they'd catch their death but had neither the heart nor the energy to restrict them, grateful they had found a way to entertain themselves while she tended to Joe and their salvation.

Now and then, Victor roamed the house like something caged—glaring at her—before huffing back out to the barn.

One day, kneeling at her sleeping son's bedside, Rose dozed off. "I have not forsaken you," her mother said, in her dream.

Rose was small again, Joe's age, sitting in her mother's lap before the fire, leaning her head on her broad shoulder, inhaling the smell of white flour and lavender that clung to her skin; her nest of yellow hair. And then Rose was falling, as if from a tree, every muscle in her body contracting in fear of impact, until she opened her eyes and saw the wraith-like figure of Saint Catherine floating before her, bony hand extended. Rose grasped the surprisingly solid form.

"Mama," Joe said, as Rose opened her eyes for real to find herself clutching her son's hand. "I can move my legs Mama—help me up."

Rose pursued the task of unearthing the circumstances of their son's death as she had once launched the mission of teaching him to walk again, tirelessly subjecting the War Department to a barrage of written inquiries. The Army rewarded her efforts with sketchy dispatches light on details and heavy on excuses, apologies, and promises of referrals through the lengthy chain of command. At last a response came from the Catholic Chaplain who had laid Joe to rest in a United States cemetery in Northern Italy.

"Joe was well liked and admired. His comrades will miss his companionship and friendship," he said, in a way that made Rose's throat contract with the certainty that the Chaplain had not known her son at all. People flocked to Joe, their deepest hopes and fears tumbling from their mouths. He lit up a room, left a calmness—that could only be described as grace—in his wake. He would have entered seminary upon his return; she would have found a way to make it so. If only Victor had not lied.

Then came a copy of a unit citation describing the battle in which Joe had perished the same day he'd been reported missing.

… Committed to attack along Highway 65 in the drive beyond enemy Gothic Line, the 3rd Battalion in seven days of continuous fighting over rough, mountainous terrain, decisively defeated elements of three German divisions and captured the town of Livergnano … successfully repelled several strong enemy counterattacks, and advanced continuously through the heaviest type of enemy mortar and artillery fire … This small force of only eighty men gallantly repelled fanatical, tank-supported enemy counterattacks for eight hours, even after every machine gun had been destroyed by enemy fire and the ammunition had been exhausted …

Victor sat erect on the couch as she read; his eyes moving up and down and all around as if following his son's hillside progress on a moving picture screen. He flinched, his own nerves registering the mine that took him.

The enraged voice in Rose's head competed with a whisper of compassion. For a moment, watching her husband, the two voices vied for her attention, words jumbled, unable to speak over each other. She shut her eyes. Saint Catherine appeared looking exactly like that painting in the book Mother Trambeaux had given her, ascending the stairs of her home in Siena, hands clasped, feet dangling above the earth; eyes rooted in heaven. With relief Rose realized the other voice—the accusing voice that held Victor responsible for their son's death—had somehow vanished.

Her hand waded through the air and settled on her husband's shoulder.

Franklin shot up out of his chair. "I'm going back," he said.

Annette sucked on the paintbrush of her braid. Honora hung her head.

"The hell you are," Rose heard herself say.

"The hell you are." It was Victor then, his fist splintering the delicate pedestal table.

"I have not forsaken you," whispered Saint Catherine.

May, her favorite month, the month during which she and Allen had once taken to the river hand in hand, a bundled lunch swinging between them and the fields embroidered with violets. Through the open windows the doctor's cart clattered up to their porch. She went to fetch Victor.

The doctor smiled, ducking down the stairs back into the kitchen from Joe's room. "He's fine," he said. "He's going to be fine. You're a free man, Victor, your milk is cleared."

Rose had not cried, not when Joe came home from school that day, not when he passed out on the kitchen table, not when she and Victor had tipped can after can of milk into the field that first morning. She had not cried. She did not plan to start now.

"Rosette," Victor said.

She shook her head and raced upstairs, grabbed a handkerchief from her dresser drawer. She stared into the mirror at her seamed face, struggling to equate the girl she started out to be, the picture her mother carried in her locket to her grave, with the woman gazing back at her. The spring had given her son back his legs. But it had taken the last remnants of her youth.

"Mama," said Joe, striding toward her into the rockets' red glare of his future.

Colleen

The Winter of My Discontent

I have taken to thinking of those lost months after completing my bachelor's degree in Boston as the winter of my discontent. After working my way through college, pushing myself to my physical—and, occasionally even mental—limits, I found myself adrift in the tract home I grew up in in Rocky Ledges, New York. My parents had recently reunited following my father's classic midlife dalliance with the twenty-something secretary who dumped him soon after they decided to cohabitate. My younger brother Timmy had boomeranged back home after flunking out the first semester of his freshman year at Potsdam, a perpetual wave of marijuana smoke breaking against his locked bedroom door, my parents' olfactory senses mysteriously debilitated. Everyone raw, silent, and checked out, oblivious to my mounting panic as I aimlessly combed the classified section of *The Times* for entry-level publishing and advertising positions without any real clue as to what to do next.

After years of working the night shift at the Athenian Kitchen and pulling all-nighters to write yet another treatise on the psychological implications of the cloistered nanny in 19th century literature, I found myself plagued with perpetual insomnia no amount of warm milk or cheap wine could salve. I had graduated a semester early and the few high school friends I'd stayed in touch with were still in school. Notably Leigh, who had just written from D.C. to announce she'd been accepted into George Washington Law School next year. She would not have to risk straying from "the vortex of civilization as we know it," to further her education. Ha!

And so I found myself alone; finally drifting off to sleep in the wee hours to the sound of my father snoring next door. Awakening long after my mother and father had left for work, my bedroom windows frosted with ice that seemed as impenetrable as my future. Beating only Timmy to the kitchen where I whipped up waffles and pancakes and muffins as I flipped through the morning paper trying to figure out how I could possibly make it in Manhattan on $9,000 a year; flabbergasted that the only jobs for female college graduates seemed to be secretarial. (What if Gloria Steinem got wind of this?) Traumatized by a succession of unstable roommates into thinking I could not possibly consider sharing my living space with another potentially psychotic stranger. Shoveling caloric morsels into my mouth in imminent danger of porking out completely when I was literally saved by the bell as they say in the form of a phone call from Christina Woods, a high school acquaintance with whom I'd lost touch after quitting the cheerleading squad junior year in a little huff of inner self-righteousness over the shallowness of it all. Her mother had spotted me at the drugstore—Oh, my God; was I *really* home for good; I just had to join her for drinks that night at Jerome's, yes, that's where everyone hung now, *everyone*; she would not take no for an answer, she would swing by for me around eight, couldn't wait to catch up, Coll, what fun!

I hung up the phone, marveling at the fact that I had not uttered a single word, wondering who *everyone* might turn out to be when there was no one in this godforsaken burg I could remember hoping to catch up with—what fun!

I occupied myself for a while primping in the bathroom after dinner, repeatedly pinning my unruly hair up and letting it fall back down to my shoulders, brushing on blush and lipstick and rubbing it off with a towel. I still had that adolescent look about me, my features seemingly oversized, their growth outpacing that of my face. I squinted at the image floating there, trying to discern myself through the eyes of a person who had not seen me in nearly four years. Searching for signs of maturity or flowering beauty or intimations of wisdom to no avail until a horn beeped outside and I gave up, pulling on my Navy pea coat and rushing toward the living room door past my mother grading papers on the sofa.

"Did I tell you I'm having drinks with Christina Woods," I said, wrapping a scarf around my throat.

"The *cheerleader*?"

I nodded.

She cocked her head and studied me.

I had nearly forgotten her talent for communicating so much without ever contracting a single facial muscle.

"Have fun," she said.

Christina screeched as I settled into the front seat of her yellow Impala. "Look at you," she said. "You haven't aged a day."

I was twenty years old. I hadn't realized the term aging was already on the table but from the looks of Christina—a good 25 pounds heftier than the curvaceous girl I recalled—I made a mental note to knock off the starch.

Jerome's Bar & Grille, a blonde brick storefront with a narrow band of smoked glass window brandishing a listing neon martini glass, sat in a small strip shopping center on Route 210, sandwiched between a dry cleaner and a Carvel ice cream store. I had been there once or twice with my Dad. It was the kind of place people's dads and even granddads frequented after work or during feuds with the wife but the new owners had started marketing to the battalions of young people who graduated from North High School, nabbed an associate's degree at the County Community College if they were lucky, and took jobs at the Gypsum Plant or managing produce at the A & P. Christina, a receptionist in a pediatrician's office, was about to marry one of them—Jimmy Doyle, the famous linebacker for the Panthers my sophomore year when our team took the state championship. A year ahead of us, he'd landed a full scholarship to Oneonta but dropped out after he blew out his knee. I remembered him swaggering around in his red and white letter jacket, guzzling Budweisers at pep rallies and peeing on things. He and his over-stuffed buddies had crashed the surprise sweet sixteen party I threw for Leigh in my parents' basement. Now he apparently worked for the town police force, a revelation that made me choke on my vodka tonic.

Christina didn't seem to notice. "You could be in the wedding. I have five bridesmaids but I'd really like six. We have these lavender gowns. You'd look great in lavender. Besides an even number is good luck, don't you think?"

I nodded, as if I knew from luck. Really, I could not tell what horrified me more, the thought of getting married at my age, the idea of asking a nearly perfect stranger to join your wedding party, or the way I'd look in lavender.

We sat side-by-side at the fake wooden bar in a cloud of smoke. A couple of people said hello to me but I didn't recognize anyone. Every now and then, the door swung open to admit a blast of frigid air and another knot of paunchy, flat-headed young males or expertly made-up Italian girls with perfectly blown-dry Farrah Fawcett dos. The new owners had knocked out a wall and added a small dance floor complete with strobe lights. Girls started doing the Hustle together and soon Christina was drawn into the undulating fray.

I drained another drink and sat chewing ice cubes, wishing I had had the sense to drive, so I could bail. The music switched to Motown finally and I found myself humming along.

Baby I need your loving, I hummed. I got up and headed for the bathroom, intending to find a pay phone and see if I could talk Timmy into picking me up when a face in the crowd stopped me in my tracks. He sat hunched over one of those giant beer mugs, alone at a little table. Swirls of dark hair hung over his eyes but I couldn't mistake that profile. After all, I'd studied it for two solid years. "Drew?"

He reared back at the sound of my voice as if startled, head bobbing, eyes widening and narrowing and widening again in an effort to focus in the gloomy light.

"It's me, Colleen Shea." I came closer; extended my hand.

His hands flew to the arms of his wheelchair, as if poised to flee. His *wheelchair*.

"Collie?" he said, uncertainly, as if I must be putting him on. He was the only person who had ever called me that, the only person I would ever allow. Four years older than me, Drew had spent summers lifeguarding at the town pool after Matthew Baker went off to college or the penitentiary or whatever. He lived in a crumbling stone mansion upriver with a lawn the size of our high school's football field. (As a little girl, I'd imagined his family royalty in their gigantic castle overlooking the Hudson, the rest of us lowly serfs; kept waiting for an invitation to a ball to arrive in the mail à la Cinderella.) His great-grandmother reputedly had been instrumental in the Underground Railroad, his grandmother had been a suffragette, and his mother—who wore black pedal pushers and ballet slippers even in winter and went braless long before fashionable—exhibited her wild oil paintings in the Guggenheim. He had gone to some fancy, New England prep school and on to Dartmouth. He had even attended Woodstock, and challenged all my bourgeois thoughts with every fiber of his impossibly forbidden being. I had worshipped him. My mother had mentioned he'd been injured in Vietnam, but I had no idea.

He smiled up at me, threw up his hands as if to say he had no idea either. "Buy you a drink?" he slurred.

I sank into a chair, trying to resist staring at his wasted legs, tongue-tied; an unprecedented development.

"To what do I owe this pleasure," he said, over-annunciating in that way drunks do, his disobedient tongue placing one syllable in front of another in a pathetic effort to talk a straight line.

"I finished school in December. I'm home for a while, until I figure out what to do next."

He barked a laugh. "I'm home for a while until I figure out what to do next," he repeated, and laughed some more.

"I'm sorry," I said. "I didn't know."

"I had only a week left," he said. "Did you know that? One more fucking week. Have a drink, Collie. Barkeep!"

He was shouting, not that anyone noticed, but I couldn't get my head around the sight of Drew Phillips drunk and dirty and broken and raving beside me.

"I was about to call my brother for a ride home," I said. "Want us to drop you?"

But he was already nodding back off into his beer.

I didn't sleep much that night. I kept seeing Drew Phillips, not the way I saw him at Jerome's but the way he used to be—all wiry and muscled and tan; those round, wire-rim, John Lennon sunglasses; coils of dark hair spiraling around his square jaw, throwing his head back and laughing at me. He liked to ferret out hypocrisy (his words; not mine) and I suppose I offered him fertile hunting ground. I remember him asking me what I thought about homosexuality. I couldn't tell the truth, of course, that at fourteen I had never given the subject a moment's attention. Instead I launched off on a long ignorant monologue about how we evolved to procreate and therefore relations between members of the same sex made no scientific sense. Drew countered that women evolved to bear children and therefore wasting their energy (their libido, if you will) pursuing a career, made no scientific sense. I wanted to throttle him. I wanted to French kiss him. I wanted to die in his arms.

My mother rapped on the door the next morning around ten, still in her housecoat. I had forgotten it was Saturday—every day had become a Saturday for me. I pulled on a sweatshirt and wandered into the kitchen to the phone on the wall.

"You up for lunch?" Drew asked. "I've gotten pretty good at cooking. You could come here."

"Are you asking me out?" I said, because, really, that was too much to even wrap my head around. All those years I'd done everything short of begging him to have his way with me and now ...

"It would be statutory rape, you and me, Collie," he'd said, back then, referring to our age difference in that philosophical voice of his, as if rules had ever been of any concern to him at all. He didn't want me; that's what I remembered. I had never really gotten over his spectacular, overwhelming indifference.

"No," he said. "I'm asking you in."

I could feel my mother's eyes on me as I set the phone back in its cradle.

"Drew Phillips?"

"I ran into him last night."

"Ah. How's he doing?"

"Crippled," I said, pouring myself a cup of coffee.

Her eyes fell shut a moment—her version of a wince.

I sighed. "He's in a wheelchair; did you know that?"

She shook her head. "No—how awful."

"He invited me over to his house for lunch."

I sat down at the table, sawed off a small slice of Entenmanns's Apple Danish and—a Kodachrome snapshot of Christina's surprising girth developing in my head—began tearing it into little strips to make it last.

"Where's Dad?" I asked.

But my mother had already slipped on her reading glasses and disappeared into her stack of ninth-grade essays on *The Scarlet Letter.*

Anyway I already knew the answer. He was out in the garage disassembling old appliances and putting them back together again in the freezing cold that seemed warmer, no doubt—in his mind, at least—than the air in this kitchen.

I had squandered so much of my adolescence fantasizing about the interior of the Phillips' home that it seemed almost anticlimactic now, standing here on the threshold gazing at Mrs. Phillips who had traded in her pedal pushers for a black tunic and matching flowing skirt as if intent on impersonating Morticia on the old *Addams Family* TV show. We had never met and my appearance seemed to have rendered her speechless, even as I thrust out my hand and introduced myself. "Drew invited me for lunch." Still, she stood silent, puzzled, until Drew wheeled toward us with a grave salute.

"I met Collie at the pool years ago," he said.

"I just graduated from B.U. I'm looking for a job in New York."

"Really?" she said. "And what kind of job would that be?"

"Book publishing."

"Really?"

"Really." I nodded as emphatically as I could.

"I know a few people. I'll have to ask around."

I smiled. It was the most progress toward possible employment I had made in four weeks. "That would be so great."

And still she stood there, staring, as if struggling to somehow integrate my ungainly presence into the whitewashed hipness of these high-ceilinged walls, this sleek leather and metal furniture, gigantic canvases entirely covered with a single wash of color— red and orange and brown.

"I'm making omelets," Drew said, rotating around and heading for the kitchen.

"Nice to meet you." I turned my back on her, feeling about as uncomfortable as I could ever recall having felt, regretting having accepted this invitation, and already plotting my escape.

"Pour yourself some coffee, Collie, you look pale," Drew said. "Grab a mug right there."

I did as I was told; taking in the butcher-block island, wooden and glass cupboards that reached to the ceiling, cobalt-tiled counters, and buffed hardwood floors. Through the skylight the milky clouds oozed into the room, rendering every object oddly iridescent, as if seen through the cool mist of a dream.

"Drew, I'm leaving," his mother called. "Back around five. Nice to meet you." The last sentence came to an abrupt halt. She could not remember my name.

Drew had set the long, rough-hewn kitchen table, and assembled omelet ingredients—mushrooms and spinach and grated cheese—on the counter. He sat at the table breaking eggs into a glass bowl and beating the hell out of them with a fork.

"What can I do to help?" I said.

He grimaced. "Know how to make an omelet?"

I nodded. Years of tending to helpless roommates had finally paid off.

"Thank God," he said. "I may have slightly exaggerated my cooking talents."

"Is that so?"

"I know how to chop things and beat things but I have never made an omelet in my life."

"This pan here?" I asked, raising a wrought iron skillet on the stove.

He nodded.

I turned on the gas, cut off a lump of butter, and dropped it in the pan. "Anyway, how can you reach the stove?" I asked.

"The chair moves up and down, Collie," he said, a tone from last night creeping back into his voice.

"Sorry." Really, I had no vocabulary for this; my every word a blunder. I took the bowl of eggs and poured it in the pan, grateful for something constructive to do. "Watch, I'll give you a lesson," I said, half expecting him to flip me off. Instead he wheeled over and ratcheted his chair up.

"You just run the spatula underneath the edges and tilt the pan around like this," I said, all Julia Child. I scattered the fillings about and folded the omelet onto a plate as Drew set out a loaf of French bread and glasses of juice.

"Cheers." He clinked his glass against mine.

We ate in silence until I could bear it no longer.

"When are you going to tell me what happened?" I blurted. My fork rattled against my plate. I had not meant to bring it down so hard but it was, after all, the major reason I had come. I wanted *drama*, to find out his story. To figure out how and why its script had run so horribly amuck.

"I drew a number three in the draft that year," he said. "I tried for conscientious objector but for some reason Uncle Sam wasn't buying it, given my family's lengthy and consistent history of atheism. I suppose I could have gone to Canada, but I guess I still thought I was invincible, a reasonable assumption—God knows I hail from lucky stock. I convinced myself it would make an interesting story one day, something to enthrall the grandchildren with. I would just do my time and then go back to school and on to Harvard Law School and la-di-da."

"You wanted to be a public defender." I remembered now.

"Yup, Collie, that was the plan. I stepped on a fucking mine. I didn't even really feel anything."

"And that was almost five years ago?"

"And what have I done lately, you might ask?"

"That's not what I meant."

"The hell it isn't," he said. "You were never a good liar, Collie; I always admired that in you. Must be that Catholic thing. I, au contraire, have gotten very good at lying. For example, I have convinced my parents and sometimes even myself that there is nothing I can do in this world given my current circumstances, nothing of any value I can contribute. Nada thing."

My eyes stung. I felt like slapping him—I have secretly always wanted to slap a guy in the face—but it seemed monstrous, attacking a person in a wheelchair. "Maybe I'd better go."

"No, Collie, please," he said. "I'll knock it off, I will. We can build a fire; play Scrabble or something. I bet you're one hell of a Scrabble player."

He reminded me of kids I used to babysit, pleading with me to play just one more game. He wanted a babysitter, I realized, unsuccessfully struggling to absorb this unexpected reversal of our roles. Well, *available* just happened to be my current middle name.

"We can go for a walk, so to speak," he said. "My mother had the paths shoveled out this morning. The sun's supposed to come out."

And so I stayed that afternoon and returned the next and the next, but it never really did.

He didn't sleep anymore, he told me that first day by the fire, lighting up a joint. The nightmares had started almost immediately after he moved home. Oddly he didn't dream about the explosion that disabled his legs but the doll-like faces of the figures in the rice paddies. The tiny people they passed in the jungle with empty, ancient eyes—stooped over old men and women with children on their backs; whacking their way through the same minefields he had—continued to haunt him. And even though he had no feeling below the waist as a result of his spinal injury, he had this phantom pain shooting down his legs. Copious amounts of marijuana did not deaden it completely; but it helped.

I had not lost my knack for babysitting. We played a lot of Scrabble and smoked a lot of pot over the next few weeks. To be more precise, Drew smoked a lot of pot and I kept him company, more than a toke or two still sent me into fetal position ducking imaginary chopper fire. Timmy got involved, first as a marijuana supplier and later as an occasional drop-in in our little dropout club. My brother had quite a business going as it turned out, the income from which enabled him to buy a barely used Mustang, stumping my parents but at least uniting them now and then for whispered discussions over the kitchen table when they thought I couldn't hear. Mostly I stayed away, grateful for the refuge of the

Phillips' sprawling fortress, literally ducking the silent missiles lobbing between Mom and Dad.

Drew's parents were almost never around. They had a similar relationship to mine, according to Drew, only my parents had once seemed happy while his never had. Their home's vastness fortunately allowed for separate suites on the rare occasions when Drew's father did not spend the night at his apartment in Murray Hill. He worked on Wall Street and actually set me up for an interview to write something called a "house organ," a kind of employee pep rag for Morgan Stanley, my first and only foray into the World Trade Center that emerged in my memory like a perfect photograph blooming in the liquid of some hidden internal dark room after the events of 9/11. I would have gotten the job, too, except that they wanted someone also schooled in photography and I had never even heard of an F-stop.

Somehow I became a kind of social project for the Phillips family but I didn't really mind. It kept me from watching my parents eyes recede into their heads like my old Tiny Tears Doll Timmy buried in the snow one winter. I found her the following spring, her plastic eyes nested inside her head and appearing, once extracted with my mother's eyebrow tweezers, to have developed something along the lines of cataracts. She never shed another tear. I never forgave my brother.

Now and then Drew's mother summoned me upstairs to try on Diane Von Furstenberg dresses she'd purchased but never worn. We were almost the same size and she would grit her teeth when I emerged from the bathroom having tied the wraparound concoctions that were all the rage in the city into incoherent knots. Without ever really engaging in conversation, I understood quite clearly my role as her little failed charity case.

Drew seemed highly amused by the whole thing. One night I was actually invited for dinner during which Drew and his father engaged in an entertaining battle over the recent addition of Drew's mustache, a development that clearly irked his father although apparently not as much as his son's "mispronunciation" of the word.

"I was referring to your mus-TASH," he said, with a strong emphasis on the second syllable.

Drew grinned. "You mean my MUS-tash," he said, with a strong emphasis on the first syllable.

"Mus-TASH," his father repeated.

Drew shook his head. "Collie, what does your brother Timmy drive us around in?"

I sighed. "Mustang," I mumbled into my bisque.

"Mus-TANG," his father corrected.

I was beginning to appreciate and reconsider the value of marijuana.

It was all quite platonic; Drew and I lounging around watching TV and pontificating on the lapsed idealism of the '60s, denouncing our generation's strobe-lit lurch toward the superficial, the government's slide to the right. Our steady commentary on the foibles of popular '70s culture ironically distracting us completely from facing how washed-up this war and its casualties actually left us feeling, from confronting *anything* remotely real within ourselves. It was all quite platonic, even though his physical presence still left my stomach churning. I walked a tightrope around him, struggling for balance, ever on the brink of quite literally falling for him but he never made a single move on me. I blamed it on his condition. I blamed it on mine. And then one day as I lay sprawled out on the couch in the Phillips' den watching the *Monty Python* show he reached over and rested his palm on my cheek. Every nerve in my body converged on that point of contact. Even now, writing this, I can feel the heat of that touch. A heat that has never been replaced in all these years. I stood up and climbed into his lap. He buried his head in my chest.

"Collie," he said.

I started to cry. I cried every time he lay his hands on me, fat, delicious, salty tears. We did it over and over, day in and day out. I cried and cried.

It wasn't intercourse exactly but it was still sex, the best I ever had. And like all sex, it changed everything. Like Sleeping Beauty I awakened from my coffin of suspended animation. Living from moment to moment was no longer enough. I wanted to get inside his head, you know? Coax him into spackling the hole in me.

All too soon I began to throw little silent fits; just like Mom. He didn't know what to do. He would ask me what was wrong and I would sit hugging my chest. "Nothing," I would lie.

He would shrug and light another joint.

I would seethe. I wanted a future for him, a future for us.

Finally, I couldn't stand myself any longer and decided to take matters into my own hands. I took the bus into the city and rode the subway to Columbia. When I came over late that afternoon, the hit movie of our life together still reeling in my brain, I could barely contain myself.

I pressed my hands against his cheeks.

"You're freezing," he said. He held them to his neck. "What is it, Collie?"

I explained I'd met with the assistant dean and told him all about him. They would have to see his transcripts, of course, but they had no doubt he could transfer his Dartmouth credits. He could start that summer. They had a whole dorm specially designed to accommodate handicapped students. Or we could rent a flat together, something on the first floor. I would find a job and he would go to school and ...

"What are you, crazy?" he said, wheeling forward and backward the way he did when he watched the news or argued with his father. "What in hell makes you think I'm going back to school?"

"You can't stay here forever," I said. "Christ, you're almost twenty-five years old. You're brilliant. You have a life to live."

"I'm living my life," he said.

"You call this life!" I shouted. "This isn't life. This is treading water. Barely, even."

"Spinning wheels," he said, trying to be funny.

"This isn't you," I said. "You have gifts to give this world."

"Had," he said. "I *had* gifts."

"You have more than most people will ever have," I said, struggling with the volume knob on my voice.

"Yeah, like what?"

I couldn't believe him. "Like idealism," I shrieked. "Like intelligence and potential. Like me!"

It wasn't until I crumpled to the couch, biting into my fist, that I realized who I was *really* talking to.

Drew had already swiveled around as if ducking the blows of my words and sat, his back to me, a few more excruciating seconds before wheeling away.

I let myself out.

I stayed up all night, thinking about paralysis—Drew's and mine; Timmy's and my mother's and father's—the literal and the figurative.

In the morning I called Leigh. She was delighted to have me come stay—her roommate was graduating and moving back to Connecticut and she was just about to put an ad in the college paper to replace her. Kismet, she called it. Ha! We would take on D.C. together, just like we always said we would. She could get me a writing job—she had a contact in this congressman's office where she'd interned last semester. I had to smile at that. I could only imagine all the contacts she had already made.

My mother said Drew came by one day a couple months after I skipped town. (My father referred to my sudden move to D.C. like that for years.) He'd gotten into Princeton for the fall (just like Daddy—Prince-TON!) and planned to move down that summer to find a place and get a jumpstart on navigating his way around. He asked for my phone number but he never did call and really, I had nothing left to say to him anyway. There are people in your life that come in for a reason—to wake you up or move you along one way or another—and then are gone forever, along with their heat on your skin. I didn't know that then, but I know it now. His father dropped dead of a heart attack the following winter and his mother moved in with her sister in Bronxville. I never heard what finally became of him.

Sometimes, though, he still pops into my dreams. The old Drew, that is, brash and irreverent and staring me up and down, undressing me with his eyes in a way that can still leave me breathless. Standing on the high springboard and taking three swift steps and a leap before somersaulting twice, his long body unfolding like a giant Swiss Army Knife; puncturing the turquoise water without wounding a single molecule; leaving it perfectly, miraculously intact.

John Lennon Is Dead

Welcome to another freaking day in paradise.

I had spilled Calistoga water on the original copy of the Erickson's irrevocable trust and spent most of the afternoon hanging its pages laundry-like on a makeshift clothesline strung up in the copy room and blow-drying them into an almost reasonable facsimile of their former selves. Now I planted myself in front of Val's desk; parched hands lost in the pockets of my trench coat. "Go get a beer?"

Val lifted one plucked brow. "Looks like somebody could use one."

But I was in no mood for an editorial from Val. I had had it with this job, had it with the partners' medieval edicts—requiring secretaries to address attorneys by surname while addressing their secretaries by given name, I mean; give me a break! There are chiefs and there are Indians in this world, Mr. Grimes had explained in his effortlessly condescending manner just the other day, peering down over his reading glasses after dictating a memo to his wife and children regarding an upcoming trip to their condo in Lake Tahoe. If only Teddy Kennedy had won the goddamn primary I might have landed a real job by now instead of being forced to toady up to a bunch of emotional cripples who communicated with their family members via dictated memos.

Val stared up at me. "Looks like someone hates this fucking place," she said, nodding her head triumphantly as though having won a private wager with herself. She had ten years and a Southern accent on me and claimed to have been born hating whatever fucking place she might find herself in.

"You want to get a beer, or not?" I studied the stains on my boots. I hated the freaking rain in this town, too.

Val tapped the stack of probate papers against her desk like a huge deck of cards, anchored them with a metal stapler, jumped up, pulled on her blazer, and knotted a bolt of turquoise chenille around her throat.

The new receptionist, Hallie Concord, trotted over on her impossibly high stilettos precariously secured with leather straps wrapped around and around her ankles, ballet-style.

"Oh, my God," she said, wringing her hands and rolling her walleyes. "Jesus F-ing, Christ," she chanted, prancing around and around in little circles like one of those tiny, hyper dogs I couldn't help but imagine dropkicking across the tea garden in Golden Gate Park.

Hallie shook her lengthy painted fingers in apparent disgust as if she had no idea what they might recently have been up to.

I yawned. Only another of Hallie's crises could make this day any better.

Val crossed her arms over her chest and watched Hallie, expressionless, as if waiting for a traffic light to change.

"He's dead," Hallie pronounced, blinking, after executing a few more seemingly involuntary pirouettes; a kind of kinesthetic Tourette's syndrome. "They shot him dead. I'm going home." She trotted down the hall, arms flailing; straps of her shoes slapping the gift of her protruding anklebones.

We headed for the elevator nonplused, assuming the requisite, lobotomized, Financial District employee position: staring straight ahead at the metal door, jaws slack. Out on the sidewalk, we raised our collars like everyone else against the sudden chill.

Val slipped an arm through mine. "Admit it, you hate that fucking place."

"I hate that fucking place!" A few heads swiveled around but I didn't give a you know what. The truth will set you free.

We fell in line with the dense, rush-hour current of fellow worker bees.

"I can't believe it," a man walking in front of us was saying. "It's like the end of a generation, you know? Can you believe he was forty? Forty; man, it feels like the end of the world."

Val tugged at the guy's sleeve. "What happened?"

He glanced down over his shoulder at her, swatting at the arm of his flannel coat as if attempting to remove lint. "Haven't you heard? They shot John Lennon. He's dead."

"My God; sorry," Val said.

The guy nodded and turned away.

I had already stopped in my tracks, forcing the sea of people to part around me, annoyed by yet another obstacle to their exodus. Val grabbed my arm again, steering me a few more doors down toward our favorite watering hole with its dark plank floors and walls roughed up to resemble a turn-of-the-century saloon. A stained glass window suspended above the carved bar caught a wayward beam of light, scattering purple and orange shadows across gleaming mahogany. And still I said nothing, trying to wrap my head around what we had heard; delayed reactor that I am.

The jukebox blared. The bartender had vowed to play Beatles songs all night long to honor John Lennon.

My eyes felt gritty. I considered calling James, my on-again, off-again boyfriend, but thought better of it. He claimed to be working nights on some project. Running guns or laundering money no doubt all for a homeland he'd visited but once. He didn't want me involved, he said, but I suspected his motives had less to do with the IRA and more to do with a roving eye for the ingénue du jour at the University of San Francisco where he taught Irish history.

"Val! Colleen!"

Jay Rabinowitz, one of the firm's young associates, sat across the room at a table with a couple of other people bent over their beers. "Come on over!" he shouted, face igniting at the sight of Val as if someone had flipped on a switch in his groin. Val pushed me in front of her toward the sound of Jay's voice.

He leapt up and dragged over two chairs from a nearby table. We sat down as he scurried off to the bar for another pitcher and two more glasses.

"I'm Cole." A guy in his early thirties extended his hand, flashing a mouthful of oversized teeth. His starched white shirt accentuated a serious tan.

"Stephanie," breathed a stunning blonde draped over the chair beside him in a low-cut, crepe dress. What kind of woman went to work like that?

Jay returned and poured us each a beer. "You've met Cole and Stephanie, then? We went to law school together—NYU." He let out a great rush of air, seemingly overcome by the excitement of running into us; the obligation of introductions.

Val tamped out a Tarreyton and Jay seized her Bic lighter. She watched him patiently—the way a cat watches its latest catch—before reaching out and calming his errant thumb with her hand. She lit it herself, tilted back her head, and blew a tower of smoke rings toward the ceiling.

We downed a couple beers mostly in silence, basking in the score of our lives. "John Lennon is dead," I said, after a while, as if hearing it again might help it register. "It's impossible to imagine." As if on cue, those haunting lyrics issued from the bartender's speakers.

We all started singing, then, except for Val, who continued smoking, sculpted features inanimate as a mannequin's.

Cole made a little teepee of his long, tapered fingers and slurred into them. "I feel like I knew him, I mean, knew him *personally*, you know?"

He sounded really drunk. I suddenly really wanted to call James.

"Let us not be melodramatic," said Stephanie, softly. In the dim light, her eyes sparkled like chips of ice.

Cole shot her a pleading look.

"Do you remember the *Ed Sullivan Show*?" Jay asked. "The first time the Beatles sang on TV? I was thirteen and my sister was fifteen. She fell down on the floor in a kind of swoon. My mother thought she was having a seizure."

Did I remember? "I was only seven," I said. "They sang *I Want to Hold Your Hand*. Our priest was there; the one that left the priesthood the following year to organize the farm workers. He shook my hand before he left and said the world would never be the same. I remember feeling something had shifted forever."

In an astonishing breach of corporate etiquette, Jay Rabinowitz started belting it out.

Val rolled her eyes and laughed. "You get down, Mr. Rabinowitz."

"You can call me Jay. What do you remember, Val?"

"I was in high school. We didn't have a TV but my best friend, April Fisher did. I watched it at her house. I liked the way their heads looked, like a matching set of mushrooms. No one in our town had hair like that. They would have been lynched."

Stephanie yawned. "I think I've had enough fun for one night. Cole?"

"Call a cab, will you? I want to stay."

Her eyes narrowed. She flipped her hair over her shoulder. What did men see in hair-flippers? It has always mystified me.

Jay rose. "I'll catch you one, I've got to grab a sandwich and get back to the office. I've got a brief due in the morning."

Val snorted. "After how many pitchers? I am seriously impressed."

"I'm used to writing half drunk. How do you think I got through law school?"

"Curiouser and curiouser," I said. I had always wanted to quote that phrase from *Alice in Wonderland*. The time finally seemed right.

"Don't be too late," Stephanie sniffed, clearly annoyed.

Cole saluted.

"You guys married, or what?" Val asked, after they'd gone.

He shook his head. "We were high school sweethearts."

"Let me guess, she was head cheerleader," I said.

"Pom-pom squad."

"Christ," I said.

"Look who's talking," said Val.

"I quit when I realized the girls were only interested in flaunting their dubious superiority."

Cole laughed. "Dubious superiority. That's rich. I've always wanted to say 'that's rich' in a sentence. It's so Joan Didion, don't you think?"

Who was this guy? I loved this guy.

"What the hell is that supposed to mean?" Val said. "We were talking about your relationship with stick-up-her-butt."

"Right," Cole said. "We'd lost touch over the last ten years but then I got a job out here a few months ago. She has this great flat in Twin Peaks and she invited me to stay until I could find my own place. We just kind of drifted into couplehood." He shook his head. "Excuse me." He rose and headed for the men's room.

"Drifting out of couplehood," I said. "I wouldn't give them another month."

Val refilled her beer. "Of course not; he's gay."

"Shut up," I said.

"I'm telling you, I have a built-in fag detector."

"But he looks so—"

"Ever tell you about the quarterback I dated in high school? Larry Bind, a minister's son. I blamed his daddy's sermons for him never touching me but it wasn't that. I walked in on him one day in his own basement butt-fucking the paperboy."

I winced. "Jesus, Val."

She shrugged.

But, of course she was right, of course he was gay. All the good ones in this town were.

Cole carried over another pitcher of beer and refilled our glasses.

"We really should eat something, don't you think," I said. I was starting to get a little preview of that whirly thing that happens when I drink on an empty stomach.

"Hold that thought." Cole reached into his pocket. "I have a little treat for you ladies, if you'd care to join me." He pressed something into Val's palm.

"Come on Colleen," Val said. "Time to go potty."

In the bathroom, she shoved me into the handicapped stall. "Honey, your bad day just took a one-eighty turn for the better." Val unscrewed the tiny vial of coke and shoved the spoon toward my nose. I did not do well on coke. The few times I'd tried it, it had only emphasized my penchant toward senseless musings and left me climbing the walls for hours after contemplating the possibility of a literal hell. I had vowed never to indulge again. Still, it had been a very bad day, month, almost a year here in everybody's favorite city. Besides, John Lennon would only die once. I covered one nostril and snorted into the other.

We strode back into the bar to the rhythms of *Here Comes the Sun*, swinging our arms like schoolgirls.

The room was crawling with people now, sitting and standing, drinking and smoking, crooning Beatles' tunes. My feet felt springy as we sat back down. I squeezed Val's hand. "So where did you grow up Cole," I shouted.

"Upstate New York," he said. "Rockland County."

I couldn't believe it. "I'm from Rocky Ledges!"

"Easy girl," said Val.

"New City," Cole said.

"Ever been to the Gum Drop?"

Cole beamed. "I practically lived there."

"Oh my God," said Val. "What are the odds?"

"The Gum Drop was *the* disco when I was in college. It had these great DJs and the best Singapore Slings."

Val gave a little gag-me gesture.

"Do the Hustle," sang Cole, treating us to a little, seated demonstration.

"Listen, John Travolta," Val said. "I think we need to go potty again."

Cole dug into his pocket and handed her the coke, mid boogie.

Penny Lane was in our ears and eyes as we headed back to the restroom.

"Don't you think we should have waited until he offered?" I was trying to whisper, but nonetheless felt like I was shouting.

"I don't see you turning it down."

I laughed, and followed Val back out the stall door. I ran icy water over my wrists and dried my hands. Val applied lipstick and handed it to me. "You're awfully pale. Try some."

I ran the tube of fuchsia tint over my lips. It made my skin look green. I rubbed it off with a paper towel.

Back at the table we found Cole still grooving in his chair, eyeing the crowd. "Why don't we do it in the road," he sang along, strumming an air guitar.

I couldn't stop rubbing my mouth. "I can't feel my lips," I said.

Val rolled her eyes. "Have some more beer, sweetheart."

I continued to interview Cole. Turns out, we'd both gone to school in Boston and must have crossed paths a dozen times at the Gum Drop, taking the Greyhound home for Thanksgiving and spring break. I found myself recounting the time, freshman year, when I'd tried to surprise my parents with a President's Day weekend visit only to get stuck in a blizzard on the Thruway, my bus the third vehicle in an eighty-car pileup that left the uninjured passengers stranded for hours. I arrived at Port Authority at one in the morning. The roads were hellacious—I could still hear my father shouting into the pay phone receiver—what in hell was I thinking? He didn't even know if the bridges were open; I would have to stay put among the lurking murderers and junkies until he could figure out a way to come get me. "And that's when I knew Tom Wolfe was right," I concluded. "You can never go home again." Who was I kidding? I had never fit in, not in my family, not in my town, and I could never go back. I was homeless, really; when you come right down to it; always had been. I had come all the way to San Francisco to find my place in this world. Where did I go from here? To the bathroom again with Val, I hoped; and soon.

"I'm the homeless one," Cole said. "Stephanie and I are finished. We have nothing in common, never did. She's just so damn beautiful, I felt like I could do anything with someone like that on my arm. Be anything anyone wanted me to be." He grabbed one of Val's cigarettes and lit it.

"I didn't know you smoked," I said.

"I don't. I quit. I've got to find my own place. I've got to tell her I just can't do this anymore. You really *can't* go home again, I know what you mean. Don't you just *love* Tom Wolfe? I love Tom Wolfe."

"I had never seen snow," Val said. "Once when I was eight years old, my Uncle Renny who used to drive all over the place in his old Pontiac selling vacuum cleaners brought me a snowball. He balled it up himself in Pennsylvania and kept it on ice in one of them foam coolers and presented it to me as an early Christmas present. I don't think I ever had a better present in my life; even though it only lasted ten minutes."

"You have to tell Stephanie," I said. "It will only hurt worse and worse if you keep on stringing her along." The words rang out in my ears. Was that what James was doing with me? Whatever had flared between us had expired; the latest victim of my overly high expectations that had snuffed out everything important in my life. Too high-strung, passionate, idealistic; parents and teachers and boyfriends had pronounced again and again. I could already hear the little speech James would utter any day now. But then, I thought about snow, the spun sugar of each uniquely perfect flake, how a person could grow up without ever experiencing snow; how an uncle could capture the sheer joy of it in a foam cooler and carry it four hundred miles on the interstate. "I'll take you home with me for Christmas," I told Val. "It always snows in Rocky Ledges at Christmas."

"No it doesn't," said Cole.

"I thought you couldn't go home again," said Val.

They got up and danced and I followed, swept up in a passing conga line, tapping spoons swiped from the kitchen together as makeshift castanets to the tune of *Hey Jude*.

Cole spun off, knocking hips rhythmically with a slight, wiry teenager with cropped, mowed-looking hair, cheekbones like buffed seashells, and a metal-studded collar he might have swiped from a pit bull.

"What I tell you?" whispered Val.

I shrugged. "I was thinking I should call James," I said, hands on Val's waist. "You think I should call James? Tell me not to call James."

"Do not under any circumstances call James."

"Meet William," Cole said. "Come on, we're going down the street to Martine's."

"Isn't that a gay club?" I asked. But they were already heading out the door.

I had never seen such resplendent male specimens in my life—dozens of Williams and larger versions completely clad in black leather. There were men in drag, Brooke Shields and Cheryl Tiegs look-alikes, and a bevy of Bette Midlers. Here, too, Beatles' music ruled and began to fill me until I found myself awash in a wave of well-being, twirling around the dance floor in the arms of very polite and beautiful people of unknown gender while bubbles—steadily launched from a machine in the corner—rained down on our heads and Val and I made a couple more trips to what passed for the little girls' room.

"It's just like he said. The world really can live as one."

Val laughed. "You're such a wuss."

"Aren't you just the cutest little thing," said Cole, who had stepped out of the closet before our very eyes and now stood, jacket abandoned, Oxford shirt buttoned down to reveal tufts of light brown hair and a dazzling gold chain.

"I think I should call my boyfriend, James; did I mention James?"

"Don't call James!" Val and Cole chimed.

"Where's William?" I asked.

"He went home an hour ago, remember?"

"Past his bedtime," Val said.

I glanced at my watch. "Jesus. Did you know it's one-thirty?"

"Ready to hit the sack, are you?" asked Val.

"Are you kidding? I don't know if I'll ever sleep again. And we have to *work* tomorrow."

"It's going to be one fucking long day," said Cole. "Come on, let's get out of here."

"Where we going?" asked Val.

"To the beach—clear our heads."

"I'll be right back," I said, pretending to head for the restroom but veering off toward the payphone in the corner. I fed it with coins and dialed. The phone rang three times before the machine picked up. "James here; only not at the moment. Leave a message at the beep."

Son of a bitch. I slammed down the receiver.

"You called James didn't you?" said Val, when I rejoined them at the front door.

"He wasn't there. That's what I get for dating a criminal."

"All men are criminals."

"Except Cole," Cole said.

"You don't count. You're gay," Val said.

His eyes widened. Then he smiled. "That's right," he said. "I'm fucking gay. How do you tell your girlfriend you're gay?"

The question hung in the air as we headed out into the fog. On Val's recommendation we did a couple more lines in the car, just to ease ourselves down. At an all-night supermarket Cole bought a giant plastic bottle of Coca Cola, I picked up a six-pack of Orange Nehi for the Vitamin C, and Val nabbed a carton of glazed donuts—because they were so gorgeous and efficient looking, we all agreed; like tiny life buoys—in case we ever felt like eating again. After that, we drove to Ocean Beach in Cole's rusty little Fiat.

He pulled a bag of pot out of his glove compartment and a blanket out of the trunk. We climbed the cement barrier, shed shoes, socks, and pantyhose and stumbled toward the shoreline to where you could just make out the waves clearly crashing but still nestle down in dry sand. The fog had lifted. Beneath a three-quarter moon we stood a moment, silhouetted in the silver light. It was four o'clock in the morning.

"So Val," said Cole. "What about *your* love life?"

"Men are not her forte," I said.

"Really?" He raised his brows.

"Not like that, doofus," Val said.

"Well, men are not exactly my forte either," Cole said. "I haven't actually had what one might call a relationship."

"How long have you known you were gay?" I asked.

"I guess I've always known. I just couldn't face the family thing, the friend thing, the what-will-people-think thing." He laughed. "Here in San Francisco, it's just so easy. The only people who care are three thousand miles away."

"Except for Stephanie," said Val.

"Jesus, Val," I said.

"It's OK," said Cole. "She doesn't love me. I just fit her profile for a while. She can write another one."

"Just promise me you won't go to any of those bathhouses," I said. There was some new virus infecting gay men and he looked so suddenly fragile in the semi-light, unweighted by his recent admission. I could tell we would be friends. "Promise me," I said.

To the north, you could just make out the bared teeth of Seal Rocks, plunked down as if on purpose by a divine travel agent for the express enjoyment of tourists sipping cocktails at the Cliff House. Cole spread out the blanket and lit a joint. Val and I strolled down toward the water's edge where an elephant seal had beached itself and lay akimbo on its stomach, sick and bellowing, struggling to right itself.

"Come on fella." I inched toward him. "You can do it."

"What are you crazy?" said Val. "That's a wild animal."

"He's not going anywhere." The wind shifted, blowing the rotten stench directly into my nostrils. The moon spun like a wayward strobe light. I rushed away down the beach, until I spotted an empty oilcan swept in by the tide. I rested my arms against it and vomited for a solid five minutes. After a while, I could feel Val's hand on my back.

"Your period still late?"

"Three weeks."

Val handed me a tissue and I wiped my mouth.

"I'm never late," I said. "Not ever."

"We'll figure it out, OK? Don't think about it now."

I nodded. My teeth began to chatter.

"Let's warm you up."

Imagine there's no Heaven, I thought, chattering against Val's shoulder. Or hell.

We rejoined Cole on the blanket like bookends, pulling the threadbare wool up around our shoulders and tucking it under our bare knees.

"There's no one left to shoot," I said, after a while.

"What?" Val said.

"I mean, think about it. They got John and Martin and Bobby just like in the song. And now, John Lennon."

"There's plenty of people left to shoot," Val said.

"They didn't even have to shoot Ted," said Cole. "He shot himself with that whole Chappaquiddick thing."

Well said, I thought. I rested my head on his shoulder.

"You were a Paul girl, weren't you," said Cole, after a while.

"Paul and John. I appreciated John's intelligence. His vision."

"Bull," said Val.

"It's OK," said Cole. "I was a Paul man, myself. How about you, Val?"

"Ringo."

"Get out," said Cole.

"I'm a sucker for drums."

"All right, Lucy," said Cole, handing her the joint.

We passed it around.

I did my best to hold it in my lungs but choked a little like I always do. It had no effect. "I think I'm pregnant," I said, after a while. I suppose I needed to hear that out loud, too.

Val patted my arm.

"I know I'm gay," said Cole.

In the silence, a gull cackled, swooping down to retrieve an early breakfast from the garbage-strewn kelp.

Val sighed, "I'm still just white trash. Easy, gay boy; you're grinding your teeth again."

She disentangled herself from the blanket and rose, arms outstretched, crucified by the lilac light of dawn. She threw off her jacket and fell straight backward on the sand as if into invisible arms; lay there for only a moment before she began flapping her limbs.

"By George, I think she's flipped her wig," said Cole.

"She's making an angel," I said, entranced. "It never snows in South Georgia. She never got to do that, remember?" We'd had that conversation, hadn't we—but weeklong hours ago?

"Who couldn't use an angel," Cole said.

The beached sea lion let out one last bellow before rolling over on its side for good.

I shivered and pressed my chin against my knees. "I just can't believe John Lennon is dead," I said.

Annette

Colleen

Safe Haven

Annette

It has been almost a year and I still wake up from my fitful sleep reaching for him; a pillow wedged between my knees to cushion my creaky hips I tell myself but *really*, no more than a sorry stand-in for my lover's thigh. My *lover*. It took me 50 years to work up the courage to utter that word, even in my head. We used to sleep like Picasso subjects, our limbs as if dismembered and reassembled. All jumbled up, cubist components of two human forms melded into one.

When we met six years ago—after Gerry died and I moved to Denver to be close to Colleen and my granddaughter Catherine—I knew I had no right to find a love like this at my age. But there he was, a retired philosophy professor from the Iliff School of Theology wearing shorts and a hooded sweatshirt; posing in some weird tai chi position in Observatory Park. I passed him every time I walked my dog Bathrobe (so named by Catherine for the chenille-like fur afflicting her coat), muscled legs bent, arms extended, erect spine supporting a shaved head that made his features—mouth, nose, eyes, and bushy brows—pop out at you like the plastic ones on Catherine's Mr. Potato Head.

I walked by him for two solid weeks that spring through the vacillating gusts and snow and copious sunshine that characterize April in Colorado. Always to find him frozen in the same half-squatting position, staring at a giant cottonwood tree, its buds tightly fisted.

One day—the temperature creeping into the fifties following a storm of heavy wet snow that left the trees' taxed branches lobbing piles of slush—he startled me. Raising his long frame in slow motion like the tin man in *The Wizard of Oz*, joints miraculously anointed by an invisible oilcan, he walked over, extended his hand, and with a little forward, bow-like thrust of his shoulders said: "Can I get you a violet?" As if offering me a glass of wine.

Bathrobe raced in frantic circles toward the perimeter of her leash like those volleyballs tethered to metal poles in the park where my kids grew up. Just another torture device disguised as playground equipment in the 1960s.

I nodded, mesmerized, as he knelt in the tufted, snow-crusted grass, plucked a single, perfect, embryonic flower from its stalk, and handed it to me. Bathrobe stopped barking, collapsed on her haunches, and studied us. I was just like that violet, Hank Lieberman told me, months later, "ethereal, albeit hearty."

Now Bathrobe scratches against the door and I am up and out of bed and smoothing the comforter, yanking on my sweats and padding into the bathroom to brush my teeth, gather my recalcitrant hair up into a topknot, and secure it with a stretchy cloth. For a moment I study the woman in the mirror with the recessed eyes and caved in cheeks. Squinting to see the little flower Hank saw peeking out to no avail.

An NPR reporter rattles on about the latest Iraqi body count. *Insurgence.* A word I cannot recall reading or hearing until we "liberated" these people on the other side of the world. A word that has become paramount in the public relations vocabulary of this ongoing war the administration insists is no longer a war. The longer I live, the more events repeat themselves. Vietnam, for example, seems to have returned, along with a bevy of ill-conceived fashions.

Bathrobe nearly trips me on the curved stairway in her determination to whisk me out the door. I plant a kiss on the bull's eye of thinning hair on Timmy's head. Reminding myself that he is my forty-four-year-old son, not the ex-husband whose pattern baldness he inherited along with a genetic inability to place a stack of anything in a coherent pile.

Timmy sits at the drop-leaf kitchen table staring into his mug of black coffee, an unlit (I will not permit him to smoke in my house—I *do* have my limits) skinny brown cigar-like cigarette pressed between his fingers, home from the night shift at Sam's Club.

"Hey, Mom," he says, without looking up. Purplish, horizontal crescents underscore his green eyes—inverted, abstract violets.

He moved in here last year after Hank died in his sleep beside me, ending mine. Unable to make it on his own anymore, marriage trashed—as Colleen put it—high-powered sales job with the country's leading HMO long a thing of the past. Shattered by memories recovered to what purpose? Shattered.

In the alley, just past a bed of daffodils squashed by melting snow, Bathrobe barks and tugs on her leash like a mongrel half her age, nearly strangling herself in a fruitless effort to launch her loaf-like frame into the air. And then I hear it, a kind of chirping sound; little bird noises emanating from somewhere inside. I yank on Bathrobe's leash to rein her in, peer over the metal rim of the open receptacle expecting to see a stranded starling only to suck in my breath. A bundled-up baby stares back at me. In my peripheral vision, the high hedge protecting the Sherman's yard from unwelcome inspection absorbs a life-size smear of dark fabric; the snap and rustle of churning limbs.

"Holy Christ," I say, because things like this do not happen in real life, at least not in my neighborhood. And that baby—perhaps responding to the look of horror on my face or sensing its impending guest appearance on the six o'clock news—opens its tiny beak and wails.

Like a quarterback (I am still a strong woman, walk five miles a day, take Pilates at the university fitness center) I rush inside with it nestled against my forearm, Bathrobe yapping at my heels. I lay it down on the couch and carefully peel away the plaid woolen car blanket to reveal a beautiful white satin gown tied with red ribbon. The outfit looks familiar and it takes me a moment to realize it is an American Girl costume, part of Kristen's Santa Lucia outfit like the one I gave Catherine the Christmas she turned eight. Beneath the doll clothes the little girl has been wet a while, her diaper quadrupled in size with moisture. Although someone has cleaned her up she has that scalded, cone-head, newborn look. My eyes sting as I fold her in my arms. She swipes at my chest, lips pulsing.

"Jesus Christ," says Timmy, hovering over us.

"I need you to run out to Safeway," I tell him. We would need diapers and formula, a couple of plastic bottles.

"Aren't you going to call the police?" he asks, a quotation mark embedded between his brows, sounding for all the world like the sane one in the family.

"Not yet. She's in shock. I want to calm her down first."

I can't say why I have no intention of calling the police right away except that I have asked as I am wont to do the question that has kept me placing one foot in front of the other this past year: *What would Hank do?* (Ha—you thought I was going to say Jesus? Not a chance.) I have asked, and he has answered.

I converse with Hank about it. I do not actually hear voices or anything like Timmy used to. It's more of an interviewing process in which I ask a question and wait until the answer comes in the form of a thought in my head. Not unlike the texting thing Catherine and her friends are so keen on that drives Colleen crazy. Hank, of course, can read my mind and already knows the suspicion growing there.

In my lap the baby has stopped crying. Her fist latches onto my index finger.

It's like riding a bike, really. I change the wet diaper and squirt a drop of milk on my wrist before plunging the plastic nipple in the baby's mouth.

Timmy watches, biting down on his unlit cigarette. He runs his palms up and down his bare forearms as if trying to warm himself up.

"I can take it from here," I tell him. "You need some sleep."

But he just sits rocking back and forth like the autistic boy who used to live next door. I wonder if he is thinking about Cecile as a baby. He has not seen his nineteen-year-old daughter in more than three years and neither have I. My daughter-in-law Regina's grudges against her ex-husband had quickly expanded to envelop us all.

The baby sucks away at the empty bottle in her sleep. Her eyelids are scribbled with tiny purple veins, fringed with black, showgirl lashes. She carries seeds of striking beauty. She relaxes all at once, doubling in weight against my arm. Her thighs fall open, frog-like.

My mind slips back as it does more and more lately. I am descending the steps of a nondescript Brooklyn brownstone with Edie Twardowsky. She leans against me; asks if we can stop for a roast beef sandwich. I am thinking about burning in hell for my role as accomplice in this act and the thought brings with it an unexpectedly welcome whiff of freedom.

Now I am thinking about the baby I lost all those years ago; ironically the only pregnancy Gerry and I had actually planned. I was only four months along but the doctors said it was a girl. I planned to name her Sylvia, after the dead poet. She had always reminded me of my best friend, Alice; so beautiful and talented; so impossibly lost. (Fortunately Gerry did not read poetry.)

"Sylvia?" Timmy repeats, edging toward fetal position.

"I've always liked that name." I am thinking about the day I found out I was pregnant with Colleen. Gerry and I had not yet married. There was this doctor in Albany the girls in my dorm whispered about over little nips of rye whiskey from a tin flask. I have never told anyone this: I thought about it.

"We can't go around naming her," Timmy says.

"Sylvia," I mouth.

As if in solidarity, the baby spits out the nipple and beams up at me, a ribbon of soymilk inching down her neck, both arms flying up in a kind of cheer.

Colleen

"What's that noise?" I ask, sitting at my mother's kitchen table pushing a slice of banana bread around my plate with my fingers. Resisting the urge to smash it down and form it into little mock communion wafers, the better to practice swallowing the body of Christ without touching it with our teeth as the nuns once instructed. My daughter Catherine has no idea how much I have spared her.

"I don't hear anything." Mother rises to refill my coffee.

I cover the mug with my palm. "I've got to knock out the caffeine. I'm not sleeping at all with these night sweats. Did you have them, too?"

My mother sits back down and cocks her head in that way of hers, as if consulting some invisible attorney. "I really don't recall," she says, after a moment; as usual taking the fifth.

It is just such a typical Annette statement I can barely restrain myself from reaching over and shaking her. My mother does not seem to recall experiencing anything in this life, awakening each morning a regular Tabular Rasa. Sometimes I think God placed her on this planet specifically to make my own runaway emotions appear all the more out there.

At my feet, Bathrobe stands and shoots me a penetrating look, as if she, too, would like to give her a piece of her mind. She executes a couple of rapid twirls before settling back down and resting her muzzle on my clogs.

It is just hormones talking, I remind myself, stirring up all I have left unresolved these many years, recently exacerbated by my ex-husband Edward's decision to finally marry his twenty-two-year-old former student and my twelve-year-old daughter's decision to forever exclude me from her life. It is just hormones talking, I remind myself, summoning forgiveness I rarely feel, begging the universe for deliverance from the anger that bubbles up out of nowhere these days. (My mother does not plan her day around ruining mine, I remind myself, sanity, however briefly, restored.) And then I hear it again, a muffled whine emanating from above. Bathrobe's ears lift.

"Excuse me a minute." Mother dabs her lips with a paper napkin embossed with teacups, rises, and disappears upstairs.

Timmy shuffles up from the basement, the usual filthy sweats riding down around his narrow hips, face creased by pillow seams; his resemblance to my father in his younger days momentarily shocking me anew with a little jolt of grief for us all.

"Where's Mom?" he asks, opening the refrigerator, unscrewing a bottle of cranberry juice, and knocking it straight back.

"Upstairs. What's up with her?"

He shakes his head and sighs, slumps into a chair, and plucks a cigarette from behind his ear.

I head upstairs toward my mother's bedroom.

"Shhhhhh." She presses her index finger to her lips, and I am transported back in time and space to our kitchen in Rocky Ledges. My mother—the perpetual librarian—constantly admonishing us to lower our voices, finger to lips, eyes roaming invisible stacks.

She sits with her back to me in the Shaker rocker she bought along with a whole lot of other spindly blonde furniture after she and my father separated years ago. Before Janine abandoned him to join a band in California and he came crawling back on his knees. The way I keep expecting Edward to. Not that I would ever take him back.

Mother rocks back and forth in the chair holding a tightly swaddled infant in her arms. The baby struggles to keep her eyes open against the soothing motion.

"What?" I mouth.

My mother inches up out of the chair, a movement reminiscent of Hank, the paramour we'd all come to love in spite of ourselves. He introduced us to the Unity Church where nobody went to Purgatory or Limbo. We held hands and sang songs. I felt like one of the Whos in *The Grinch Who Stole Christmas*. Mother—having renounced religion completely after Timmy's ordeal—still had her doubts, but it was my kind of place.

I follow her into the guest room where she lays the bundle down in the little bed she has fashioned from a dresser drawer. She holds her finger to her lips as I follow her downstairs.

"Whose baby is it?" I ask when we have seated ourselves once more at the table.

Timmy pushes his half eaten cereal away and leans back in his chair, a dreamy, unfocused look about his eyes.

The smoke of something hot and unspoken smolders in the air between them.

Annette

"Did I ever tell you when I was carrying you I had this sensation of little bubbles exploding inside me that kept me awake at night?" I say, a hiccupping Sylvia splayed against my shoulder. She began to cry right after I told Colleen the story, as if she could hear the silent scream forming in my daughter's head. At times Colleen resembles that Edvard Munch painting, *The Scream*, horrified by the madness of this world. It has never met her expectations and yet she somehow can't help believing it still will. I swear to God she came in this way; I refuse to accept responsibility for this particular trait.

"The doctor said it meant you had the hiccups in utero. You hiccuped more than any baby I've ever seen. Timmy never did that. It's so interesting how each child is so completely different."

Colleen sits beside me on the couch one arm drawn to her chest, its palm supporting her other elbow, chewing on her knuckles; eyes widened into perfect Cheerios and looking for all the world like the black-and-white photo of her I keep on my dresser. Sitting in her booster chair at her fifth birthday party wearing a frilly sundress and one of those pointy paper hats, surrounded by laughing, screaming children; absolutely appalled. News of Sylvia seems to have left her speechless, an unprecedented turn of events in our decades together. I am not a chatty person by nature but her silence leaves me clamoring to fill it.

"Really, Colleen, I know this looks pretty outrageous but I just have a strong feeling about this child."

I also have a hunch I know who abandoned this baby, the person who disappeared into the Sherman's yard past a weathered Bush for President sign. A girl I'd seen many times with long, stringy hair and the requisite low-slung jeans and baggie hoodie shooting hoops in the alley with her siblings. Melissa, Vanessa, something like that—the Sherman's oldest, not much older than Catherine. They had seemed a regular Norman Rockwell ensemble—two girls and two boys who moved together across the summer days as a kind of unit—tossing water balloons and sucking Popsicles. Bowing and saluting as I inched through the alley into my garage—sufficient unto themselves—not unlike my brothers and me growing up on the farm. But *these* children lived in central Denver; home-schooled, someone said. I had seen her a couple of times, a faded woman in a sack-like denim dress with a fixed stare, lips pleated tight as the mouth on a laundry bag. Religious zealots, someone said. I had not cared to further our acquaintance.

It could not be, I told myself, but Hank just shook his head. If my neighbor's *child* had given birth to this child it was not just a crime, but two crimes. I needed to find a way to help them both. It wasn't too late to make up for my failure to protect my own children from the blows life had dealt them as a direct result of my highly ambivalent mothering.

"I think I saw something last year on Channel 9 about some kind of new law that lets mothers abandon their newborns without getting prosecuted," I say.

"They can't throw them in *dumpsters*."

"I think I know who the mother is. You know those kids across the alley Catherine sometimes shoots hoops with—their oldest girl?"

"Jesus," says Colleen. "The Christians?"

"I think I saw her running away when I found Sylvia. The baby was all cleaned up and everything. She was wearing Kristen's Santa Lucia gown."

"What?"

"She had dressed her in doll clothes, American Girl. I think she was watching to make sure somebody responsible would rescue her."

Colleen presses her index fingers against the spot where the bridge of her nose meets her brows and draws a breath on the verge of a wheeze.

"I know this has been a difficult year for you, Mom," she says, after a while, in the flat voice she gets when she has absolutely had it with you. "I may have underestimated what a blow it was, losing Hank like that in his sleep, just like Daddy. Maybe we should have gotten you into some kind of support group or something."

How dare you compare Hank with Gerry? I would like to shout. But he *is* the father of my children, after all. *Her* father. "This is not about Hank." But even as the words slip off my tongue I can see him materializing across the room, limbs twisted into one of those pretzel positions; wagging his finger at me.

Colleen runs her hand down my forearm. "Are you sure about this, Mom? That girl's like Catherine's age."

"I can't be sure it's hers but I know I saw her running away."

She winces. I swear to God she was born wincing at the injustice of a world so out of whack with her vision. She yanks a cell phone out of her pocket and stabs away at it. I listen to her telling Edward there's been an emergency—could he pick Catherine up at soccer?

"Maybe there's a way that law you were talking about *can* help," she says, snapping the phone shut. "I can't remember the details but I'm thinking I could call Don Garcia."

"The D.A.?"

"Remember that day-in-the-life-of piece I wrote about him for the *Post*? He sent me a thank you note—told me to call him if I ever needed anything."

I draw Sylvia a little tighter into my ribs, tears I did not shed even at Hank's service suddenly backing up in my throat. "Please don't give her to the police."

As if at the word *police* Sylvia's eyes pop open. She starts making those little breathy groans of hers—like someone having a bad dream—that mean she's ready for a change.

"Hold her a minute." I hand her to Colleen and head upstairs for a diaper and some wipes; stopping a moment to compose myself in the mirror. "Please, Hank, please help us, *please*," I whisper, in my head. Because wherever he is, he is a whole lot closer to God than I will ever be.

Downstairs Colleen, clearly smitten, has the baby propped up on her knees. Dressed in his blue and orange Sam's Club uniform that conveniently doubles as a Bronco's outfit Timmy leans against the wall, eyes fixed on his sister as if watching a movie. He has smoked a lot of pot in his life, enough to slip back into a doped-up state seemingly at will. I sometimes envy him that. Sometimes I regret not trying it years ago with Edie who had gotten a joint from God knows where and whipped it out that day I drove her back from the doctor in the city.

"Patty-cake, patty-cake, baker's man, bake me a cake as fast as you can." Colleen is making tiny symbols of Sylvia's palms.

Timmy drifts out the door, raised hand opening and closing over his head in a wave.

"Pat it and roll it and mark it with a V and toss it in the air for Sylvia and me," croons Colleen, flinging Sylvia's arms into the air.

Colleen

Colleen will know what to do.

It is like a mantra for my mother and my brother, I think, backing into a parking space on Logan, climbing out of my Jetta, and feeding quarters into the meter. I tug my rain jacket hood up over my head to try to stop my recently blown-straight hair from swelling up and frizzing out, Brillo-like in the sleet.

Colleen will know what to do.

That's what my mother and brother have been thinking for decades. I can almost remember myself at that baby's age beaming my youthful parents the reassurance they craved. A pattern I tried to break by fleeing them right after college. A pattern the change in venue did nothing to disrupt, instead drawing the likes of my husband and a long parade of other needy souls before him to me—moth to flame.

I hurry down hill to the City and County Building, dodging the backsplash from barreling SUVs that have no respect for the environment or pedestrians (sometimes my heart still aches for the civility of a San Francisco crosswalk), pass through security, and take the elevator up to the D.A.'s Office. A secretary calls me *honey* and brings me a cup of decaf as I sit waiting for Don Garcia, gazing out the tall windows at sheets of rain that leave me feeling displaced—it never rained day after day like this in Denver.

I sometimes think I traded the coast for the mountains not so much for Edward but to wipe my slate clean. To release the burden of the mortal sin I had committed as a young girl. Not a child like this mother, but not a grownup either; just scraps of cloth in a still unassembled quilt. Not that I believe in mortal sin. Not that I'm one-hundred percent sure I believe in anything at all even after bouncing from church to church when Catherine was little hoping to find my moorings. Involved for a while with a leftist Christian group still fond of chaining themselves to things. Spending a whole week at a Buddhist monastery in the mountains training to qualify as a Friend of Zen. Nevertheless unable to master the complexities of walking meditation and chanting or refrain from sneaking bacon and squashing spiders. After all that seeking this is *still* what I do when I'm nervous: rattle on in my head.

My boot taps against the hand-woven Indian area rug—a habit I inherited from my father no amount of meditation has been able to quell. I survey the neat towers of manila folders on Don's desk; the framed professional certificates and vintage ski posters on the wall. Odd for a man my age—the glaring absence of family photos. Married to his job he confessed in the interview, and left it at that.

And how did this girl get pregnant in the first place at twelve years old? I cannot get her out of my head. My daughter started middle school this year and suddenly veered from teaching her American Girl dolls Haiku to wearing T-shirts emblazoned with suggestive messages—*CONTENTS UNDER PRESSURE!* Conveniently located to highlight teenagers' boobs in case anyone hadn't noticed. Writing passionate love letters (I do not pry but, Jesus, she leaves them everywhere, that means she *wants* me to find them, all the books say so) to so-called "boyfriends" she never sees outside class except on the long bus ride home from her magnet school. (My imagination has a field day with that!)

I want my daughter back.

I press my fingers to my gritty eyelids; careful not to dislodge the swipe of mascara I'd given my lashes hoping to divert attention away from my fatigue. What on earth will Don Garcia have to say about this baby, about my failure to immediately notify the authorities? I can't help picturing myself and my seventy-three-year-old mother and this alleged peer of Catherine's sharing one of those horrifying cells at the Denver Women's Correctional Facility; heckled by the meth heads that had verbally assaulted my fellow journalists and me when we toured the prison last year.

Their words echo in my ears—my own little Greek chorus—egging me on. I will just have to make Don realize we have acted for the highest good. We are mothers ourselves. Grownup mothers who want nothing more than to spare this baby and her child-mother the harsh fate that surely awaits them.

He strides into the room swinging his arms, lankier than I remember, slightly hunched over as though to soften the blow of his full height.

"What an unexpected pleasure," he says, grasping my hand.

He has kind, wide-set, triangular-shaped eyes. Years of smiling have gouged deep parentheses on each side of his mouth. His skin is the color of a soy chai latte. I remember asking him why he decided to become a prosecutor because he didn't look or act the part.

He'd steepled his hands against his mouth before explaining that he'd had a sense of justice, even as a child; had always tried to make things right with other kids, to intervene when kids were being bullied on the playground and so forth. It was like staring into the eyes of the male counterpart I never knew I had.

"To make things right, one person at a time," he said, the quote my editor had pulled out and enlarged. A mantra I myself had come to live by having traded the battles of my youth for the far more challenging cause of making peace with my family day in and day out.

He gestures for me to sit and settles into his leather chair. He had been instrumental in launching a highly successful victims' rights program some years ago; worked with the juvenile courts to help young offenders make restitution for thefts and other petty crimes. When he talked about these efforts, they actually made sense.

"You're looking well, Colleen," he says.

He called to ask me to lunch after the article came out. To thank me, he'd said, but something in his voice hinted at more. The ink hadn't dried on the separation papers Edward and I had filed and I couldn't entertain the idea of anything remotely resembling a date.

Well, times have changed, I think, noticing his eyes briefly skimming the buttons of my silk blouse before refocusing on my face. I had thought my ability to magnetize a man pretty much annihilated along with a bunch of brain cells and the possibility of ever again regulating my personal thermostat.

I sit up straighter in the chair; finger an amber earring. "You said to call if I ever needed anything."

He leans forward, elbows on the desk, listening intently as I relate my mother's story.

"There's that law," I say.

"Safe haven."

Such a catchy name; no doubt crafted by some government spin-doctor, young and ambitious enough to believe his own rhetoric.

"You can abandon a baby in a safe place—a police station or a firehouse—within seventy-two hours of birth without prosecution," he says.

"My mother thinks the girl intentionally slipped the baby into the dumpster when she heard my mother coming."

"The law is really clear on this Colleen."

"She didn't plan to harm her. She knew my mother would take care of her. She can't be more than thirteen years old."

He rubs his forehead.

"To make things right, one person at a time," I say, sealing the deal.

Mother fusses about the kitchen, nervous about delivering the greatest performance of her life. Sticking to the script we have agreed on after my meeting with Don. She hands me cups and saucers—the bone China with flamboyant pink roses she inherited when Grammy died—peels store-bought molasses cookies off their parchment squares, places them on a plate in concentric circles, and pours milk into the creamer.

Catherine sets the table, folding the linen napkins the way I taught her to make a little pocket for the flatware, the way Grammy taught me.

I stopped home after I left Don's office and told my daughter the whole story. It seemed a much more efficient way to get a point across than my usual lecturing. She was quiet for a long time, wrapping a hank of my father's reddish hair around her index finger. Her innate stillness—the effortless focus she displayed even as a child kneeling in the grass to examine a ladybug seemingly for hours—has never ceased to amaze a me who spent years in meditation and many thousands of dollars on tapes and seminars in a futile attempt to silence my chatterbox mind.

"Her name is Vanesssa," she said, at last. "She's in seventh grade at Metro Christian."

My daughter started talking then. There was a sixth-grader in her school that got pregnant and her parents made her have the baby. Another "very Goth" eighth-grader slit her wrists when she missed her period. Catherine insisted on coming with me.

Senses aroused by the commotion, Bathrobe paces the length of the galley kitchen, now and then pausing to lift an ear to the front door, until the doorbell rings and she charges it.

Don has brought a social worker named Mariah Trujillo and a detective named Tony O'Brian with him. I lead them into the kitchen and make our introductions. Catherine, with a poise and graciousness that makes me proud, takes orders for tea and lemonade. Mother slips into her chair and Don clears his throat.

"Your daughter filled me in, Mrs. Shea," he says. "But detective O'Brian and I need to hear the story from you, to take your statement. We have a report to file, an official report, you understand?"

Mother glances at me before straightening her shoulders, staring straight back at Don, and nodding. "The child, Vanassa Sherman, brought me the baby early this morning," she begins.

I listen to my mother warming to the fabricated story Don advised us to deliver with a pang of admiration I have not felt in years. Not since watching her stand up at a Vietnam antiwar rally and unfurl her banner. Not since hearing the slap of her sandals behind me the day I walked out of church for good. The day Monsignor McGowan decided to bless us with a slideshow of fetuses instead of a sermon in case the church's position on legalizing abortion had slipped our minds.

"Did she say it was *her* baby?" the detective asks, rubbing his shiny pink face that does not yet seem to have required a razor. Obviously a complete rookie—Don is no fool.

The social worker watches skeptically, narrowing her black eyes. An overweight nose-breather whose chest heaves with every breath, cleavage battling a floral, boat-necked top.

"She was very upset and I didn't press her on it. It seemed most important to take care of the baby. Also, I wanted to get in touch with my daughter to find out what to do but I couldn't reach her for a couple of hours."

Catherine has dissected her cookie into bite-size pieces, a technique for eating sweets inaugurated by my grandmother that has now plagued four generations. Listening to our lies, she methodically places them on her tongue and mashes them against the roof of her mouth, allowing them to dissolve without touching her teeth like a communion wafer.

We retire to the living room, mother carrying a sleeping Sylvia. (The name seems to fit her; I have taken to using it, too.) Timmy wanders in explaining it has been a slow night at Sam's but we all know he cannot bear to miss the ending of this story. He turns on a *Law & Order* rerun and we all curl up on the horseshoe couch with the multiple, lap-size quilts mother is fond of rescuing from garage sales.

Lying on her side, Catherine rests her bare feet against my hip. Timmy presses ever so slightly into my ribs, the way he had during thunderstorms when we were little. The way he had when mother would put on the *Peter & the Wolf* album and we would nestle under the covers together in delighted terror.

When the program has finished and they're still not back, Timmy gets up, rummages in the refrigerator, and returns with a carton of Rocky Road ice cream and four spoons. Even mother takes a dip, for once declining to admonish him about his essential piggish nature, and we launch into a collective fantasy that we will raise Sylvia ourselves—our own little village.

"I could quit my job," I say. Only how would we live?

"You don't have to quit your job," says mother, setting Sylvia on the couch beside her. "I don't have a job. I can take care of her."

"We can all help," says Timmy.

"You have me, Mommy," Catherine says, in a small voice without a trace of sarcasm. And it seems more than enough, being called Mommy again, to actually consider rising to the challenge.

Annette

Don raps on the side door and Bathrobe, asleep at our feet, goes ballistic as the children say. Dashing around in circles and yapping. Timmy rises as I tuck the blanket tighter around a snoozing Sylvia.

The girl tried to deny it at first, claiming she had no idea how she had gotten pregnant. Finally the story came gurgling forth. They were at a barbecue at Mr. Sherman's brother's house in Colorado Springs. Her cousin Robert jumped her in the garage. She hadn't known what was happening. Afterwards she was afraid to tell. He was head of the church youth group, top of his class, star quarterback on the freshman football team. Everyone loved him, *everyone*, who would believe her? Her parents planned to send her and the baby away to live with maternal relatives in Nebraska since they couldn't very well force the father to marry their daughter.

Catherine—who climbed into Colleen's lap midway through the story—rests her head on her mother's shoulder.

"I'm sorry," says Don. "We need to take her now."

"Timmy, can you please go gather up her diapers and formula?" I gaze down at Sylvia, trying to prevent my mind from conjuring up a childhood involving evangelicals and the state of Nebraska.

The Shermans stumble in, the parents' faces dazed and ashen, Vanessa's blotchy from crying. She hangs her head, hiding behind a drape of asphalt-colored hair. As if at a wake her parents inch toward the couch to view the baby. Her mother nibbles at her hand. Her father rubs his eyes as if to dislodge the sight of her.

I struggle to link the dark-eyed jewel lying beside me with this milk-toast pair.

Don rests his hand on Vanessa's shoulder. "Is this your baby?" She nods.

"Did you give it to Mrs. Shea?"

The child hesitates.

"Vanessa, did you ask Mrs. Shea to watch your baby for you?"

"Yes," Vanessa says, fitting the final piece down into the puzzle of lies we have crafted for ourselves.

"We'll take her now," says Mrs. Sherman.

For a moment I imagine seizing Sylvia, sprinting outside, jumping into my Volvo, and driving off into the sunset. She might have been a poet, after all, a *poet*. Across the room, Hank winks at the thought.

"I wanted to thank you for taking our grandchild," Mr. Sherman says, after a while.

"I can't believe you're going to make Vanessa keep the baby," says Catherine. "She's only a child herself." She has risen and stands grimacing, arms stiff at her side. Fists clenched in her defensive fullback soccer position. But a larger version of her mother at her age—*outraged*.

Mr. Sherman's perfect wasp face, marred only by a pebbled history of acne, swivels toward her.

"I'll take her now," says Mrs. Sherman.

I stand, easing Sylvia's bundled form toward Vanessa's mother.

"This just totally sucks," says Catherine.

Mrs. Sherman's eyes roll back in her head at my granddaughter's foul language.

This time it is Timmy as a child she seems to be channeling—my mouthy nine-year-old son.

The grownup version returns with a shopping bag and hands it to Mr. Sherman.

"She's a good baby," he says. "She never even cries. My daughter cried all the time—colic."

I have to take it as a good omen, this sudden interest in someone other than himself.

"She likes to play patty-cake," says Colleen.

Don beams down at my daughter as if he has never heard anything so adorable.

Across the room, Hank raises an eyebrow.

I shrug, but I am secretly rooting for them.

"Really she's very advanced," says Colleen. "You'll need to sing and read to her a lot. I could ship you some of Catherine's old books and toys if you like."

"Thank you but I have four children," Mrs. Sherman says. "We have plenty of educational materials."

"I bet," says Catherine.

I loop my arm around my blessedly irreverent granddaughter and draw her rigid form to me. My arms seem so empty, so light without Sylvia.

Hank blows me a kiss and is gone. Hank.

"She makes this little breathy sound when she needs to be changed," I say, but no one seems to hear me.

ABOUT THE AUTHOR

Susan Dugan is a freelance writer writing everything from newspaper and magazine articles to advertising copy, radio scripts, and fiction. Her short stories have appeared in literary magazines including *eclectica*, *JMWW*, *Carve*, *RiverSedge*, *Prosetoad*, *Amarillo Bay*, *The Saint Ann's Review*, *River Oak Review*, and *Echoes*. A collection of her personal essays about practicing the spiritual psychology *A Course in Miracles'* extraordinary forgiveness in ordinary life, **Extraordinary Ordinary Forgiveness**, was published by O-Books in 2011. A Course student and teacher, Dugan chronicles her personal experience with its transformative mind healing in her popular blog: **www.foraysinforgiveness.com**.

14649457R00144

Made in the USA
Lexington, KY
13 April 2012